SCEPTRE

Also by Valerie Blumenthal

Knowing Me
Benjamin's Dream
Homage to Sarah
The Colours of her Days
To Anna: About whom Nothing is Known

Chasing Eagles

VALERIE BLUMENTHAL

First published in 1996 by Hodder and Stoughton
A division of Hodder Headline PLC
A Sceptre Book

10 9 8 7 6 5 4 3 2 1

British Library Cataloguing in Publication Data

Blumenthal, Valerie, 1950–
Chasing eagles
1. English fiction – 20th century
I. Title
823.9'14 [F]

ISBN 0 340 65406 6

Typeset by Palimpsest Book Production Limited,
Polmont, Stirlingshire
Printed and bound in Great Britain by
Mackays of Chatham PLC, Chatham, Kent

Hodder and Stoughton
A division of Hodder Headline PLC
338 Euston Road
London NW1 3BH

Acknowledgements

Thanks to:

RSPB: Jackie Day and Stuart Gillies – for their invaluable information. Anne Brooks, St Edwards School, Oxford – an insight into a boys' school. Margaret Alice Stewart-Liberty – a happy walk across Port Meadow. Dr Robert Graham – for his dental tips!

The extract on p 142 is taken from 'My Mother's Sister' by C Day-Lewis, reprinted from *The Oxford Book of Twentieth Century Verse*.

'Does the Eagle know what is in the pit
Or wilt thou go ask the Mole?
Can Wisdom be put in a silver rod,
Or Love in a golden bowl?'

William Blake. 1757–1827. [Thel's motto]

1

'I think my mother's having an affair,' Wiz says to his latest friend, Frederick, who's collecting up glasses in a rather languorous way from the tables outside the Trout Inn.

'Your mother?' Frederick, tall, pimply, bespectacled, slowly sets down the glass he was holding. The red lipstick smeared on its rim has transferred to his index finger and he wipes it on his pullover. 'She doesn't look the type. I don't believe it.'

He met Wiz's parents as well as Wiz for the first time two months ago, on Wiz's fourteenth birthday.

'Everyone's the type.' Wiz, serious-eyed, pale-cheeked, gives a wise jerk of his chin and stares towards the weir.

Frederick comes to sit beside him and they swing their legs in silence over the edge of the wall for a bit.

'Well why do you think she is?'

Wiz picks up the binoculars hanging round his neck (a camera on another long cord rests below them). 'Canada geese,' he murmurs, focusing into the sharp sunlight on some distant dots, whose honking soon becomes audible along with their forms sharpening into definition.

'I just think,' he says enigmatically, in a tired tone. 'I have evidence. It's almost conclusive. I can't talk about it.'

'OK then.'

Wiz lets the binoculars hang loose – second-hand Zeiss

8×20s he bought with his birthday money and savings – and turns to him, suddenly anxious: 'You're not offended or anything, are you? It's just – it's just kind of private. Not *that* I know, but *how* I know. That bit's kind of private, if you see what I mean.'

'Yeah, I do.'

'I mean I hate to offend people, I really do.'

What with Frederick being so much older – four years – *and* a new friend, he's still treading cautiously.

'You haven't offended me.' Frederick runs a hand over the stucco of his acne, which no amount of unctions seems able to restrain. 'To tell the truth something happened to me a couple of nights ago—'

'Hey Frederick!' The landlord emerging from the umbral depths of the pub. 'I pay you to work, not chat . . . even to our better customers,' he adds more tolerantly when he realises it's Wiz. 'How're your parents?'

'Fine, they're fine,' Wiz mutters tightly, getting up and wiping down the seat of his jeans.

But nothing's fine, is it? Everything's a mess.

'Tell you when I next see you,' Frederick says, and goes back to collecting the glasses.

Wiz goes to fetch his bike from the car park. All the cars have gone now. Only the chef's battered Lada remains, and the landlord's jeep. And Wiz's bike, padlocked to a drooping-leafed tree. The pet peacock screeches from somewhere, and Wiz imitates it, cupping his hands, clambers onto his saddle and sets off. He can go wherever he wants. At fourteen the old constraints have been lifted. He can legally be left on his own. He can legally babysit. Were his parents to divorce, and he wished to live with one of them rather than the other, his wishes would be taken more seriously. Wiz knows his rights.

He cycles out of the car park. At Wolvercote he turns into Port Meadow and takes the path that cuts through all the way to Osney, stopping occasionally to peer at some sighting through the binoculars. The wide expanses of meadowland, traversed by the canal and the railway and bounded by the river, have completely dried out after the alluvial winter; the ponies concentrating on grazing are barrel-sided with the rich perspiring grass. Dogs weave and leap in and out of them, barking, provocative. In another group a little further away, the cows glance up, more wary. In the distance the green-tipped, Byzantine-style spire of St Barnabas Church glittering silver . . .

Wiz, a slight, tow-headed figure on his bike, pedals with the absent-minded air of someone who is burdened with problems. He dismounts when he comes to the small gate and the path that crosses over the rail bridge and then the canal, via Aristotle Bridge. On his left are the allotments – and an old man in a peaked cap is toiling over his lettuces – and on his right, the small recreation ground where he and Ben used to play. It seems an aeon ago.

He'll get a video out from the video shop in Walton Street, he decides. *Edward Scissorhands* will take his mind off things. And it's got Winona Ryder in it.

Wiz opens the iron gate to his garden. Sunk on its hinges, it grinds painfully against the York stone, which has a rusty line worn into it from continual friction. The gate has to be shut to prevent the spindly lurcher, appropriately named Lowry, from going next door. The last owner didn't mind. For two generations she had let animals and children alike play in her garden. The stone air-raid shelter had been a hide-out for little gangs of small boys and girls. They had furnished it with scraps of carpet and logs. Wiz had been one of those children. The elderly woman had brought them soft drinks and currant buns on a metal tray with ring marks all over it. Then she had died. The new owners had put up festoon blinds and frilly pelmets, and everyone knew the days of the air-raid shelter games were over. The dogs took longer to persuade.

He wheels his bike over to the dilapidated timber shed beneath the walnut tree. Last year the swallows nested there. This year they've discovered the carport which Alastair, his father, had built especially for his Austin Healey that he plans to restore in his spare time ('What spare time?' Liz, Wiz's mother, said). They squat, alert, sequin-eyed, on the rafter, in between constructing the netball-goal sack of their nest; scattering shit and pebbles onto the gun-metal blue bonnet – until Alastair is forced to move the car into the road where it remains unattended, next to the family Golf, gathering dust and fly dirt. Alastair cycles to his dental surgery in Beaumont Street. Everyone cycles everywhere in Oxford, not just the students. A city of bikes – soon to become even more driver-unfriendly if plans to ban cars from the city centre go ahead . . . They've kept Ben's mountain bike as a spare. It was his last birthday present – in his possession for perhaps a couple of hours. He had planned to try it out that evening. Nobody else has used it yet. Gleaming maroon with electric-blue zigzags, it would somehow be sacrilegious. Liz offers it occasionally to guests or students, but quickly follows with the bike's history, and they always decline.

Ben would have been seventeen in two days. His parents are priming themselves for the grim double anniversary. Nobody says anything, but Wiz knows it. It's going to be awful.

Life in the Miller household can be divided into Before and After. With Ben and Without Ben. You can say, This is how it was; and, This is how it is. In one way or another his presence never goes: memories, words, mementos – the tangible, the abstract – are there for the summoning. And then there is the accident itself, and the aftermath; well how can those horrors ever go? Wiz knows things will never be all right. Before the accident. After the accident. That's how it is. And now his mother . . . Counselling altered nothing. He froze, sitting there on the rigid sofa. He clammed up with self-consciousness and was resentful of this invasion into his privacy. And when all was said and done, no amount of counselling could banish the photographic images, the screaming in his head that played and replayed; nor could it restore the old atmosphere – the ease, the laughter, the *love*, the normal family life. And there were some things Wiz could not say. Like: Did my parents wish I'd been killed instead of Ben?

Liz hears the grating gate and creaking of bicycle wheels with her usual sense of relief. She is so used to experiencing this tension and its release within her body that she accepts it as normal, and doesn't even realise she has been feeling tense until that mind-clearing sensation washes over her and her shoulders and ribcage drop. Whereas once there was a light of irony in her eyes, as though a match flame flickered in their Sioux' blackness, now there is the opaqueness of anxiety. Nowadays she has a tendency to lift her narrow-tipped finger to the corner of her lip to hide an involuntary trembling, like the beating of a wren's heart. Before, her lips had always seemed to be on the verge of a smile, as though it were an effort to repress her humour.

It is natural to worry, natural to become overprotective; All that she is experiencing is *natural*. And is that really supposed to help? It is also natural, apparently, to go off sex under such circumstances. But he, her husband, turns to it. She, away from it. The dichotomy of their needs has created a divisive chasm between them.

Her foreign students help her, unwittingly: the pleasure of having young people about her without the accompanying maternal anxiety that mars her pleasure with Wiz. Sometimes she can joke almost in the old way with them, chivy them, even scold them, asp-tongued, as she had used to do with her own sons. Now, with her single remaining son she is too gentle, too softly-spoken. They have been through too much together to joke.

Liz grasps the chrome rail of the Rayburn, and using it as a ballet bar, does some leg lifts. For a very brief time she was a dancer, until she hurt her back when she was barely twenty. She teaches it twice a week at a preparatory school. Her face and body are a dancer's; even her head shape: round, neat, small; pale ears pinned close to her skull. And her hair, once down to her waist, shorn like a boy's. She'd cut it after the accident, in her own act of penance; an act of harshness she herself could control.

Up and down, sideways, forwards, backwards . . . Raises her leg – muscular-calved and thighed in shorts to above her hip level, holds it there, taut, before slowly lowering it to the ground. Ten times one leg, ten times the other; pointed-toed. The comfort of discipline and repetition. And when the ringing of the phone suddenly cuts the silence she doesn't budge, doesn't divert her attention. It is not the phone anyway. It is the parrot: the Archduke Ferdinand, repulsively bald, except for his head, which he can't reach to pluck at, and one iridescent green wing which for some reason does not interest him and is left as a reminder of his former glory. Perched on top of his cage, he tilts his vivid head and maintains a perfect imitation of the telephone ringing.

Five minutes have elapsed since she heard her son return. What's he doing? she wonders, intrigued, and goes over to the sash window, dully glazed with dust. He is standing with his back to her, perfectly still, facing the canal at the end of their garden. And as she watches, tender-hearted, he lifts his hand to a passing group of people waving from a brightly-painted barge. Oh Wiz. Oh Ben. Oh God. And she longs to run to him, there in the garden (does he not know he's standing on the poor, struggling tarragon?), and gather him up to her, crying, 'Where were you? I expected you an hour ago. Where *were* you?'

The train from London tears past, and the window vibrates. The boy turns, and she ducks as he heads indoors. The thud of the front door, and the squeaking overhead of his trainers on the quarry-tiled floor; the yelping of the lurcher; and the Archduke is abruptly stilled from his ringing, head inclined to one beaky side.

'I'm in the kitchen, darling,' Liz calls, in a normal mother's normal tone. So careful. They are all so careful not to upset one another.

She is dreading Saturday.

Except for Wednesdays, when he finishes work early and gives his amiable tennis partner a bashing at their North Oxford club, the first place Alastair goes when he arrives home at around seven, is his 'Lair'. Ben called it that. Dad's Lair. He hibernates there increasingly often nowadays. At first he gave the pretext of paperwork as an excuse. But he has ceased to offer excuses. Does anyone really mind where he is, or how long he is gone? Apart from paying the majority of the bills, what is he needed for? He'll give Wiz's curly head his bi-daily ruffle, bestow a cursory kiss on his wife's pale cheek, then off he goes. Any discussion will be deferred until dinner, an hour or so later. The door clicks decisively, quietly (forbiddingly, Liz thinks), and that's it. Who knows what he's up to behind it, what this tall, thin, diffident man is doing or thinking?

In here Alastair feels completely self-sufficient. He has his views across to the canal, his small upright piano, his gardening books, his computer chess, his newspaper, his desk with all the appropriate contents. He has installed Ben's old hi-fi system in here – the other is in the main sitting room – and sometimes silence reigns; at others music filters through, though never obtrusively loudly: anything from Sting or Eric Clapton, to Britten or Brahms. Sometimes the music might be his own piano playing.

This Thursday evening it's the strains of Erik Satie's *Gymnopédies* – courtesy not of himself but Glenn Gould – as Alastair lies on the Victorian chaise longue which is disgorging horsehair from the old green leather. His sensitive face with its fleshy, sensuous lips and powerful nose (a warrior's nose, a Saracen's nose, Liz once observed, tracing its sabre curve) is yearning. His pale grey eyes like Wiz's, and which can go from vulnerable to stern in a trice, are distant. Focused on distant places. He is dreaming once again of escape. These fantasies started out as an occasional, flitting thought, usually prompted by something he might have read or watched on television. He is a man of habit and has never been particularly adventurous when it comes to travel. For years he has been entrenched in his way of life – the North Oxford, Liberal Democrat, upper-intellect life, and all the things pertaining to it. But lately he has begun to question everything. Yes, *everything*; and the urge to flee is becoming increasingly strong in him, and taking the more real form of travel books and magazines, sequestered from prying eyes: Nepal, the Solomon Islands, Polynesia, the Hebrides, the Spanish mountains. . . A year away from all this. Just zap off. He would not tell a soul; just lock the door on his dental practice, where all hell would let loose. His lips part in a smile at the thought of the ensuing chaos. So wonderfully irresponsible . . . how he longs to be irresponsible. He would leave a note for Liz, of course.

He can hear her preparing dinner. The house has an odd layout. The dining room and kitchen are downstairs, down a dark staircase that is like descending into a dungeon. It's a kind of dug-out house on account of its sloping site. The kitchen is below his Lair, and he can smell the casserole cooking. The clatter of pans, the sound of the tap running, the chuckling of the pipes carry comfortingly upwards, breaking through Satie's lugubrious meanderings and diluting his own dreaming. He cannot hear his wife moving about now. Liz is silent as a cat on her feet, and she is barefoot as usual. He strains to hear some movement, but hears nothing and feels a sudden pang. A hankering for her stronger than his wanderlust. He still mourns the loss of her hair. One evening he had come home to find an androgynous stranger with a black, cropped head. But it took more than a haircut to estrange them.

He can hear the Archduke chortling away. It's funny, he muses, how each animal seems to know to whom it belongs. Ben's lurcher, Lowry, is now his loyal companion. The parrot is definitely Liz's. And Schrödinger, the cat, is Wiz's. Between the latter two creatures there exists a strange symbiotic respect.

A wave of guilt sweeps through him as he reviews his little family unit. The responsible man in him reasserts itself for the moment. The long Bank Holiday weekend stretches ahead. He has promised to take Wiz to Symonds Yat on a bird-sighting jaunt on Sunday. And on Saturday evening they are going to the opening of his brother-in-law's first sculpture exhibition. Architects are all resorting to alternative ways of living, it seems.

Alastair is not looking forward to Saturday. It would have been Ben's seventeenth birthday. He died on his birthday.

Oh I am a confused, middle-aged man. Oh Ben.

2

The birds in the roof guttering wake him up before the alarm. The fluttering and scraping of starlings and sparrows. And from the walnut tree branches beneath his window comes a combined happy chirruping. He can sense what kind of day it will be from the extent of all the activity.

Wiz lies in his bed, absently massaging his erection inside his pyjama trousers, and making shapes with his eyes so that the finger of light filtrating the gap in the curtains expands and contracts. If he squeezes them into millimetre slits the finger becomes rust-speckled on a buff ground, like a woodlark's egg. Wiz knows just about every bird's egg there is, even the more obscure ones. His memory for these sorts of facts is astounding. When it comes to remembering to give someone a message, or learning chemistry formulae, or dates of battles, or names of former prime ministers, these all elude him. His eyes will glaze as he pores over diagrams of the earth's crust; but provide him with an article on the habits of the red-backed shrike, and his mind will snap into computer efficiency. *Lanius collurio*. He knows all the Latin names too. His aptitude for Latin in relation to ornithology does not stretch to Caesar (Gallic Wars VII), however. The boys at his last school used to rag him. Bird-brain, they would quip, egghead; then, after Ben died they kept their respectful distance. At Rivers School there's an ornithology club, albeit poorly attended. His friend Josh gives him street cred: Big, soccer-loving, carefree – all the things Wiz is not. For some reason he selected Wiz to be his friend when they were both new boys in 'Shell'.

Shrouded in blank-sheeted sleep, Wiz lies here slowly absorbing: the light and shadows; the birds; a gargling sound; a weight on his legs. Little by little, like the unfolding of a frieze, one segment at a time, awareness unfolds: the gargling is the pipes; the weight on his legs is Schrödinger. And now snippets of information about the day ahead feed through to his brain: it is half term; he must get up soon to do the paper rounds; today is one of the days Klaus comes for his bi-weekly lesson. And Wiz intends to hang about.

Schrödinger was so named by Ben. Wiz had found him in the shed when he went to check on an orphaned sparrow fledgling he was rearing in there. The tabby cat yowled in pleasure when he entered. He was totally, remarkably, uninterested in the bird. The cat came apparently from nowhere and was unclaimed. An unneutered Tom, he had obviously been in some sort of accident and his jaw was completely out of alignment, so that his lower left canine tooth had been pushed into the middle of his mouth, jutting out like a unicorn's horn. Half his tail was also missing. The first thing Liz did was to have him neutered. But he still disappeared for days at a time – always to return. For this reason, after a month of answering to 'Cat', he was renamed Schrödinger by Ben, Schrödinger's cat being the was-he dead-was-he-alive protagonist in an experiment by the great Austrian physicist.

'He's my cat,' fumed Wiz, nine at the time. '*I* found him. *I* want him to be called Cat. Who's heard of Schro-whatever? I hate the name. It's stupid.' Close to tears. And outvoted. His mother abstained and his father took Ben's side.

To Wiz's relief Schrödinger retained his peculiar apathy

towards birds, saving him from divided loyalties; and nowadays the cat's maraudings do not tend to be beyond the boundaries of the garden.

It was Ben who had come up with the nickname 'Wiz', to replace his real name of Oscar. He used to love to play with words. 'Oscar, Os . . . Oz,' he said when they were respectively aged about seven and ten. 'Oz . . . Wizard of Oz . . . Wizard . . . Hah! Wiz! Wiz and Liz!'

He was clever, was Ben; verging on brilliant, according to his teachers. He commanded respect from his peers and superiors alike. He was tall for his age, whereas Wiz is small; and good at sports. He excelled at tennis, and could make a skateboard leap almost shoulder-high and land properly. Wiz is hopelessly ill-coordinated. He can't play tennis as he can't serve, because he finds it impossible to throw the ball up straight. His father becomes exasperated with him, which only makes him worse.

Wiz hoists himself up with his elbows and pulls Schrödinger onto him. The cat drapes itself round his neck, its purrs vibrating against Wiz's throat. The alarm goes off in a victorious crow, and he pushes down the pop-up cockerel, and gets out of bed – simultaneously pulling over the duvet: the bed is made. He has no trouble getting up. His hobbies are morning pursuits as much as nocturnal ones: bird-watching, film, photography. Sunrise – and the birds just rousing; sunset – and birds settling for the night, duck flying off to another destination . . . And a small dark formation in the pink sky is revealed as a sute of mallards . . . And besides, getting up to do the paper rounds has a real purpose. He is saving for a camcorder.

He showers, dresses, drags a comb through his thick curls and goes down the three flights of stairs – his is an attic room – closely followed by Schrödinger.

'Morning all,' his father says from the depths of his muesli and bran – and raises his hand towards Wiz for the routine first hair-ruffle of the day, before going back to his article on a new technique for inlays.

Wiz opens a can of tuna flavour for the cat and spoons it into the plastic bowl.

'Talking of which,' says Alastair, removing his gaze from the illustration to fix it on his son. 'You've been scrubbing again. I went into your bathroom. Your toothbrush is like a hedgehog after an encounter with a juggernaut.'

'It takes ages the other way.' Wiz: putting a cap on the cat tin and pouring himself some orange juice, wiping the spilled drops with his finger and licking them. He'll have breakfast when he gets back. Sometimes Bert has something interesting to eat.

'Don't come running to me when you're twenty for a gingivectomy.' Alastair tries to sound light-hearted and jocular, but Wiz's hands are already clenching up into fists. Alastair adds, irritability creeping into his tone, 'If you would only use the electric toothbrush—'

'I've told you. It feels funny. It tickles.'

'Oh for God's sake.'

'Well it does.'

His son. His son is so *eccentric.* Alastair tries to feel benevolent, but it is too early in the morning, and last night Liz, well Liz . . .

Wiz gulps down the orange juice – 'Bye Dad' – outside he goes, leaving the glazed kitchen door to rattle shut behind him, and to the shed to fetch his bike. It's leaning against Ben's, and for a moment he toys with the idea: what if he took that instead? Who would know? Who would dare say anything? He stares at it, fingers the sleek saddle, and recalls his brother's pleasure at the present. His fifteenth birthday. Soberly he wheels his own bike from the shed. It's ten to seven and a silver haze hangs over everything, rests soft on the hair, on the skin, on the grass, which squeaks sweet-smelling under the rubber soles of his trainers. It hides the beginnings of a pale sun, washes over the dark canal, enshrouds the barges moored nose to tail like huddled lovers, conceals the birds calling to one another from the willows on one bank to the fruit trees of suburban gardens of the other.

He goes over to the bird table to inspect it: the sunflower seed and raisins have gone, as well as the nuts. The chaffinches like the former; and Wiz feels a little glow of satisfaction. He had to entice them at first, and they are still rightly suspicious of next door's ginger, who crouches amongst the herb bed, making seductive throaty sounds to lure them. Opens and closes the gate as quietly as is possible, relieved to be away when his father's like that. As Saturday draws closer, so he senses the build-up of tension. And does his father know about his mother? Only now does this thought occur to him. Oh God, how awful if he does. If he does not know, then he must never find out.

Before mounting his bike, he clambers onto the wall surrounding the house, trampling on an overlapping branch of spreading rosemary, and inspects the progress of the swallows' nest. It is very nearly finished; a mound several inches long, of mud, pebbles and saliva. The metallic crown of one of the swallows is just decipherable from the central rafter, and even as he watches, its mate swoops low over his head, returning from a foray with a live worm clamped in its thin black bill. As it alights on the rafter, the bird already there issues an excited 'Tswit, tswit, tswit' call.

Do they recognise him, he wonders? He checks on them several times a day and they have ceased to be bothered by him. And now he climbs on his bike, whistling tunelessly, momentarily happy and forgetful, up Kingston Road. It's like a complete self-contained village here, in this part of Oxford where Wiz has lived all his life. He knows all the shops, all the shopkeepers. It is a friendly street with an atmosphere all of its own. At Party Mania it suddenly becomes Walton Street, but it is still the same road; and the Phoenix cinema is his haunt, although so many of their films are '18'. There's no way he can pass for eighteen, with his elfin face, unbroken voice and height of five foot three. But he has big feet. His big feet give him hope that one day he will be tall. And meanwhile he slips through with Josh, and more recently, Frederick, by hovering just behind, head down.

. . . Past the dry-cleaners, the Grog shop, the bookies; the Jericho Café on the other side of the road; the cycle shop . . . The bursar at Wiz's school had to organise a work permit for him. It's all very proper. He's not allowed to start before seven, since he is under sixteen. If he could, he could earn double, as he could do two more streets given another hour. As it is, there are about eighty houses. That makes two rounds he can squeeze in before school chapel at eight-thirty. It's a long day. He doesn't get home from school until around five-thirty. But he makes £19 a round. That's £38 a week, paid in cash each Sunday. Sundays are more work, as the Sunday papers are so heavy that the same two streets take a couple of extra trips to Mr Singh's. During the week he races about to fit everyone in. Most of the houses take the *Guardian* or the *Independent*. Only one person takes the *Sun*. And Wiz always stops to have a peep at page three in a disused builders' yard a few doors up the road. The mischievous faces and the fleshy balloons with their nipples like babies' *moued* lips, make his penis tingle and harden. It was how he met Bert. Bert sleeps rough on a pile of sand beneath the archway in the yard, with his husky draped over him like a grey rug. Lately Wiz's dreams are an extraordinary amalgam of free-floating pneumatic breasts, dentures, and his mother's eyes. Then Ben, who will at some stage change into Bert, will appear and take charge like a film director, ordering all the disparate components into their apposite compartments.

He padlocks his bike to the lamppost outside Mr Singh's newsagent's.

'You're early, young Wiz.' Mr Singh, tall, dignified in his pristine white turban. 'What's happened to your half-term lie-in this morning then?'

Klaus has happened. He wants to make certain not to miss a single revealing second of Klaus's arrival.

'I woke early,' he says, rubbing his right foot against his left calf and smiling his beatific smile.

'Time for some tea?'

'We-ell.'

'I have only just made a pot.'

'OK then.' Adds, 'Thanks.' Calculates: five minutes won't hurt. Klaus won't be there until nine.

Mr Singh has known Wiz's family since he took over the shop ten years ago. He and his wife came to Ben's funeral and wept. Their only child, a son, had been killed three years previously in a racial attack.

He likes to talk, and to air his grievances, in particular against the Hindu shopkeeper next door.

'I'll get back at that good-for-nothing rogue, He's got absolutely no right to do this to me. He makes life hell for me.' He gulps down the weak tea.

'But Mr Singh –' Wiz always tries to be fair, '– you started selling the fruit and stuff first.' He blinks, and shifts his bottom on the stool next to his employer behind the till.

Mr Singh glares, not at the boy, but in the direction of his enemy with the sub post office and greengrocer's next door.

'Bah, a few lousy apples. What do they count?' And oranges. And tomatoes. And potatoes. 'They weren't on display outside, were they? They were just there for my regulars. Not for the world to see. He has papers on the *rack* outside. He – has – no – *right*.' Mr Singh's voice rises and he makes a pp-ing sound with his lips. 'They're all the same, his lot. You can't trust them.'

Mr Singh is a Sikh, and Wiz's father has explained to him that the war between the two men has its origins not in fruit and newspapers, but in gods.

He collects his first wad of newpapers, puts them in the sack provided, hoisting the strap over his shoulder, and cycles off.

The first few houses are still asleep; curtains pulled across their Victorian windows. The frenzied barking of dogs comes from several homes. He can hear a row going on in one house; through the open mouth of the letter box as he rams the paper through; yelling: 'You said –' 'I didn't.' 'You're so unreliable . . .' And then the paper is tugged through, pulled from him by an invisible hand.

Will his father yell at his mother when he finds out? Would he murder her? Oh God, it is too awful to contemplate.

He fishes out the *Sun* in readiness. But first he comes to the house of one of his father's patients. She's an elderly archaeologist or something, watering her plant pots now, in her dressing gown and a pair of wellingtons.

'Good morning, Wiz,' she calls.

'Hi,' he says back, walking up to her and handing her the paper.

'I don't think this is mine dear,' she tells him mildly, handing him back the *Sun*.

'Oh . . .' Flustered, eyes downward and watering in embarrassment. Passes her the *Guardian* from underneath it. 'And your bill's inside,' he mutters. The rims of his ears are inflamed as he cycles away, and he feels her eyes on his back. He'll have to turn into Southmoor Place to read it.

. . . Pulls over at the edge of the road. Nobody about. He turns impatiently to page three . . . Oh God, she's so beautiful. Oh God he wants to touch her. Put his face there.

Put his . . . Wiz groans in pent-up pleasure. Fourteen, and the smallest boy in his class. Half an inch shorter than the other shortest boy. And no sign of his voice breaking. But the urges are all there; assuaged somewhat against the saddle of his bike as he cycles off on the rest of his round and in the direction of Bert.

Bert, grizzled-haired, mottled red-veined complexion, is in the middle of shaving by touch, pulling at the loose folds of his skin with dark-stained fingers that poke twig-like through cut-off grey woollen gloves. Wiz comes to sit beside him and waits respectfully. The razor sounds like sandpaper scraping against the white stubble. Wiz fumbles in his anorak pocket for the chocolate biscuits there; one for Bert and one for George, the odd-eyed husky.

'I brought these,' he says, when Bert's put the razor back inside the ancient rucksack that contains all his belongings and also serves as a pillow.

'Thanking you,' Bert says, taking them and giving one to the dog.

He first encountered Bert a month ago. He'd stopped in the yard as usual, and there he was; curled up with George sprawled across him. They stared at each other in surprise.

'And who might you be?' Bert, possessive of his patch, mumbled through sleep-parched lips, and sitting up.

'Wiz. My name's Wiz.'

'Funny name.'

'It's a derivation.'

'What?'

'A derivation. You know. Derived from something. A nickname.'

Bert grunted, and opening a tin of tobacco, started to roll a cigarette.

Wiz persisted. 'From *The Wizard of Oz.*'

'What?'

'The film. *The Wizard of Oz*. You know.'

'Can't say I do,' Bert said, licking the rim of the paper, sealing it, and striking a match. Wiz admired his expertise. He did it all so naturally.

'I like your dog.'

'Old George. He were given to me when he were a pup.'

'What is he?'

'A husky. Same as them dogs pull them sledges. He were given to me,' he repeated.

Wiz stroked the dog's thick ruff. The animal growled slightly and moved closer to his master. Wiz noticed the mouth organ then.

'Do you play that?'

'Yep.'

'To get money?'

'Yep.'

'It can't make you much. Just doing that.'

'I gets by . . . You doin' the papers then?'

'I've been doing them for nearly three weeks.'

'Ain't seen you before. But then, I been laid up with lungs.'

'Lungs?' Wiz queried.

'Me lungs. Couldn't breathe.' The old man inhaled and exhaled in an exaggerated way, his breath emitting in fetid wheezes.

'Oh I see,' Wiz said. 'Lungs.' He copied the breathing to show he understood, and Bert nodded. After rifling around his rucksack he brought out a sandwich.

'Want a bit?'

Since then their friendship has developed. Bert has taught Wiz to play the mouth organ. Wiz, in turn, has shown Bert his slides of birds. He reads him pieces from the papers.

'Bert, what happens in the winter, when it's really cold?' Wiz asks him now.

'There's an 'ostel I can go to if I likes. Then there's the day centre.'

'Where's that?'

'By the station. Well it's a change. Somebody to talk to, like. And a warm cuppa.' He clears his throat and spits on the ground. Wiz stares at it glistening there.

They never have a very profound conversation, much as he engineers it and tries to read innuendo and philosophical wisdom into every one of Bert's remarks and pauses. But he bides his time, convinced that Bert has 'hidden depths', that his simplistic language disguises the mind of a sage. He hangs on every word, waiting for the moment of revelation. Has seen *Down and Out in Beverly Hills* with Bette Midler and Richard Dreyfus, and Nick Nolte as the tramp, four times. Only a few weeks ago there was Jean Renoir's *Boudu Saved From Drowning* on television, a 1930's black and white about a tramp who tries to drown himself. And what about Charlie Chaplin's tramp? And meanwhile, Wiz can see the light of a savant behind Bert's lashless, bloodshot eyes. Imbues every lengthy hiatus between sentences with the weight of contemplation, accrediting to this stinking, wretched figure the mind of Nietzsche.

He returns to Mr Singh's for the second lot of papers, and cycles off again with this new load.

Ben had done the same rounds. He had been saving for a scanning electron microscope . . . Retracing his brother's tracks . . . Peering through the same curtains . . . The same dogs barking at him . . . Milk bottles by the various doors, waiting to be taken inside. Seeing as his brother saw. Through his brother's eyes.

Ben is never far from his thoughts. Ben confuses him constantly. Ben shadow-trails him. Shadow-boxes. He did used to shadow-box Wiz – goading him, provoking him, always smiling. Innocent, harmless play that had incited Wiz to bellow in frustration, evoked in him feelings of fury he had never felt towards anyone else; and he would hurl himself at the good-humoured laughing wall of his brother. He recalls how when he was six or seven he had been given a new toy gun, and the wholeheartedness with which he had 'shot' his brother was more than mere role-play. And then, for maybe the last three or four months, there had been signs of an unspoken détente. Ben's teasing became gentler. He sometimes showed more of an interest in Wiz's pursuits. The jibes were more often tender than mocking. Wiz, mistrustful, wary, was slow to respond.

Memories jab at him. Wherever he is – whenever – Ben, with a Jack-in-the-box irrepressibility, springs up. Clever-me Ben. The world-loves-me Ben. And Wiz remembers how he was forever trying to appeal to him, to show that he too could be clever, funny, original, act the fool, play sport . . .

So there they were, perhaps four years ago, in the waiting room at his father's practice; why were they there? Wiz, absently posting papers, cannot remember the reason; but he can remember nudging his brother: 'Come on.' Emboldened; adrenalin high, because *he* was the instigator of a game. And downstairs they stole, into the laboratory, where they were immediately enveloped by the various strong, mixed smells: the sickly odour of ether, the acrid smell of the impression material, the pungent meths. It was a cool room, about twenty feet in length, the linoleum floor stacked with different-sized boxes. To one side was a freestanding bench with equipment for making the moulds: the centrifuge, bunsen burner. The walls were lined with shelves, upon which were arrayed dozens of bottles of ether, chloroform, mouthwash and sealed packets. There were also rows and rows of plaster dental moulds, sets of dentures and plates. Wiz and Ben both wore plates.

'Hey!' exclaimed Wiz, grabbing a couple of pairs of false

teeth and holding one in each hand. 'How do you do? I'm fine . . . You're looking very old . . . Well, so would you if—'

'I don't think you should do that Wiz,' Ben, usually the outrageous one, cautioned.

'Wimp,' Wiz jeered gleefully, as his brother had often done with him. 'Who's being wimp-y? It's because it's *my* idea. You don't like it because it's my idea.'

He began to dance round with the teeth, play-acting different roles, assuming funny voices, whirling round excitedly, cheeks becoming flushed; carried away. And his wild gesturing arms swept over the shelf, knocking off all the grinning teeth that had been in careful order.

'Shit, what've you done? *Idiot,*' shouted Ben.

'I didn't mean to. It was an accident. I didn't mean to.' Wiz, close to tears at the havoc he'd just wrought, stared at the jumble of obscene mouths on the floor. 'He'll go mad. Dad will go *mad.*'

'In concentration camps they had that,' Ben said suddenly. 'Piles of false teeth from all the dead. I saw a picture once . . . Well, get on with it then. Don't just stand there gaping.'

They put them all back on the shelves. Lined up neatly, they looked the same as before.

'He'll put all the wrong teeth in the wrong patients now,' moaned Wiz plaintively.

'They're all labelled, idiot.'

Wiz faced his brother, pleading eyed. 'So it'll be all right then?'

'Probably. It'll probably be all right.' He looked back at Wiz and relented with a smile. 'Yes, it'll be all right.' And he pretended to punch him playfully in the stomach.

Wiz started to giggle then. Relief. Release of tension. Tears and giggling simultaneously. 'Imagine if he put the wrong teeth in the wrong people. *Imagine.*'

Ben laughing too. The pair of them creeping upstairs again, returning to the waiting room as if nothing had happened.

Wiz arrives back home. Eight-fifteen. He's been longer than on a schoolday. I must buy a mouth organ, he thinks, letting himself into the kitchen by the back door. His mother hasn't come down yet. He heads upstairs to his room, passing his parents' bathroom on the way. From it comes the gentle splashing of his mother in the bath. The scent of some sort of oil she has put in the water drifts past the door. Perfuming herself, like he's seen in films. Isn't that conclusive evidence?

'I'm back,' he says, miserable again.

'OK darling. I'll be out soon. Help yourself to breakfast.'

He hovers for a moment; has a clear image of her body that she's never kept hidden from him: bony-shouldered, slim, taut, small pointed breasted . . . and a neat bush of black pubic hair. Nothing like the girls in the *Sun*. Or the two magazines he stole from Mr Singh's shop and he keeps folded inside his cricket pullover at the top of his wardrobe.

He trails upstairs to his room to fetch *Empire*, the film magazine, to read with his breakfast.

3

Liz lies in her scented bath letting the purple oil soak into her skin. The mirrored wall behind it has almost steamed up. And there, in the condensation, in ghostly vapour, is an imprint of her husband's hand. He must have rested it there as he stood up. Her husband's hand: that used to run – light as a fly's legs – down her spine; fondle her hair; caress her breasts; explore with minute attention between her legs . . . And herself wet and voracious for him. For years it was like that. Now she feels shrivelled and dry as an old woman. Now, when he pushes inside the rigid block of her body she only just manages not to shout out in protest.

Last night he had tried to make love – or was it have sex? – with her for the first time in a month. Her silent frigidness had made him go limp. The first time ever. He blamed her angrily. But he blames her anyway, and the knowledge of his blame inhibits her and constantly punishes her.

'I told you to check the tyres,' reverberates through her head whilst his penis gets on with its business.

And the sad, the pitiful thing is, that the more estranged she feels from her husband, the more helplessly locked she becomes sexually – the more painfully she loves him.

She stands up and lays her fingers on the wide spatula fingers imaged in the mirror. Water slithers down her oily skin in long rivulets. She lies back once more and squeezes the sponge over her face so that the water drips in slow globules over its aching cheek muscles. Thinking back. Shutting her eyes. And that hand reaching for hers at a particular moment at a concert, so that they could share it.

In the early days of their relationship she would find hidden cards with messages from him dotted all round the flat she shared with another dancer: found you . . . Act 1 was great. Can't wait for Act 2 . . . Watch this space . . . Save the splits for me . . . He called her his llama-eyed sprite, read Shakespeare sonnets to her and recited Yeats. Alastair compensated for the deficiencies in her life; for all the bad. He caught her at her most promiscuous and pinned her down. Two years into their marriage, when Ben was one, they exchanged London for Oxford. When his father, a wealthy Harley Street surgeon, died, Alastair could afford to buy the practice in Beaumont Street.

Contentment. It can be shattered at any moment. Does this therefore mean that one should not permit oneself to feel it, she wonders? That one should always temper it with caution, if not downright pessimism? What sort of eventuality for the day must one be prepared for, just in case it should happen? A burglary? A rape? A plane crash? A murder? A car crash.

A second is all it takes for the reversal of contentment, for ordinary, unthinking calm to transmute into constant anguish.

Liz reflects: I've had three stages in my life so far: bad, good, bad.

Meeting Klaus has made a difference. Someone coming in from the outside. Someone who appreciates her without judgement. She has started making more of an effort. Not for him, nor even for Alastair, so much as for herself. It is all very recent and slight, this slow transitional process. But little things – the oil in the bath, reading the papers thoroughly, wearing lipstick, buying exotic fruits – little things like that, that she had stopped bothering about, she is doing again. And she's down five cigarettes a day, to ten instead of fifteen. Alastair hates her smoking.

Alastair. Wiz. And once there was Ben. When Ben was alive it was Alastair and Ben, Wiz and herself. They all loved each other of course; but that was the pattern. She has deprived her husband of his son and for that he blames her bitterly; and – apart from that single remark that is constantly replayed in stale refrain – silently. Alastair is a true Capricorn, a meticulous man who needs stability. She has deprived him of that, too. And herself. But she does not count. They cannot even talk of him together without strain, without her feeling the unspoken rays of animosity radiating from him.

He needs her sexually, she needs him emotionally. If she satisfied him with the first, could he satisfy her with the second? Who will venture down the other's road? But his unwelcoming eyes deter her. She simply cannot feel womanly. It is a father's love she craves at the moment. But what would Liz know about a father's love? and meanwhile, she presumes that in his heart Alastair bears her a deep grudge and possibly dislike. If she had deliberately planned the tragedy, the outcome would have been no different. His sense of deprivation could be no greater.

But she has never voiced these thoughts and suppositions to her husband. Bed apart, they exist as if nothing is wrong, acting out normality; shying away from potentially damaging self-revelations. Her husband's gentle detachedness, tense quick-and-it's-gone smile, the mat, joyless grey of his eyes, the side-stepping politeness, all preclude her saying, 'Talk to me. Tell me what you're feeling.' And besides, she dreads hearing the hitherto unuttered words: It's your fault. She never dares say, I love you, for fear of nothing in return.

And so, in their efforts to behave as a normal family, on a Saturday the three of them might stroll down Parks Road and peruse the paintings on the railings; in the evening there could be a concert or recital at any number of venues. On a Sunday, after his tennis, Alastair mows the lawn and she weeds. Also on a Sunday she cooks roast lamb. After lunch he might work on the Austin Healey. But the old ease has gone. They try too hard; so that like a long-sighted person threading a needle, the thread keeps just missing and stabs instead at empty air.

On the wall behind their bed is a portrait of her naked, lying in abandoned pose on a pile of Indian cushions, one hand resting on her stomach, black hair like a puddle around her; as depicted by her artist friend, Anna. The picture harks back to those halcyon, sensuous days of her thirties. She is forty-one now, but looks at the most thirty-five, despite everything. Liz describes herself in French terms as *'belle-laide'*.

At her dressing-table she massages moisturiser into her cheeks. She has a tendency to bags beneath her eyes, and a white filigree scar, about an inch long, runs diagonally just above the thick arch of her left eyebrow. When she is tired it becomes raised and pink and itches her. The habit of fingering it, even when it is not troubling her, has never quite left her. Her face is small, wide at the cheeks, pointed at the chin. Wiz has her features with her husband's colouring. She puts on the red lipstick she has started to wear, thoughtfully blotting it on a Kleenex; and her whole face seems to spring into focus. Now – naked, crop-haired, red-lipped and round-buttocked – she moves with her dancer's grace around the room. Making the bed: the pillows indented with the burden of their disparate dreams, creased from their tossing-turning heads; the duvet strewn half over the floor, hauled from one zone to another; and there in the middle of the exposed sheet – the reproachful crisp-dry stain.

She covers it up quickly.

'Wiz,' she calls at the doorway. 'Darling, can I borrow your new black jeans?'

'OK.'

She will paint her toenails red and wear her mules.

'And your white t-shirt with the black panther on it?' she calls out again. Then hurriedly puts on a pair of knickers and a bra. Wiz seems to have become embarrassed by her nakedness recently.

'What are you up to today?' she asks her son, downstairs in the kitchen.

'Oh nothing much. I thought I'd hang about. You know.'

'Not seeing any friends?'

'Maybe later. Maybe I'll go through my photo albums or something. I might do some revision for exams.'

'How was the round this morning?'

. . . The homely rising smell of the toast doing . . .

'OK. I'm halfway there. Two more months and I'll have enough for a camcorder. There's this shop in Little Clarendon Street. He does some really good deals on second-hand ones. And he's got second-hand Swatches. I might get one of them, and trade in my old one you and Dad gave me – you remember the one – three years ago. Would you mind if I did that?'

'Of course I wouldn't.'

'Would Dad?'

'No darling. Of course not.'

'Only this one's – the one I really like – is a diver's one.'

The toast pops up. On cue, so she can take it to him

and hug him at the same time. She never used to be self-conscious about hugging him.

'You're doing really well,' she says, setting a plate in front of him on the pine table. And bending forward, wraps her arms round him. Clamping him. For a moment he leans his head back against her, into the hollow where her ribs meet. It feels like a warm comfortable bowl, he thinks, closing his eyes. She strokes his thick hair and releases him before he has time to tense up.

'I'm really proud of you.'

'I saw Bert this morning.' Wiz spreads peanut butter thickly on his toast, and his mother sits down opposite him and pours them both coffee. 'He was telling me about this day centre he goes to.'

Wiz tries to inject their limited conversation with something deeper.

'He was talking about the need for change,' he embellishes to his mother.

'That sounds very profound,' she comments gratifyingly, tilting her body towards him, elbows propped on the table, knuckles supporting her chin. Gently smiling at him. They have the same slightly gummy smile, the same mouth. How can he avoid noticing the lipstick, and the red toenail varnish? His jeans, loose on him, fit snugly over her small round bottom.

'Is Klaus coming?' As if he doesn't know.

'You know he always comes on a Friday. He's been coming for over three months.'

... Fiddling with his spoon, biting into the toast. 'I mean, would you say he's good-looking?' he mumbles, mouth full.

'Goodness, what a question!'

And Wiz, hyper-perceptive, detects an artificial lightness in her tone. She's playing for time, he thinks.

'Well I've never really thought about it ... I suppose

he's all right,' his mother says, giving a high little laugh that he recognises instantly as false. 'Now the Archduke—' she laughs more naturally now, pointing to the bald parrot. 'I'd say he's quite splendid-looking, wouldn't you?'

He smiles wanly. Well, she's evading the issue, isn't she? Classic. It's classic. All the signs are there.

'Now I want to know about *your* day . . .'

'I've said. I've already said.'

They sit for a further quarter of an hour discussing general things; but each senses the awkwardness of the other. Liz lights up her first cigarette, then they stack the dishwasher together. The dog licks the plates voraciously.

'Shooh now,' she tells her son, when everything is put away. 'I've got to sort my books for Klaus.'

'Dad could've been a pianist instead of a dentist.'

'I don't think so.' Liz – sifting through the two piles on the chair in the corner.

'He's as good as Klaus.'

'No he's not. Anyway Klaus isn't just a pianist. He's a musicologist.'

'Well Dad could have been a musicologist,' Wiz says desperately.

'What – and deprive Oxford's dowagers of their favourite heart-throb dentist? Be fair. Now, what is all this, eh? Scram, will you. I must get ready.'

For Klaus. And at that point the door rings.

4

Everything about Klaus is exaggerated: his Swiss-German accent, his sudden enthusiasms followed by sombreness, his odd humour, his grand, rather old-fashioned gestures, his good looks – for yes, he is outstandingly handsome. He is also immensely rich, both from inherited wealth and his own electronics business which he sold to a well-known Japanese company. Now, aged thirty-five, he is doing a doctorate in music. Music is his overriding passion, and to this end his ambitions are also not far short of grandiose: to be considered the leading authority in his field and to be invited to lecture all over the world on his subject. But first he must improve his spoken English.

'Hello Klaus.'

'You look marvellous today. Very marvellous,' Klaus tells Liz in return, throwing his arms wide and stepping into the hallway, where rainbow reflections are cast on the white walls by the stained-glass door panel.

Wiz, hovering, mutters sourly, 'You forgot to shut the gate. Lowry has just shot through.'

'Well go and fetch him darling, quickly.'

'But Klaus—'

'Yes, it's very bad of me. I must be sorry.'

'I must apologise, not I must be sorry,' Liz corrects

him, smiling briefly, then raising her eyebrows at her son. 'Wi-iz.'

'OK. OK.' Disgruntled, he leaves them. Now he'll miss whatever happens next, he thinks, chasing down the path, and up the road, where a spaniel bitch is on heat. Its owner let everyone know in advance, and for good measure stuck a notice to several lampposts: 'All male dogs please note: Bonnie is on heat from now, May 20th, to June 10th. Your presence will NOT be welcome.' An eccentric woman. There are quite a few of those sort of types round here, Wiz thinks – before remembering his father called him eccentric. Eventually he captures the lurcher, and hauls it back home against its will, spluttering in its resistance as he tugs the chain round its neck. He closes the gate firmly.

They have already retreated to the kitchen, and his shoulders sag in defeat. From inside come their mulled voices.

He'll go in. No knocking. No excuses. Didn't Klaus's flattery and his whole expression give everything away? And his mother, she couldn't wait to get rid of him – Wiz – could she? He never interrupts her lessons normally. It's a rule. Unless something is urgent she is not to be disturbed for the duration of the lesson; in this case an hour and a half.

He hesitates, bracing himself for the scene which may greet him, and opens the door. They turn in surprise as he enters – he scans their faces for signs of guilt – his mother at the end of the table, Klaus next to her at an angle. Several text books, a tape recorder, pens and file paper lie haphazardly in the middle of the table, and pushed to the other end is all the usual clutter: a box of matches, Liz's cigarettes and lighter, a sketch pad, a novel, a cardigan, a cotton reel, a brooch, the muesli packet from breakfast . . . And Wiz's camera. He has his pretext, conveniently handed to him, even though he had been quite prepared not to have one.

'What is it Wiz?'

'My camera. I think I left it in here.'

'Oh – yes you did. Now – scram, darling. You know not to interrupt.'

Klaus appraises him with curiosity and a small smile, as though Wiz belongs to another species.

'Could I sit in? I'm really – I mean it might be really interesting to sit in. I never have done. I'd be quiet. Well I could even help. You know – help, sort of thing.'

'What *is* this, Wiz? Of course you can't. Now here's your camera.' Her voice, sharp at the beginning of her speech, is soft-toned by the end – albeit firm. Her whole face is soft (he notices Klaus's gaze is now glued to her).

She pretends to throw the camera to him. 'Catch!'

'Don't!' he cries out. 'You'll break it.'

But it hasn't left her hands. His mother's smile is gentle and questioning. And he takes the camera from her and, blushing, leaves the room. Where he positions himself outside; for an hour and a half if necessary.

'I could never to have children,' Klaus remarks to Liz.

'The infinitive is in its basic form after "never" or "not", Klaus. You know that. No "to". You've written that down dozens of times. The same applies to "could".'

'I forget because you distract me. I am distracted *by* you. Active and passive, huh?' He jerks his chin forward teasingly.

'*Huh*. So, why don't you want children?'

'They are too demanding. And my music – you see for me my music is very . . . exclusive. I will not to want—'

'*Would* not: conditional. You are talking about hypothesis. And *no* "to", Klaus.'

'You see how I am distracted? So, I *would* not *want* children to be interfering with my music.'

'Klaus, why have you used the present continuous infinitive instead of the ordinary one?'

'Because it will be going on, their interfering. Continuing for many years.'

This, she has to grant him, would appear to be a logical argument; however, 'to be interfering' is the gerund, she explains; a verbal noun.

Patiently he listens, his eyes roving towards the painting over the dresser – a naîve oil of a naked pubescent girl and a ewe in a cornfield – and then continues his own conversation as if she had not interrupted. 'Also, what would to happen if my child, he will grow up and he will also have a musically inclination? I want for music to be mine alone. I want for my ideas to be mine. And you see I then must discourage my child and that would be a terrible thing. So you see how it is better I am able to recognise my selfish inclinations and therefore not to have a child who I will not be generous to.'

Liz does not correct his peroration this time. So close to him – their hands resting on the table are an inch or so apart – she is acutely aware of him. Never has she met anyone like Klaus before. Unrealistic, self-centred, brilliant, fixed in his opinions and impressionable, impassioned and given to extremes, he is intensely romantic. His brown eyes spill sexuality. They remind her of liquid praline. Lately she has found herself wondering what it would be like making love with him; but flits quickly away from these little fantasies which have no place in her life. His shirt sleeves are rolled up to just below the elbow and the hairs on his lower arm – silky and brown – make her want to lay her own arm against them. He is stockily built, muscular, much shorter than Alastair, who can look awkwardly gangling.

'Well, you will have to find yourself a woman who

doesn't want children,' she says. And he fixes his head-tilted, knowing smile on her, then startles her with one of his abrupt mood switches.

'Tell me about your other son.'

'Ben? Look, Klaus, it's your lesson now. We must get down to some work. You don't pay me to talk about myself,' she jokes feebly.

'I will pay you anything,' he says fervently, staring into her eyes.

She pulls a wry expression. 'I could misinterpret that.'

Outside the thick old door Wiz misses words here and there; tries to interpret what the innuendo might be; guess their expressions, how close they're sitting. He tries to remember how Lee, alias Barbara Hershey, was, in *Hannah and her Sisters.*

'So?'

'My two sons were very different. Ben was brilliant, extrovert, uncomplicated . . . Tomorrow will be two years since he died. On his birthday. We were on the way to London, to the Science Museum. We were a very close-knit family before. Now . . . I can't tell you what something like this does to a family. Our lives are shattered. It's something you can never get over. You don't expect your child to die before you. And that you – oneself – have been the cause of the death . . . To quote Samuel Johnson – you do know Samuel Johnson because you read to me from Boswell's account—'

'I remember.' Klaus gives one of his Germanic little nods.

'Well he wrote, "Human life is everywhere a state in which much is to be endured and little to be enjoyed." That about sums it up.'

In return he quotes Rilke: '"Be patient toward all that

is unsolved in your heart and try to love the questions themselves like locked rooms or books that are written in a foreign tongue. The point is to live everything. Live the questions for now. Perhaps you will then gradually, without realising it, live your way some distant day into the answer."'

He stops speaking and for a moment there is a heavy lull between them.

'That's very beautiful,' she says finally, with the flicker of an embarrassed smile. 'And you recited it in perfect English.'

'I learned it in English. Rainer Maria Rilke – for me he is symbolising great optimism in the decaying world. *I* am an optimist also. Liz—' He reaches over and strokes her arm, before she moves it away.

'No, Klaus, don't.'

'*I* can make you enjoy again. Not endure.'

Smiling, straightening her back. 'No, Klaus,' she says again.

'I love you,' Wiz hears Klaus clearly proclaim, from outside the door. This is followed by ear-splitting silence. And his ears are ringing with it, ringing with Klaus's declaration. What are they doing? Are they kissing? And he charges upstairs, unable to listen to any more. He has heard sufficient, anyway. The evidence is CON-CLU-SIVE.

'Tape-recorder time,' Liz says with artificial cheerfulness. 'You know the score.' He has to speak uninterrupted for fifteen minutes, then she plays back the recording and they analyse it together. 'I want you to tell me about the development of the piano over the last two centuries.'

'Liz, did you listen me?'

'Hear me,' she corrects him. 'Or listen *to* me. But hear is better in this instance. Hearing is an unconscious thing.'

'Hear me. Did you *hear* me?'

'Yes of course. But I don't think you should have said it.'

'It makes me feel good. That I say it.'

'Saying it. Gerund.'

'Please, Liz? Please be serious.'

At the sight of his tender, serious expression she can no longer be jocular. What does she feel? What does she *feel*? Surprised? Grateful? Flattered? Excited? Happy? Confused? Sorry for him? A reciprocal attraction? Later. All to be considered later . . . or maybe not. Aren't things quite complicated enough already?

'Klaus, I don't know what you want me to say back. Whatever it is, I can't say it. I'm married. This is my home, my kitchen you're sitting in now. We're a family. Ben's dead, but we *are* a family.' And even as she says it, a jolt of something, a recognition, acknowledgement, call it what you will, grabs at her unawares, leaving her on the point of decision or understanding. She cannot say what either of these is, but for a flash she is illuminated with it. Then it is gone and is replaced by seeking darkness. Tears come to her eyes and the scar on her forehead becomes livid and raised and begins to irritate her. Turning away from him she rubs at it with the side of her hand.

Briefly he touches her arm in a conciliatory gesture. 'I'm sorry. I have not – I do not wish to upset you. So . . . The piano . . . Prior to the invention of the piano there were already in existence the clavichord and the harpsichord. The harpsichord can be played more louder, more brilliant than the clavichord, however the clavichord it has the greater – expression – and contrast of the tone . . . And so, it was necessary with continuous evolving of composition and more sophistication in style, that a new instrument must be produced, that has more greater possibilities. And thus it is, in Florence, in the year seventeen hundred and nine, a genius with the name Cristofori has produced a "*gravicembalo col piano forte*". This means literal: "a harpsichord with soft and loud." It was, in the effect, the first piano, having hammers instead of . . . Liz? Liz. Please do not to be sad, Liz . . .'

After Ben died Wiz moved up to the attic room, where once the Scalextric had occupied half the floor space. He had always been drawn to this room, with its views across the garden and canal and the wide expanses of sky. In this quaintly-angled room his mind could wander randomly. He could dream. Just the other side of the canal is a large empty site, at one time occupied by a light engineering business. But the three adjoining metal-roofed buildings have been dismantled for years, and periodically planning permission is sought to erect a housing development there. Whenever this happens the local residents unite to protest and campaign vociferously against it, and so far all applications have been refused. Beyond this overgrown wasteland the railway is glimpsed as a broken line behind a screen of trees. The trains chuckle or hurtle past, depending whether they are local or inter-city, every half hour or so, the last one being at 12.10 at night. Sometimes he might be awake; and it offers a soothing rumbling sound as he lies in his bed in the patchy dark, picturing people seated in the carriage compartments, with their own lives, heading off to their own destinations and dramas, for their own reasons. Infinite permutations. A thousand stories. And sometimes, staring out over Port Meadow, to the grazing ponies and piebald cattle, the flying kites and bouncing dogs, the cyclists and walkers, children and adults, he fancies he can see himself, cutting across on his bike; himself in the third person. And to others, *he* is just someone else.

The walls of his room are completely covered: two bird

calendars, sighting charts, posters and photographs: of birds and of films; and a couple of pictures of Winona Ryder. An enlarged photo of a common snipe caught in mid zig-zag flight and taken by himself, framed in glass and clip, hangs over his bed. The duvet and pillow have a navy-and-red diamond pattern, and his door and window frame are painted with red gloss. The floor is scarcely visible beneath the mess of photo albums, scrapbooks, Young Ornithologists' Club magazines, film magazines, files . . . He always seems to have some project on the go, and has just commenced one on the mammals of Great Britain. His previous one was on birds: 'The Breeding Patterns and Inter-relationships in *Passeriformes*'. But lately he's been toying with the idea of becoming a vet when he grows up and is necessarily broadening his horizons. It was his father who put the idea into his head. Before that he wanted to be a professional ornithologist, maybe write books and lecture and all that. For a few months he wanted to be a film director, but Josh told him he wasn't tough enough for the film world, and he should know as his father is a Channel 4 producer. So he reverted to ornithology or possibly zoology.

'You'd earn more as a vet,' his father said.

'Why must it always come down to money?' Wiz said.

'Well most things do in the end,' Alastair replied.

And actually, if it weren't for having to do the sciences, he would be quite sold on the idea.

He opens the window and breathes in the newly-mown grass of next door. Its honeycomb freshness drifts in the air, as though tiny fragments have spiralled upwards and are floating in the atmosphere; and suddenly he is urgent to be outside, to be lying on a quiet spot of the river bank, where nobody can get to him.

The Cherwell Boathouse, at the end of suburban-leafy

Bardwell Road, has a holiday feel to it. The kiosk attached to the separate terrace is already busy with people buying soft drinks and ices. Up on the terrace Japanese and American tourists are snapping the green stretch of river with its dark, cool shadows and overhanging weeping willows. Pulled up on the hard-standing are banana-shaped punts and other assorted boats. Several others are on the water, occupied by hilarity-struck groups with individuals amongst them trying to grapple with the pole and stand up at the same time. Those looking on are busily engaged with their cameras.

'Hi Geoff.'

'Hi Wiz.'

He knows the youth in charge. He's a prefect in the upper sixth. An easy-going sort of guy. So he pays no attention to Wiz hovering about, fiddling with one of the punts (£6 an hour). Preoccupied as he is with the mirthful tourists, one who is in danger of capsizing his craft, his back is turned for long enough for Wiz to untie a punt, push it down the concrete slope into the water, step inside and drift several yards with the flow. When he finally looks round, Wiz's rear view figure could be anyone's.

To start with, until he has covered a safe distance, Wiz tries using the paddles, never having quite mastered a pole before, but these, too, are harder to manipulate than he supposed. The punt is long and the breadth of two people. His arms cannot span both sides and hence it's impossible to use the two paddles simultaneously. The pull of the river is left-biased and the upstream current – towards Marston – quite strong, so he can just manage by using his right paddle and drifting. But he won't get far at this rate, and the obstacles are many – boulders, bridges, keeling trees, branches which form tunnels – reminding him of the St Giles Fair ghost tunnel; spits of land . . . not to mention all the other boats.

By now it's mid-morning, and everyone is out and about

in droves: in their gardens, fishing, walking, sunbathing in the long grass, necking in it, boating. Lazy hazy silver day. Swallows flit past, sweeping insects from the mottled surface of the water. *Swallows and Amazons* by Arthur Ransome used to be his favourite book (a holiday on the Norfolk Broads never measured up to it. He and Ben rowed solidly. Ben was at his bragging worst). After that – even now, actually – it was *Jonathan Livingston Seagull.* He has the video of the film and cannot watch it without shameful tears springing to his eyes as the white bird soars gloriously in perfect ever-higher flight. His throat becomes blocked by an aching node. God he wishes he were a seagull. '. . . A seagull is an unlimited idea of freedom . . . Your whole body from wingtip to wingtip is nothing more than thought itself.'

But he is merely human, and meanwhile he is getting nowhere, and everybody is having to skirt round him as inadvertently he finds himself forming a crossbar with the opposite bank; people are starting to shout and gesticulate. 'Do you think I'm doing this on purpose?' he shouts back. He has no option, and reaching for the pole resting along the floor of the boat, crawls to the rear and tentatively tries to stand up. He succeeds in doing so – with his bottom sticking out awkwardly – and manages to straighten the punt, enabling everyone to pass round him, either side. All smiles now; waving and smiles and cheers. Some of them have picnic hampers with them. In one crowded punt a blonde girl lolls at the back on a pile of cushions, wearing white shorts and a bikini top. God, she's fantastic. Tiny-breasted, but still fantastic. His third ambition, after becoming a vet and sighting a golden eagle, is to kiss a girl and touch her breasts. Or maybe the latter is his fourth ambition. Probably the other will happen first.

His progress in this haphazard, makeshift way is extremely slow and erratic, but so far without mishap. For possibly an hour he keeps going at his snail's pace. Cow parsley has overtaken the bank and fields on the right. On the left the gardens and houses peter out. Then a distressing incident occurs. Two boys on the bank, probably a couple of years younger than himself, have caught a fish and are torturing it, throwing it up and catching it. He can see it twisting and flapping and is sickened.

'Don't do that,' he yells at them, half standing and gesturing with his arms. 'Stop it immediately or I'll report you.'

The punt rocks precariously and he is thrown to his knees against the seat in the middle.

'Oh yeah? Go on then, cunt-face, you do that,' one of them mocks.

'I *will*.' Wiz, temper inflamed, powerless, watching them shaking the fish, whooping noisily and jeering at him: 'Cunt-face. Cunt-face.' And himself drifting towards them, unable to punt quickly away; cheeks burning; eyes watering.

'Here – you can have it.' Laughing, the other boy hurls it towards him, aiming at his head. It soars in an arc through the air, and he ducks; but it misses, falling into the water to float motionless and pop-eyed on the surface.

What do they care about its dying? About *anything* dying? What do they care about anything at all? Some of the boys at his old school were like that. His parents scrimp to send him to Rivers School. Ben never went to public school. If Ben were alive he wouldn't either. They could never have afforded two lots of school fees . . .

Mustering up the dregs of his dignity, driven by the adrenalin of anger, Wiz forces himself to stand up, and for the first time feels properly balanced and stable. Digging the pole firmly into the ground with the expertise of an old hand, he moves the boat away from them. And now he gets into the motion of the whole thing: plunging, drawing up, and plunging again, never allowing his body to be left behind with the action of his arm, feeling his shoulder muscles, his stomach muscles, other muscles he never knew he had, all being put to use. Oh this is marvellous . . . Elation floods through him. He wants to shout out and laugh with it. And now he is making real progress; passes the Victoria Arms pub, or the Vicki Arms as it's known locally . . . Look at me, look at me. I can punt! Time becomes a protracted shimmering pattern of minute insects and diffused green light, and he is light itself, and weightless with freedom; like a bird, like a gull, like a—

His pole is stuck. Just by a small island. In vain he attempts to extricate it, willing it to come up with his tugging, imagining the suction noise it would make; but the punt is veering to the left and the blessed pole is forming a widening 'A' with it towards the island. He can do one thing or the other, but not both. He can retain the punt without the pole, or retain the pole but end up like a monkey stuck up it. Or he can vault onto the island. He has seconds to decide – and opts for the last. Watches the punt drift folornly away like a love-lorn swan.

Robinson Crusoe. *Blue Lagoon* and Brooke Shields. *Castaway*, and Amanda Donahoe. And who amongst his friends didn't fancy one or the other of those women rotten? *Desert Island Discs* . . . And this conjures up an image of his mother listening to it on the radio on a Sunday morning, maintaining a commentary along with the choices of music: Oh God that is *so* naff . . . Listen to that would you? . . . Doesn't he have any taste at all? . . . OK, he's vindicated himself with the Saint Saëns . . . Let's guess what the luxury will be . . .

Dudley Moore had been interviewed once, he remembers. Dudley Moore gives him hope because he isn't tall or macho, but he's made it.

And what about his mother? Liz will more than likely be starting to worry. He didn't tell her he was even going out. He was so upset, he just went.

Now here he is lying on the elliptical little island with its scrubby grass, and lapping greenish-brown water patterned with silver and black whorls and slivers of fallen willow leaves. Birdsong in the trees. He can distinguish each different voice in the block of sound: a series of musical 'seeps' from a song thrush, the fluted blackbird melody, the weak, descending trill of a meadow pipit and – if he is not mistaken – a summer visitor, a warbler. At first he assumes it to be a reed warbler, with its bouts of lively chirruping interspersed with mimicry of the other birds; then with rising excitement, he realises it is more probably the rarer marsh warbler, because of the way it lingers brilliantly on its notes.

He lies back, cushioning his head on his arms, drifting into a semi-sleep of amorphous thoughts and images impregnated with balmy, moist warmth and insect-humming, water-plipping, bird-melodious sound. Dreams – or is it a dream – of his aunt and her gleaming skin. Tomorrow he'll be seeing her at the sculpture exhibition. His father's younger sister. His father then appears before him, a perplexed expression in his smoky eyes. Splendid, he says in his deep, grave tone. Perfectly splendid. It's his stock word. His father shutting himself away in his Lair. This Sunday they'll have the entire day together, and he wonders what they'll talk about, each seeking to find a common denominator. Whilst he loves and admires his father, he is a little in awe of him. Alastair in his withdrawn mood can seem a little austere.

And now Wiz broods over the implications of his mother's and Klaus's affair. Above all, he loves his mother. Will there be a divorce? Will she marry Klaus? Where does he himself come into the equation? In his mind he treads his own future with uncertain footsteps. And whom would he live with? Impossible to imagine Klaus as a stepfather, or being in the same house as him. Klaus is *weird*. And what would his father do? He has never seen the slightest hint of violence in Alastair's character. He doesn't even raise his voice, but will reprimand or subdue with a single withering look. But Wiz has seen enough films and read enough headlines to see what jealousy does. Husband murders wife in jealous frenzy . . . It must not happen. It must *not* happen. And it is for him to find a solution.

For the moment, however, a more imminent problem presses. How is he to get home, marooned here as he is on this island? And overhead a pregnant cloud is swelling darkly.

In the end he cadges a lift from a bunch of foreigners. There are four of them, a couple about his parents' age, and two kids. He flags them down, waving his arms. They all look as gloomy as Charon. The girl's face is blotchy as though she has been crying. The man punting is immensely hairy, his eyes are so close-set he reminds Wiz of a Cyclops. His eyebrows form a single hirsute ridge without a break. It turns out they are from the former Yugoslavia, and own a fast-food restaurant in Headington. He knows it actually. They've had bad news from home, the father tells Wiz. His sister, a victim of Zagreb, has just died in hospital.

So they've got every reason to look gloomy, now he knows this. And a war, so remote from his insulated world, relegated to the middle pages of newspapers he rarely reads, suddenly loses its impersonality and looms into the foreground. He does not know what to say, mumbles, 'How dreadful,' and gazes fixedly at the bank and the grazing cows until they arrive back at the boathouse.

He sort of merges with them as they climb out, hoping the boat lad doesn't spot him, says a rushed good luck, and runs off to reclaim his bike padlocked to a tree in the lane, opposite the Dragon School playing fields.

In twenty-four hours Ben would have been seventeen. He would have been taking his A levels this term as he was a year ahead. He would have had driving lessons for his birthday present.

5

Saturday has arrived. Alastair is the first up. He had woken in the middle of the night with his heart racing, and turning towards the clock had seen the luminous green digits flashing 2.07. His heart slowed to its normal pace, but after that he barely slept. If he did doze it was to slip into an unpleasant twilight domain from which he would forcibly drag himself. Wakefulness was a state hardly preferable. He wondered what it would be like to emerge from sleep one morning without the weight of concrete in his head. He thought, but could not be certain, that his wife was awake. She was too unnaturally still and silent. The seam of space between them was too deliberate. Were she genuinely asleep her legs would not have been so neatly together. One would have been askew, or straying towards him or even curled away from him; but he had the impression in the darkness that she was in a tense pencil line; could sense her eyes wide open. And what Hieronymus Bosch horrors might she be reliving that he had been spared and – however hard he tried – could never fully imagine? He had been presented with the frightful tidings (the two policemen arriving at his surgery mid-morning, exactly two years ago). She and Wiz had had the actual experience. The scar on her forehead was constant testimony. Suddenly, lying there, he perceived her shorn head as symbolic: a prisoner doing penance. But he was also a prisoner, with this block of concrete inside him that he could not think would ever go. And he no longer knew what was expected of him. By nature he was introspective and guarded; a shy, proud man with high standards and principles. He was hopeless at dealing with complex emotional situations; timid of probing and stirring and thus provoking changes which he would not know how to deal with. And here he was floundering, his roles of husband and father no longer clearly defined.

I miss Ben. I miss Ben.

He would have liked to have stroked Liz but could not be sure, groping in the dark, where his hand would alight. If she were asleep, then she would wake up. And if she were awake and his hand were to find itself inadvertently on her buttock, then she would flinch away. Whenever he touched her, her flesh seemed to resile. He felt starved of touch and of love. He recalled the days when they used to bath together and she would wash his hair, turning it into an erotic ritual, massaging the shampoo with a strong sensuous motion into his scalp, then working it over his entire body; and himself tilting back his head and closing his eyes as she showered out the soap, slicking his hair back from his forehead with the edge of her hand. It often ended with their making love. And the water would slop over the side of the bath as their legs fought with the taps.

But today – this day – these protagonists, who bore scant resemblance to those of another era, would drive to Wolvercote as a family. To visit the one missing.

They hardly discussed their son at all with any consequentiality. They never told each other if they had been to the cemetery on their own. If ever he came upon Liz sifting through photos, she would hurriedly put them away. Likewise, if he were reading letters Ben had sent from summer camp, or old essays or school reports, he would thrust them back in the drawer as soon as she came into the room. It was almost as if their grief was competitive, he realised, as the clock showed another hour had passed. By their mutual reticence, each was in effect claiming his sorrow as his alone. And the longer this endured the harder it became to cross over to the other's territory.

For perhaps the first time Alastair recognised and understood the dangers of what was happening but was powerless to intercede.

And yes, there dwells in him a latent seed of recrimination which he does his best to suppress. Hasn't she (haven't they both) suffered enough without exacerbating matters? He has entirely forgotten that in the heat of the moment he levelled at her, 'I told you to check the tyres.' In his mind any slight blame he may or may not feel (and mostly he simply feels compassion for her, for them all; but cannot communicate it because nowadays she seems only to rebuff him) – in his mind this slight blame has never been voiced. As for the caution itself: 'Don't forget to check the tyres,' he always said this as a matter of course whenever she drove any distance. 'Don't forget to check the tyres.' Uttered in the same breath as, 'Drive carefully. Wear your seatbelts.' Never dreaming of . . . After all, the chances of anything . . .

So Alastair's reasoning goes. On and on. Then his reflections will naturally turn to Ben himself. Ben was exuberant. There was no other word for it. And irrepressible. But he knew when to be sensible also. And he could grasp a fact immediately; could debate and argue a point with the maturity and intellectualism of an adult. He had shared his father's love of old cars, chess and tennis. They would watch the rugger on TV together, yelling out at the same moments and leaping up and down noisily in their chairs. During Eights Week, or 'Bumps' as it was known, on the last day, the Saturday, he and Ben cheered madly as the boats representing the different colleges deliberately tried to bump their opponents. Wiz kept his binoculars trained on sky. This Saturday it has come round again, coinciding with the date of his son's birth and death. He will cycle to Christchurch Meadow and watch some of it on his own. Homage to Ben, rather than the rowers.

He'd probably have been starting to shave . . . His voice would be a young man's. That girl he was keen on – what was her name? – would have been replaced a dozen times. I'd have been giving him a driving lesson today . . .

The knife of dawn glinted into their bedroom. For a moment Alastair's vision was so clear: himself in the passenger seat of the Golf, his son behind the wheel . . . And they eased away from the kerb, and off they set, limping down Southmoor Road.

A small choking sound rose from the back of his throat. He got up then, picked up his tracksuit from the floor and pulled it on, and went downstairs.

Six o'clock on this Saturday morning. He lets Lowry into the garden, and while the dog is peeing quickly slips through the gate, shutting it behind him. Inspects his Austin Healey despondently, rubbing a map of bird mess with his handkerchief. The city is still somnolent. The weather looks uncertain. Would it be wrong to snatch a quick game of tennis before going to the cemetery? He could be back by 10.30. He ponders over it as he trudges back indoors, stroking his stubbled chin thoughtfully.

There's no right or wrong. It's how I feel. Do I *feel* like playing tennis? It'd probably do me good.

He projects himself, imagines himself jigging on the spot to receive the ball, thwacking it. Yes, he decides. He'll call his regular partner in a couple of hours' time. In fact playing tennis brings him close to Ben, restores the link, reminds him of when they played together.

He ambles over to the dresser, where the coffee's kept, and something there catches his attention. A fan. He lifts it up and opens it out. Crafted of sandalwood, musky-sweet-smelling and with black silk tassels, it seems an exotic and useless thing in the humdrum context of their untidy kitchen. It is very delicate, with its cut-out design on each tapering segment. He fingers the tassels and holds it to his nostrils, breathing in its aroma: exciting, faintly decadent, hinting of the Orient and of massage parlours. Not that he would know. Is it Liz's? Why would she buy something like this? Liz, with her schoolgirl's short socks and floaty mid-calf skirts, her total lack of interest in fashion and frivolity, is not the sort for parasols and fans. Although for the past couple of weeks there has been a subtle change. Now he comes to think of it.

'Klaus gave it to me,' she says, suddenly and soundlessly manifested before him; thick hair sticking up in black spikes, body wrapped in a grubby, patterned kimono; feet bare and bony.

He puts it down as though caught out. 'What made him do that?'

'I don't know.' She gives a dismissive shrug. Too late, she regrets her statement. Coming upon him like that, after a night when she had lain awake and knew he had also – yet he had not tried to comfort her – she had the urge to hurt him. She wanted to make him jealous; to show him that someone cared about her enough to give her something beautiful and totally useless. A second's defiance, a second's bravado; sped. And she feels obliged to make light of it, afraid of what he might construe; consequently feels guilty towards Klaus, that she is trivialising both the gift and the rather touching little scene when he gave it to her.

'He probably bought a job lot for all his girlfriends and had one left over.'

She goes over to where her husband is standing with an expression that is either lost or aloof – she cannot be sure which – and carelessly chucks the fan in a drawer of the dresser, along with the sieves, candles and cling wrap. He observes her with a pensive frown. Her eyes are puffy, the pouches beneath them enlarged. Her skin has that look about it, a dry pallor, that would indicate she has scarcely slept.

'Coffee time.' She bustles around, suddenly hyperactive, doing everything, pouring parrot seed into the Archduke's container and opening the cage door, filling the kettle then shaking out some dried dog feed from the pack for Lowry.

'I thought I might play a spot of tennis before . . . Would you mind?'

'Why should I mind?' Liz can hear the terseness in her own voice. It belies her real feelings; in fact she is close to tears.

She pours the water into the cafetière and pushes down the plunger.

'We could have coffee in the garden,' he says. 'I'll take everything out.' He gathers up mugs, spoons, sugar, the milk jug, and takes everything outside on a tray, setting it down on the uneven stones. She follows with the cafetière and two cushions, and they sit side by side on the metal chairs, which are badly in need of a coat of white paint. The barge moored on the opposite bank still has its curtains pulled. The sun is pale and cold, a breeze tweeking at the tiny hairs on her bare lower arms. She rubs the goose bumps there, and then rubs one foot against the opposite calf.

'Are you cold?'

'A bit.'

'I know . . .' He disappears indoors and reappears with a tablecloth which he drapes around her. 'There. Better?'

'Yes. Thanks.' She smiles at him, sinking her neck into her blue gingham surplice, finger fluttering first to the corner of her mouth then instinctively to her forehead.

He hesitates and then takes her hand. And nearly, in this moment of intimacy, says to her: 'I'd have been giving him his first lesson behind the driving wheel today.' He *so* nearly says it, but being pre-emptive, doesn't; in case she should misinterpret it and it should seem as though he is blaming her. The words linger titillatingly on his tongue and can only be banished by his severing their physical contact and releasing her hand. And thus the moment of intimacy is lost.

'I expect Chris is feeling apprehensive about this evening,' he says of his brother-in-law. 'It's pretty sad, isn't it? Six years' training as an architect down the tubes.'

'He seems really happy.'

'*Seems* being the operative word. Who knows.'

'Yes. Well OK, who knows,' she agrees quietly, managing to quell a surging upwards of tears, getting up slowly and deliberately – 'I'm rather cold' – and going inside with her head very high.

He is left with the usual sense of rebuff, the sense he has failed her, just as everyone has failed her all her life and he had resolved not to; the sense that she dislikes him and that this is what it's all about. Her tight expression, the mask of taut skin across her cheekbones, her short morning-spiky hair, all seem to ward him off.

There are times when he feels like a man who has nothing to look forward to, who has been robbed of his future as a Happy Family Man.

I *will* go away. Maybe New Zealand . . .

While Wiz is doing his paper rounds and Alastair is working up a sweat on the tennis court, Liz goes into Ben's room and sits on the bed. It's more or less as it was: posters of football icons; of John McEnroe scowling demonically behind his tennis racquet; Sharon Stone's seductive blue gaze from the wardrobe door. The wardrobe is still full of his clothes. The cupboards above house his chemistry sets.

She can't bring herself to get rid of anything. The tracksuit is still stained at the knees. The trainers still have mud on the soles. His rugger ball, skateboard and tennis racket are in a corner of the room in a yellow plastic box

He had called her Ma. He was affectionately disrespectful towards her. He made her laugh. He could also infuriate her when he was showing off or trying to outwit her.

'I pity your wife when you grow up and get married,' she said to him once. 'I shall certainly side with your mother-in-law.'

'I'll be a brilliant husband. I'll make my wife laugh,' he said. 'And I'll make sure I don't have a mother-in-law.'

'How will you arrange that?'

'I won't go out with a girl unless she's motherless. Orphaned would be even better.'

'Horror,' she said, taking a swipe at him then attempting to hug him. He ducked both.

She had never come across a boy who was so completely confident, self-assured and self-sufficient. He did not seem to need her in the same way as Wiz. He did not really seem to need anyone.

Wiz is moody and overimaginative, sensitive and shy, endearingly odd, impulsive and not always rational; immature on the one hand and old on the other; eager to please and overtly affectionate. He had been eclipsed by Ben. There was always fraternal friction.

She keeps thinking that if she hadn't oversteered, if she had gone *into* the spin instead of fighting it . . .

She misses Ben's pranks, his cleverness and quick repartee; recalls how they would pore over *Innovations* magazine when it arrived sandwiched in the *Sunday Times*, giggling together over some of the inventions. 'Who on earth would use that? Can you imagine wearing that? How do they even begin to think up some of these things?'

Was I a good mother to him? Am I to Wiz? she often

asks herself. The trouble is not having had a yardstick; it makes it difficult for her to judge. There has been no one whose example she could follow, no one to give her advice. Her behaviour and reactions are all instinctive. It's a miracle she's not more screwed up. Her mother, who died when Liz was three, is a blur. Her father, an international businessman, regarded the little girl as a liability. His second wife did also; particularly when they started a new family. She migrated from one set of grandparents to another and then boarding school. One summer night, when she was twelve, the car that her father and stepmother were in left the sharp bend of a mountain road near Cannes and she never saw them again (in the slow-motion seconds of horror when her car was whirling before landing upside down, she thought of her father). Her half-siblings went to live with their maternal grandmother. She remained with hers until she, too, died. She used to go home with her English teacher for some exeats and weekends, when no one else could have her. This forty-five-year-old spinster taught the fifteen-year-old girl female sex in a fumbling inexperienced way. Liz could neither refuse nor resent her, after her initial shock, because this woman also taught her love. The teacher genuinely loved her. Without love how could she have got by? Where would she have gone? This woman imparted to Liz her own passion for the arts and culture, introduced her to musicians and actors who were friends of hers, took her on as her protégée, and encouraged her to dance. From her the girl learned not to be forever embittered, not to lose a sense of optimism, that there is always something; someone. Small reward in return, therefore, her immature teenage body beneath the older woman's frightened lips and fingers, and the tentative guiding of her hand over that craving uncherished body.

She has told nobody about this, not Alastair, not a single soul. She doesn't want other people to hate the

English teacher, who was dear and kind, confused and afraid; to accuse her of wickedness; of violating, abusing and corrupting a young girl; to express any kind of negative opinion about something they can never hope to understand.

Alastair said to her when they got engaged: 'I know it's hard to provide everything the other person needs within a relationship, but I hope I can supply the main components.' In a card she came across recently, he had written in poetic prose: I should like to parole your thoughts. Pace up and down in a moth's shoes with paper-thin tread.

They drive to the cemetery, Liz holding flowers cut from the garden.

'I could've cycled,' grumbles Wiz. 'I could've gone on to see Frederick. Now I'll have to go back home first.'

'The whole point is to go together,' Liz says, swivelling her head to look at him in the back.

'But we would've been together. I'd've met you there. We could've met by the chapel. You know – the chapel.'

'Stop arguing, will you,' Alastair says, and he shuts up instantly, pouting. Liz swivels back again. Tense-jawed silence presides for the rest of the short journey, until they arrive at the cemetery. Its imposing wrought-iron gates lend it the air of the entrance to a stately home. Wiz has always wondered about the significance of the gold-painted cows in the centre of the gates, which somehow seem incongruous.

They park opposite the chapel and get out. He trails behind his parents; his mother, head bent, clutching the flowers: iris, campanula, honesty and bellis. His father walks with his long lope determinedly ahead. 'Wolvercote' cemetery is somewhat of a misnomer, being a mile or so from Wolvercote itself – where Wiz attends Rivers School – but although the traffic from the main road is clearly audible, it is somehow not obtrusive and an aura of tranquility prevails. There's a hopeful feel about the place, or so Wiz thinks. He cannot reconcile the park-like grounds, specimen trees, neat, intersecting gravel paths, blue sky and birdsong with death. The euphemistic language on the headstones doesn't correspond with decomposing flesh and gouged-out skulls. And Tolkien is buried here, in a joint plot with his wife. He had been the English professor at Merton. The headstone's wording is pragmatic, giving nothing but names and dates, no hint of the magic this man wielded with his pen. On the grave are tubs of heather that endure throughout the seasons. And nowhere are to be heard the echoes of Bilbo Baggins and Gandalf calling to each other.

The cemetery is a busy place this sunny Saturday, with figures dotted about tending their loved ones. There is a new grave with freshly heaped soil and piled with flowers in Cellophane, in the same row as Ben's. Who has just been bereaved? Liz wonders as she lays her own flowers on Ben's grave. 'A much-loved son and brother. We remember your laughter,' is inscribed on the headstone. At the funeral a white-hot sun had glared down; she heard again Ben's voice in her head: 'Shit, what's happening?' as the car went into its spin.

Wiz is thinking, In a hundred years it'll be grassed over and forgotten. Who was he? people will say. How young, how sad . . . He can almost hear them. What will people look like in a hundred years' time? He glances at his father, stooped in silent contemplation. Again it crosses his mind, does he wish it had been me? His mother is nervous. He can tell from her stance, the twist of her body. It's all this enforced togetherness. It's farcical, like on New Year's Eve, when you all have to be jolly at the same time even if you don't feel like it. And at precisely midnight there's the kissing lark, and blowing trumpet things and being stupid.

For what purpose, this combined visit? If it is supposed to draw them close, to make them remember, then why are they all standing separately. Why doesn't his father take his mother's hand or put his arm round her? It's his father's fault his mother is having an affair. He can never ascribe any blame to Liz.

And then, as he is trying hard to conjure up an image of his brother, and to think generous thoughts, from overhead comes a loud 'Cor-lee. Cor-lee', followed by a series of trills; and looking up he sees a curlew in low flight westwards towards the river, the long arc of its bill clearly visible. He longs to say something, but refrains from doing so. They would not be interested. It's Ben's day.

The warmth of a hand covering his suddenly, fingers binding with his, massaging his knuckles. And his mother's dense black eyes shed tacit understanding.

'It's definite,' Wiz tells Frederick, who has been given permission for a twenty-minute break by the landlord now business has quietened. They sit at a table away from the few straggling diners, eating ploughmans. Wiz pushes his onions onto Frederick's plate as they make him sick.

'Well, you can't do anything about it, mate,' Frederick says, popping one into his mouth. '– How can you possibly not like pickled onions? – You'll just have to let them get on with it.'

He removes his glasses to inspect whether the black blob on his chunk of bread is a fly or a bit off the tree. Without them he's not bad looking, Wiz observes. It's a shame about the acne. That must be awful. He hopes it doesn't happen to him. Most of the boys in the sixth form seem to have it; no wonder the girls are more interested in the masters. All of the older boys Wiz knows seem to be doing a gap year.

Frederick's saving to go to Zaire to study the wildlife there, particularly the monkeys, before attending university to read zoology. That's how they became friendly in the first place, when they discovered a mutual interest in animals.

'A bit of twig,' remarks Frederick, tweezering it with his fingers from the bread.

'I *can* do something,' Wiz says.

'Oh yeah? What'll you do – murder the guy?' Frederick says, the ghost of a smile lightening his dour features.

'Oh no, nothing like that, of course not,' Wiz replies, blinking seriously at his plate and wiping round the buttery edge of it then licking his finger.

'So it's "watch this space" time then,' Frederick says.

'I guess so.'

For a few minutes they eat without speaking, then Frederick says, 'You remember the other day I was starting to say something had happened to me – and then I had to go?'

'Yes,' lies Wiz.

'Well, I saw my father. I mean I haven't seen him since I was seven or eight. He walked out on us. Anyway, he came into the pub. Up to the bar to be served. God, it felt really odd. I can tell you, I really freaked out. Of course I recognised him straight away, but he didn't know *me*. Well I've changed a lot and he hasn't much. I was only a kid, so of course I looked completely different. And I didn't wear glasses then. So I served him and I never said a word. I didn't let on. It freaked me.'

Wiz is agog with astonishment. 'But why didn't you say something? How could you serve him, I mean pour him his drink and everything, and not *say*? I couldn't've kept quiet. I'd've been bursting.'

'Well I'm older than you, aren't I? I've learned a few things over the years,' Frederick says in his pukka Oxford drawl, and with a note of superiority which makes Wiz proud to be his friend.

'He was a bastard,' he goes on. 'He dumped us. My mother, and myself. Not a card. Not a penny. Nothing. So it was like a test that night. Seeing if I could stick it out, not telling him who I was. When he left I was shaking. But I felt good in myself, like I'd punished him even though he didn't know I had. *I* had the secret satisfaction . . . You can't do what he did. You just can't walk out like that as if your family doesn't exist.'

Wiz digests all this attentively. 'So what did your mother say when you told her?'

'I didn't tell her. I wasn't going to upset her. He's not worth it. She's worked her guts out to support us all on her own.'

'What does she do?'

'She owned several employment agencies, which she sold a while ago. Now she's taking things easy. She deserves to for a bit. She plays a lot of tennis.'

'My father plays tennis . . . Your mother – what does she look like?'

'She's something. She's really good-looking. Well I know she's my mother, but she is. You must meet her . . . Want to go and see *Before Sunrise* at the Phoenix this evening? It's "15". I could get you in. Julie Delpy's in it.'

'That'd be great . . .' Wiz is preoccupied, still thinking about Frederick's mother. An idea is taking shape. '. . . Oh no, I can't. I've got to go out with my parents somewhere. To an exhibition of my uncle's sculpture.'

Actually he doesn't have to go. They're quite good in that respect, his parents. They let him do more or less what he wants; don't insist on his going everywhere with them. Except to the cemetery today; big things like that. But he wants to accompany them this evening. He wants to see his aunt. Julie Delpy's cute. But his aunt is for real.

* * *

The gallery is in the High, one of those chic, neutral places with a golden strip-wood floor and white walls. Colour is provided by the paintings, sculpture and ceramics, all carefully selected not to be too avant-garde for the Oxford palate, but sufficiently different to invite comment. The room is already fairly full when they arrive. A thin girl in a black Chinese-style top and pants and heavy black eye make-up is near the door as they come in, handing round a tray of twirly-looking canapés. She goes to Rivers School – they take girls in the sixth forms – and he knows her from the ornithology club, which has all of eight members.

He stares down in embarrassment when he sees her, but she greets him in a friendly way, not in the least patronising: 'Hello Wiz,' smiling at the same time.

'Hi Emma,' he says back, adding, 'Are you working here?'

'No. Just helping out. It's Dad's gallery. That's my brother pouring out wine at the table.'

'It's a really cool place.'

'I know.'

'I saw a curlew today in flight,' he tells her impulsively, blushing.

'Did you? Where?'

'Oh. Well, actually the cemetery. You know. Wolvercote cemetery.' He wishes he hadn't said anything. Why did he say anything. Now she'll ask what he was doing there.

Then he spots his aunt and uncle; his parents are weaving their way in that direction. His aunt stands out a mile.

'I must see –' He leaves the sentence unfinished and bolts off, composing himself as he approaches.

Nita, short for Anita, is ten years younger than her brother and Wiz is quite simply dazzled by her. Tall and auburn-haired, she is a tantalising and teasing woman with only one similarity to Alastair that Wiz can see: the ability to raise one eyebrow. On her it looks incredibly sexy. Everything about her oozes promise: the languid way she sits and crosses her legs, or strokes long strands of hair away from her face, her generous laugh, her strong teeth, her heavy-lidded eyes, the way she is so tactile, always resting her hand on you with its long fingers and long pink nails. Her air of glamour and sophistication is utterly un-Oxford. She seems to bask in her womanliness, flaunt and exaggerate it, flirting in a manner that is frowned upon nowadays; and anyone observing how she acts and behaves would probably dismiss her as an air-head. In fact she is a paediatrician at the John Radcliffe. Her husband is several inches shorter than her, a hyperactive man with a jaunty grin and restless eyes continually on the move from one target to another, and he talks with machine-gun rapidity. He is fiercely intelligent and assumes everyone else to be also, obsessed with Caesar and with Napoleon, and pours all his manic tendencies into sculpting.

'How lovely to see you all,' Nita gushes in her deep voice, hugging them in turn. 'And my favourite nephew too.' She tweaks his cheek playfully after she's kissed him, letting her finger linger there and blowing a further kiss at him for good measure, pursing her lips forward. He catches a glimpse of sleek, tanned thigh through the slit of her skirt; and his penis, which has lately been demonstrating a wayward will of its own, becomes warm and swells, rubbing against his boxer shorts.

'Glass of wine, everybody,' says Chris, leading them over to the table.

'It's an impressive turnout,' Alastair comments.

'Well it's a freebie, isn't it?' the other man says, peering across the room to some newcomers entering. 'But when the wine is drunk and the nibbles nibbled, people's pockets are suddenly remarkably distant in relation to their hands.

I've sold one, though, the girl with the cello. Let me show you round.'

'Darling, let them get their wine first,' Nita says.

'Oh yes, of course.'

'And Wiz –' she turns to him. 'Will you have some?'

'Yes please.'

He glances at his parents to see their reaction, but Alastair doesn't seem to have heard, and his mother is standing in her ballerina's pose, wearing a distant smile. She has on a white trouser outfit, which contrasts well with the little dark cap of her head. He wants to tell her she looks beautiful, not in the same way as Nita; but in her own special way she does. And he mumbles it to her as a glass of white wine is handed to him: 'You look pretty, Mum.'

'What a lovely thing to say,' she says back.

'Now for a grand tour,' announces Chris. 'I tell you, it beats architecture any day. There's none of that frustration, and always being at the mercy of someone else's whims . . . Now this is a praying mantis. I had great fun doing this one from a photograph. Do you like it? No doubt you know that the female bites off her mate's head after the act of passion. A rather literal case of love making one lose one's head . . . This one is rather special, don't you think?' He pauses in front of a graceful bronze tree standing about three feet high, with three arched branches, two having delicate leaves attached to them, the third yielding a single disproportionately large and beautifully formed apple.

'Splendid. Perfectly splendid,' Wiz, who has gone ahead, hears his father say. Something has arrested his eye further on. 'Excuse me, excuse me . . .'

He pushes his way past people to get to it, over the other side of the room. And there it is, in life-size bronze, faithful in every detail. He has no need to see the title on the plaque: 'Golden Eagle'. He crouches down to examine it more closely. Even the head and nape are lightened with gold as they should be, and the tail feathers black-banded. The massive, lethal beak is slightly parted, and above it the eyes gleam sharply. It is brilliant. His uncle is brilliant. Wiz's throat thickens and he reaches out to stroke the model.

'It's great, isn't it?' a voice says softly, and, startled, he turns to find Emma there.

He straightens up. 'It's fantastic. I mean it's my favourite bird, it really is.'

'Are you coming to the meeting on Wednesday?'

Wednesdays at 2.30 is when they have their club meetings, held in Mr Hutchinson's study. He's the English master and runs the ornithology club.

'I don't know,' Wiz says morosely. 'It's exams. I'll have to look at the timetable.'

His family catch up with him. 'Fergus died a few days ago,' Nita is saying. 'It's so sad. Dogs have such a short life expectancy.'

'So do some adults,' comes Alastair's curt response.

And after that there is a great deal of apologising and gushing, and they all split up in different directions just as Wiz is about to ask his uncle about the eagle.

'My sister can be so stupid. She was always tactless,' Alastair says in the car back home.

'She didn't mean it . . . You remember they're coming back for a snack, don't you? Wiz darling, I'll give you yours on a tray. You can eat while you revise. I've hardly seen you revise over half term.'

'I have. Lots. And we've been doing it at school as well. The whole time. Most bloody afternoons.'

'Don't swear,' Alastair says.

'Well we have. You don't know what it's like.'

'Of course I do. What do you think I did at school?'

He is in a mood. He wants – needs – to be by himself, to dive into his Lair and mope there on his own, remember his son and games of chess. For some reason the printed wording of the cards they sent out to well-wishers comes back to him: 'Liz, Alastair and Oscar Miller want to thank you for the understanding and warm sympathy you have expressed at the tragic loss of our beloved Ben . . .' And now he must be subjected to several hours with his posturing sister and her husband, who, although Alastair likes him – it was he who introduced Chris to his sister in the first instance – he can only take in small doses, and this evening not at all.

'I can eat with you and then do my revision,' Wiz says. 'I can do that can't I?' The thought of his aunt downstairs for the entire evening whilst he's stuck upstairs is more than he can stand. At this rate he might as well have gone to the Phoenix.

'You heard your mother.'

'We-ell,' Liz wavers.

'Wiz, sometimes adults just want to be by themselves,' his father says, reverting to his Moderate Voice.

'Oh, so that's the real reason.'

'Both. Both are the reasons.'

'Don't be down, darling.' His mother stretches out her arm behind her and feels for his face; leaves her hand resting on his knee.

'I hate exams.'

Back to school on Tuesday, and straight into them. His school's half term is different from everyone else's. Tuesday to Tuesday. It's a cheat really. They end up with a week instead of ten days.

'I know,' says Liz.

'I mean I could just have one course with you. And then you'd be by yourself and I'd go and work,' he says brightly. 'You're always talking about compromise. Well it'd be a compromise, wouldn't it?'

His mother starts to laugh. Even his father does. They've

relented. He imagines his aunt next to him at the table, sensing the warmth radiating from her, smelling her perfume, brushing his leg against hers accidentally. And then he could go to his room. And then after that, he would revise.

'You're taking me to Symonds Yat tomorrow, don't forget,' he says to Alastair.

'How could I? We'll have get up at the crack of dawn. Leave the second you return from your paper round. No time for learning about life's secrets from Bert. You won't have time to linger.'

Is there a smile in his voice? There is. Wiz catches him smiling in the driving mirror. And his father's arm snakes backwards too, to ruffle his hair, and then briefly collides with his mother's hand on his knee. For a moment there is accidental contact, and Wiz observes as his father's fingers seem to hesitate before moving away and attaching themselves once more to the steering wheel. Presently his mother's hand disappears also, and he senses the sadness in its gentle removal.

For a few seconds they had almost been a normal family. It keeps nearly happening, and then a guillotine blade descends, severing the moment at its inception.

But – only a few hours and the day with all its connotations will be over. And the one that will replace it, the one after that and after that: what about them? And Wiz has yet to develop his plan.

6

Bonding, Liz called it. 'You never do anything on your own with him,' she said to Alastair. She herself had lessons to plan for a new student. The girl was a Japanese graduate with an interest in nineteenth-century English and American literature. It meant routing around the dusty upper shelves for Dickens and Trollope, George Eliot, Henry James, the Brontë sisters . . . Skimming through them to remind herself at least of some of the secondary characters and even the protagonists; jotting notes for her reference. She would probably cheat and resort to using the introductions at the beginning of the books as an instant, potted source. Would the girl appreciate Edgar Allan Poe? That could liven things. Monsters, murder and madness. And speaking of the latter, Klaus, upon learning she would be on her own, said he might call round. He refused to be dissuaded, and Liz was both exasperated and a little amused. It was all very nineteenth-century and appropriate, she thought: herself having an admirer. It was something rather to relish. It warmed her. It did no harm.

At last, ten miles short of Monmouth, there is a sign off the A40 to Symonds Yat East.

'For God's sake, do we want East or West?' Alastair says.

'I'm not sure,' mutters Wiz. He hates the way his father drives, has got himself all tense, clenching his teeth and gripping his seat every time they draw close to the car in front or swing out to overtake. He's always in a sweat by the end of a long journey. Nobody knows about his fear of being in a car.

'We'll take pot luck then,' Alastair says, and veers sharply left. 'I must say, the traffic hasn't been too bad, considering . . . You're very quiet there. You OK?'

'Yes, fine.'

'I don't know why we couldn't simply have gone to Farmoor. There're birds by the thousands there.'

'That's not the point. The point isn't for it to be easy. The point of a sighting is to see something uncommon.'

'You told me a hen harrier was seen at Farmoor.'

'That was Otmoor. Farmoor was a pair of short-eared owls.'

'Whatever.'

'Dad, these are *breeding peregrines* we're going to see. It's the largest British falcon. I mean you can't compare them. A hen harrier or a short-eared owl are great to spot, but they're more widespread. Anyway we go to Otmoor and Farmoor with the school club.'

'OK, you win.'

To Alastair a bird is a bird. But he has to admit the scenery is starting to be interesting. A series of small roads lead to an iron bridge straddling the Wye, and just past it, at a fork, is a sign for Yat Rock.

'That's it.' Wiz sits up excitedly. 'We want to go up there.'

The narrow lane climbs steeply, cleaving through the forested escarpment, then levels out.

'How did you know about this place?' Alastair asks, turning into one of the car parks.

'Everyone knows.'

They get out and make towards the forest site.

'Do you want me to carry anything?' Alastair asks, glancing over at his encumbered son. The boy's expression is earnest and eager.

'You wouldn't drop anything?'

'Cheeky.'

'You could take my camera, maybe.' He hoists it off his head and passes it over, leaving him with a small rucksack and his binoculars.

'What's in the rucksack?'

'My Walkman. Spare film. Notepad. Pen. Reference book. Compass. And a bar of white chocolate.'

'You're a case, know that?' his father says, giving him one of his more wholehearted hair ruffles.

'Want a piece?' Wiz breaks off a chunk and offers it to him.

'You know I strongly disapprove.'

But he's grinning, and in front of him Wiz makes a show of biting into it.

Alastair is beginning to be glad he came, despite the hordes of people with the same idea. Discreet wooden signs point in various, baffling directions. He feels like Moses in the Wilderness. His son heads determinedly past the log cabin selling refreshments, and its queues: mostly intense-looking hiker-types; bearded, earthily masculine men and solid-calved women. They seem to occupy a lot of space with their brimming health and hearty voices. Dogs strain at the end of their leads to get to one another.

'We could have brought Lowry.' Alastair thinks he's not as fit as he should be; trying to keep pace with his son – along the sharply climbing track, over the tiny footbridge, following signs to Yat Rock, and Peregrines. He has never seen Wiz like this before: authoritative, purposeful and animated. Even bossy, which he finds quite funny. It is a novelty for him to see this other perspective of his son.

For the first time it strikes him their characters are not unalike. Both shy, both dreamers, both sensitive with a stubborn streak. It is their interests that differ. Whereas he and Ben shared similar interests, Ben's *character* – his humour, his sharpness – was more like Liz's. When there were four of them the interaction between them was a constant, unconsidered weaving in and out of similarities and disparities fusing as a unified whole.

They arrive at the top: a natural stronghold of hewn cliff rising above the valley and river, which loops around it in an ox-bow. Volunteers from the RSPB man a pair of telescopes fixed to the protective high stone wall and trained on the massive Coldwell Rocks towering over the gorge. The sun bounces off the white rock face. The valley is so lush, so deep a blue-green. The meadows are peppered with buttercups. And all at once Alastair remembers: he came here as a child. He had been – what – eight or nine? His father had brought him here. The place hadn't been nearly so crowded. There were no telescopes. But the view – this is unchanged. And, in fact, over the years a photographic image of this view has occasionally, and mysteriously, appeared before him and he would wonder: where was it? When did I go there? With whom? It was *here*. How very odd.

He feels quite weak with nostalgia, gripped in the powerfully evocative hold of reminiscence. It filters back to him in stray threads. His mother was pregnant with Nita and had remained at home; after a series of miscarriages and by then in her early forties, she spent most of this pregnancy in bed. He had gone alone with his father. How clearly he can recall the nervousness and pride to have to himself this handsome, diffident and rather remote figure whom he regarded with awe if not affection. How eager he had been to say and do the right thing, to display the apposite reactions, to appear intelligent and sensible. And it had been *his* half term! He remembers that now, also. And is almost overwhelmed with emotion, laid bare and raw as his childhood converges upon the present in a cycle of perpetuality, repetition and coincidence. He sees Wiz as himself, and in the third person, himself as his father, and fights down the urge to weep.

He turns away from the view to find Wiz studying his compass intently.

'We're facing east,' he announces. 'The telescopes are facing eastwards.' And he pulls out his pad and pen from the rucksack to write this down.

'Your turn for the telescope,' the RSPB warden says. 'Don't adjust the position, will you?'

'Of course not,' Wiz says loftily.

'You can alter the focus though, if you need to. It's the red bit.'

Wiz stoops to peer through, Closing his left eye, he concentrates his right through the lens.

'What exactly am I supposed to be looking at?

'You see the two 'windows' in the middle cliff?' the man says.

'Ye-es.' Wiz adjusts his gaze downwards.

'Right. Now just below there, on the left is a cluster of pink flowers. Got them?'

'Yes.'

'Good. Now slightly to the left—'

'Got it! I've got it. I can see him.'

'Her. That's the female. She's much bigger than the male. He's gone off somewhere.'

Even as he speaks the distant form of a bird glides into view and alights near its mate, who is perched motionless, presumably by its nest. He wishes he could see the nest with its three chicks.

'That's brilliant. That's absolutely brilliant. I don't believe it. My first pair of peregrines. I mean proper. Not ones in a falcon centre or a zoo.'

He stares through the telescope for a while longer, until his father taps him gently on the shoulder, making him start and whirl round, so utterly transported had he been.

'May I have a peep?'

'Oh. Of course.'

Alastair adjusts the focus to his long-sighted vision, then bends and fastens his eye to the lens to see what has so thrilled his son. He can just decipher a dark shape that looks a bit like an upright skittle from here. Surely that cannot be it. And another small dark thing near it. It flaps its wings.

'I don't know if I'm doing it right. I can just see these small black shapes in the distance.'

'That's them,' Wiz says. 'But they're not black.'

'They look it from here.'

'That's because they're so far away. They're a charcoal colour with a pale belly really.'

'But—' He is about to ask what the point is of having driven this considerable distance only to see them as far-off dark shapes, but stops himself. Why dampen the boy's excitement? And judging by the extraordinary reaction of the others here, his son is not unique.

'Do we go now?' he asks respectfully.

'Well – can we stay a bit? I mean usually one stays to see what they do.' The binoculars are lifted to his eyes now and he has found the spot; can just make out the peregrines as dots; is attentive to their slightest movement.

'Whatever you want.'

'You don't mind?'

'It's your day.' He feels indulgent and magnanimous since the revelation of his memories.

'Could I ask you a favour?'

'Sure.'

'While I'm looking, could you write the sightings in my notebook?'

'Sightings?'

'There's a board over there with the bird sightings written on it. Where I took the pamphlets from.' Just about every free leaflet has found its way into Wiz's rucksack. 'It's got animals as well as birds on it. I need those for my new project.'

Twenty minutes pass. Alastair marvels at Wiz's patience. He passes the time perusing the leaflets and gazing at the view, allowing his memories to get the better of him. His mother fit and slim with perfect vision and no sign of arthritis then, playing Chopin at the grand piano by the French windows. From time to time he would fall in love with one of her female students. Nowadays she is a bitter woman, half blind with glaucoma, unable to stand bright light, crippled with arthritis, so that the keys of the redundant piano are yellowed, and the sound yielded metallic-edged like something out of a pub. She would end it all if she didn't believe it to be a sin. Instead she complains, and has set herself up as the high priestess of useless and unoriginal aphorisms. And his father. In tardy retrospect he acknowledges a deep resentment towards that formal, autocratic, esteemed man who was always absent, caring for patients who took precedence over his family. How has Nita turned out the way she has? Suddenly Alastair is filled with admiration for his sister.

'Dad, quick!'

Wiz's urgent tone rouses him from his thoughts.

'One of them's started to circle. I think it's coming this way. It must've spotted something . . . I can see it. There's another bird it's after. A pigeon I think.'

'I can't see a thing.'

'Have these. There's nobody at the telescope. I'll use that.' And rushes over to it before anyone else can.

His mood is infectious and communicates to Alastair who, despite himself, is starting to feel a sense of excitement.

Through the binoculars, through the telescope, they watch together as the falcon flies into dramatic focus with a surge of speed, the sickle wings beating with a strong, shallow action between gliding, head menacingly low. Over the river it glides now – clearly visible to the naked eye – gaining rapidly on its quarry; a spear in the brilliant summer blueness, intent on a single purpose: to kill. And through the telescope, through the binoculars, they can, from this distance of perhaps twenty-five metres, make out its features: the powerful line of its body, the colouring and pattern of its feathers, the distinctive cruel form of the head, the glint in the yellow eyes. And now it is closing in on the pigeon, who makes a desperate last bid for its freedom by jinking erratically to distract its assailant. It does not stand a chance. In a spectacular high-speed dive the peregrine stoops on its victim with nearly closed wings, seizing it up in its talons and carrying it off, beating its way at a steady, more leisurely pace, back to its nest.

'I don't believe it. I don't believe it!' Wiz grabs his camera and starts snapping away hopefully and rather wildly.

'Perfectly splendid,' agrees Alastair, lowering the binoculars.

'I mean you don't know how *privileged* we are.'

Everybody is talking amongst themselves. The place is abuzz with excited commentary.

'I don't suppose it's much fun for the old pigeon,' Alastair remarks.

'Well it's nature, isn't it? I know it's horrible, but it is. And a pigeon eats worms. They must feel too. Worms. And they're eaten alive. A peregrine nearly always kills instantly, with the striking of its talons. It stoops at a speed of between a hundred and two hundred miles per hour. Isn't that *amazing*? It's the speed of a high performance car. It's the fastest creature in the world when it stoops.'

Alastair puts an arm round his son's shoulder. The boy's

cheeks are pink, his eyes sparkling with elation. 'This really means a lot to you, doesn't it?'

'Yes. In my top five sightings.'

'Then I'm glad I was with you.'

'What did you think, Dad?'

'I found it all very exciting. If this is what "twitching" is about, I could get quite interested.'

'Oh but it's not just this.' He relaxes against his father's arm, feeling the ridge of its boniness against his back, accustoming himself to the strangeness of its being there. 'There're lots of different aspects. A lot of the fun's seeing small birds which look quite ordinary but are actually scarce. Or you see them in unexpected places, out of their normal contexts, in different habitats.'

'You like the diversity, then.'

'Yes. There're so many different things to learn and to listen to and to see. Every region attracts different species, and different birds choose different breeding grounds. Then there are the summer visitors and the winter visitors . . . It's like a whole world.'

Alastair's attention is fixed on his son's fervent, glowing face. 'Well I must admit I'm enlightened,' he says. 'It's all perfectly splendid.'

'I wish – Mum could have been with us to see it.'

'Yes. But it's quite nice being the two of us, man to man, as it were, isn't it?' Alastair says.

And so, man to man, while they are strolling back, Wiz broaches the subject of affairs.

'Dad, most grown-ups have affairs, don't they?'

He had intended to lead up to it gradually, perhaps relate it to birds' breeding habits, swans mating for life; something like that, but failed to find a suitable approach. So out it comes, this extraordinary remark pertaining to nothing they have seen or discussed.

'What makes you say that?' Alastair stops walking, in his surprise. His son can be *so* eccentric sometimes. They had been ambling along quite normally, having an ordinary conversation, albeit about birds, with Wiz showing off his knowledge, when he comes up with a remark apropos of *nothing*.

'Well I mean every film you go and see, they're always having affairs and things. Going off with each other. You know.'

'That doesn't mean it's right.'

Ah! So his father disapproves.

'You liked *Hannah and her Sisters*.' He can feel the colour drenching his cheeks, and snapping off a twig from an overhanging branch, proceeds to break it into bits.

'What?'

'You know. The Woody Allen film with Mia Farrow, Michael Caine, Max Von Sydow and Barbara Hershey.' He discards the last bit of twig and pivots nervously on the balls of his feet.

'My God, you know your stuff, don't you?' Alastair says, impressed.

'Well you took it out on video. You remember.'

'Vaguely. Only vaguely.'

'You really enjoyed it at the time. And Michael Caine – he was Elliot – was married to Mia Farrow, who was Hannah. And he went off with Barbara Hershey, who was Lee. *She* was with Max Von Sydow who played Frederick—'

'Hold it!' Laughing, Alastair lifts his hand to interrupt Wiz's rapid flow. 'And I'm supposed to remember all this?'

'It's not complicated. You can remember all the names of teeth and things,' Wiz retorts, his face breaking into a rare smile.

'Huh! Touché.' His father cuffs his cheek.

'Anyway, you really liked the film. I remember you did.

And when Frederick – Max Von Sydow – susses it and says to Lee – Barbara Hershey, "Good God, have you been kissed tonight?" you yelled out in your chair, "Good for her!" You were glad that he'd sussed it, because you said that Mia Farrow – Hannah – was boring and Barbara Hershey was much sexier.'

'Did I say that?' Alastair, confounded and out of his depth, asks. 'You can recall my saying that?'

'Yes. And they ended up together. I mean it wasn't even just an ordinary affair. They were sisters. He went off with the *sister*.'

'Well if Hannah was boring—' Alastair ventures tentatively. Wiz pounces. 'So does that make it right then?'

'No, not right, but more understandable.'

'So if someone's boring and you're fed up with them, an affair's OK?'

'God Wiz, you're relentless. And remorseless.'

'I need to know,' he mumbles, his confidence ebbing from him.

'Well, people do stray,' Alastair says, running his hand self-consciously over his hair. 'They shouldn't, but they do.'

This is a most unusual conversation to find himself having with his son, but he supposes Wiz is getting to that age. Nowadays it is not enough to be told the basic facts of life and discover the rest for yourself. Nowadays kids feel free to ask their parents about everything. Affairs. Homosexuality. AIDS. The parameters have all changed. And you are expected, as a parent to give a straight answer, even if it means admitting to weaknesses of your own and risking losing respect. In his day his parents were remote beings and he would never have dared probe the veil to expose hypocrisy. And the replies he gives might quite possibly govern his son's behaviour, and *his* son's, and so on. Yes, there is right. Yes, there is wrong. But the divide is frayed; then there is the susceptibility of human emotion . . .

'One can just do one's best,' he says, almost apologetically.

Watch and pray, that ye enter not into temptation: the spirit is indeed willing, but the flesh is weak.

He has only once been tempted – by a young dental nurse – but never strayed. In those days there had been no reason. It would not have been worth jeopardising his marriage for a fling. And what about now? Would he stray now? Oddly, whilst he has dreamed of fleeing to foreign shores, infidelity has not once crossed his mind. Yet he is a man of average, perhaps even high, sex drive. He is also a man of strong principles and integrity. Only now that his son has raised the topic in this circumferential manner, does the thought (the possibility?) occur to him with some piquancy. He realises, too, that it would have occurred to most men in his situation a great deal earlier, were they to have wives who shrank from their touch.

Wiz observes a whole spectrum of expressions cross his father's face. The last is a kind of parted-lipped awareness. A light sparks in his grey eyes. No more is said on the subject, and they arrive back at the car. Wiz scuffs the gravel with his feet while his father rubs bird shit from the windscreen. His trainers are rust-stained with soil and dust, his anorak pockets bulging with pine cones. He would have liked to have tackled the three-and-a-half mile forest walk, but didn't want to push his luck with his father, who has his own ideas for the rest of the day: lunch by the river, followed by a walk across the buttercup-strewn meadows. That Alastair had gazed down at from Yat Rock with intense, inexplicable longing.

They retrace the last part of the journey in the car, down through the gorge, the sheer escarpment rising behind them, into the valley, where the pungent smell of wild garlic growing amongst the cow parsley in the verges reaches their nostrils through the open window. At the fork in the road they take the right branch, catching the odd glint of the river between trees and the occasional cottage. The trees form dark porticos across the lane and the sun infiltrates through the sieve of leaves to cast discs of light on the tarmac. A strange drilling sound is fleetingly caught – then lost. Wiz reaches for the pad on his knee. 'Woodpecker,' he writes in it. 'Heard. Unseen. Type unknown. But green, great spotted, and lesser spotted varieties all seen in locality. See: sightings.'

His father switches on the radio for the news, turning it off immediately when all he gets is a harsh crackling. Alastair is still preoccupied with their earlier conversation. Out of the mouths of babes! he is thinking. Wondering.

The village seems almost to tumble into the river and to consist entirely of whitewashed hotels and watering holes, apart from a canoe centre. Opposite is Symonds Yat West, and a line of cottages; five miles by road but a minute by the punt-like boat serving as a ferry, and attached to a cable linking East and West.

They manage to park by the ice-cream hut, manned by the ferryman keeping a sharp lookout for anyone who might be waving to him on the opposite bank. What happens in winter? Alastair wonders. Everyone is outside: at tables on the terraces, picnicking or lounging on the grass beneath the willows. Everything is green and sparkling. Canoes and kayaks are like bright punctuation marks all along the river; children wearing luminous helmets and life jackets paddle back and forth under instruction, as a group of muscle-shouldered enthusiasts skirt round them heading towards the rapids.

'I'm going to buy some postcards.' Wiz squints at so much colour, at the almost unbearable prettiness of the scene, like something out of a child's storybook which, as you grow up, you know was a lie. The limpid-sweet air holds promises you can almost believe. You yearn to believe.

'Where from?'

'The ice-cream kiosk.'

'Fine. I'll grab a table outside the Saracen's Head. See you there.'

He buys a dozen in all. One of them is of a female peregrine with her white fluffy chicks in their nest. The rest are all different. He turns away to join his father, as the roar of a powerful motorbike disrupts the peace. Heads swivel as the two leather-clad, studded, bikers dismount and swagger about. When they remove their goggles and helmets, they are old – in their sixties at least. There is audible laughter all around, and the couple acknowledge it with a mock bow and curtsy and salute. 'Good for you,' somebody shouts.

'Did you see them?' Wiz says to his father.

'The old swingers you mean? Splendid, aren't they? You've got to admire people who refuse to give in to what's expected of them; refuse to conform. No concessions. It takes a certain kind of bravery not to care what others think about you.'

Alastair says this in a tone almost of envy, and Wiz glances at him askance, seeing him in that moment of wistfulness, as a person, a man with aspirations and hankerings and fears, not merely as his father.

'I bought this for you,' he says, fishing amongst his postcards and handing Alastair the one of the buttercup-showered meadow under a brilliant sky. 'You said you liked looking at it.'

Alastair takes it slowly. 'I did. I do. Thank you. That's very sweet of you. Very thoughtful.' He gives Wiz an affectionate little punch – the same as Ben used to. He is embarrassed to kiss his son; wants to, but doesn't know how to go about it suddenly. And isn't that the fault of his own upbringing?

They order fish and chips. Alastair orders a beer.

'Could I have a cider?' Wiz asks.

'*Cider*? You'll be rolling.'

'I won't. I really like cider.'

'I suppose a small one won't hurt.'

'Compromise,' murmurs his son.

It is a companionable meal, chatting and watching everything going on: the boat – 'Hand Ferry' – toing and froing with its passengers, dogs included, the tattooed, bronzed ferryman standing upright as he jerks the rope along the line of the cable; the bank-holiday assortment of people; the boats; the children; the ducks, geese and swans pecking about for scraps between the tables or waddling over picnic rugs. A pair of white-throated dippers standing 'bobbing' on a step by the water, before plunging in.

The white flesh of the haddock is moist and fresh, the texture of the batter light and crunchy, becoming soft against the roof of the mouth and melting there. Wiz savours it as he chews. He dips each plump chip into the pool of ketchup on the side of his plate.

'I think we should get another little boat,' Alastair muses.

The last one, a tiny, ancient craft with an outboard motor, had rotted beyond repair several years back.

'That'd be great.'

'It would, wouldn't it?' Alastair had lost interest in the idea after the accident.

'We should be able to get one quite cheaply, shouldn't we? You always see them advertised.'

'Oh yes, I should imagine so. Well that's something to look forward to.' Alastair rubs his hands together. He's quite excited. Really quite excited. And in addition, contary to his expectations, he has enjoyed the day so far immensely; being alone with his son. He feels it has done them both good. A revealing day in so many ways.

'Would I be able to drive it?'

'I don't see why not.'

His father has this habit of rarely answering with a direct yes or no.

'We could take a canoe this afternoon for an hour or so. What do you say to that? And then walk, if there's time. It's years since I've done anything like this.'

'Great. And I might sight something really unusual from the water. A bittern or something.'

'You never know.'

They lapse into easy silence. Alastair is smiling at some private thought, the angular lines of his face softened with the lifting of his mouth, all traces of severity erased.

Wiz takes a deep inhalation of breath, holding it for a couple of seconds in hesitation, then releasing it. 'Dad, you remember my friend Frederick?' He tries to keep his tone casual.

'Yes, of course. The spotty boy.'

Wiz ignores that. 'Well, his mother plays tennis a lot. I mean, she's really good apparently. Well anyway, Frederick says she sometimes needs a partner.'

Not a blink does he give at this invention.

'So?'

'So, I thought you might be able to partner her sometimes.'

'I don't see why not. Give me the number when we get back.'

He's agreed! It was that simple. Oh God, now what? He'll have to fix it with Frederick. And suppose she's not good-looking at all. Suppose she's an old boot, like the school matron? Suppose she's spotty like Frederick? Everyone thinks their own mother is really good-looking. But his own is, isn't she? And her hair suits her short. It's not just because he's biased. He envisages his mother, her lithe body, her small mobile-featured face, her great black eyes – llama eyes, his father used to say, but doesn't anymore; her impulsive enveloping hugs. Is he being disloyal? He *feels* as though he's being disloyal. Why does he feel he's being disloyal, when it's for *her* sake? To protect her. Suddenly he is afraid. It all seems very daunting, very complicated, very grown-up, what he is about to become involved in. He is no longer certain that what he is scheming is the right thing. Yet it is as if he is being sucked inexorably into a vortex of his own making. No, not his own. Circumstances. And one of Ben's favourite, rather pompous little sayings comes back to him: 'It is a simple matter of balancing the equation.'

That is all he is planning. To balance the equation. But the brightness has fled from the day. It has become monochrome. The chatter all around him is in an unrecognisable language. Probably some of the people here are burglars or murderers or dangerous criminals, these people laughing and eating and drinking. Some of them are probably really bad. Everything is an illusion. But the peregrine. That wasn't an illusion. He'll get *Kes* out on video tomorrow, if the shop is open.

'It's like something by Seurat,' comments Alastair of the scene around them.

Wiz says nothing. He hasn't heard of Seurat.

'You're very pensive. Penny for them.'

'Nothing really . . . I hope Mum wasn't lonely on her own today.' The wheels are in motion.

It was a bizarre start to the day: listening to the radio, and across the airwaves suddenly hearing an ex-lover's voice. Even without the presenter's introduction, she would have recognised it instantly: the refined, measured tones, his clever analysis, his expressions – 'bowled over'; 'knocked out'. 'Ravishing'. He still used that word. He was a theatre director and was discussing his choices of holiday reading.

For a minute she was rooted to the spot, there with her heap of ironing in the kitchen, poised with the spitting iron in her hand. She set it end-down upon the board very slowly, disbelieving. He was one of those 'wild' men, the sort to whom she had been drawn before entering the sanctuary offered by Alastair. She had not thought about him, about any of them, since. Now she recalled a small episode. Once she had written that lover a passionate letter and posted it, immediately regretting having done so. She waited by the post box for nearly an hour in the rain for the postman to appear, and together they had gone through the letters until they came to hers and she could retrieve it and tear it up . . .

Remembering, she laughed out loud. Oh the relief of not being that age again, living that kind of life. Instead . . . Instead?

She was in the middle of making character study notes about Isabel from *Portrait of a Lady*, when a commotion distracted her: Lowry, frenziedly barking, hackles up, was chasing back and forth the length of the garden. She went outside to investigate. There, at the bottom of the garden where it met the canal, was a swan with her three well-grown cygnets. Each time the dog approached she let out a warning hiss and reared up, flapping menacingly. Liz ran inside to fetch some bread and returned. Initially the swan hissed at her also, but at the sight of the bread was pacified. The lurcher observed from a safe distance, skinny body trembling.

'You beautiful creatures . . .'

She watched them for a while, standing quietly about eight feet away. She thought how thrilled Wiz would be. Work. She must work. But first, on an impulse, she went to check the swallows outside the front. The mother flew from the nest as she peered inside it. A clutch of five eggs rested there: white, blotched with reddish brown.

She went back indoors and resumed her work. Except for the parrot's interjections she was undisturbed for the next couple of hours. The dog lay miserably beneath the table as though in shock, and every so often she rubbed his thin tummy with her bare foot. And then, sandwiched in the centre of *Wuthering Heights*, she came upon a papery pressed rose. She lifted it carefully. Dried to a blood red; odourless. Only Alastair would have given it to her. And it pained her that she couldn't remember the occasion. A birthday? Anniversary? Or simply a token of love. It must have meant so much at the time; she was desolate to have forgotten.

The bell rang. It could only be him. Everyone else always walked straight in. The door was never locked when she was around. He – the polite Swiss – always rang. Then the fleeting thought: that it might not be him. It might be the police come to break the news to her of another accident. It was possible. It was quite possible. She stood there, chilled, imagining. But – Liz, the realist-woman, replaced the rose in the book, fluffed up her hair. Went upstairs to meet Klaus.

7

'Bert, do you believe in reincarnation?' asks Wiz.

'In *who*?'

Bert is particularly the worse for wear this drizzly morning; redder, more rheumy-eyed than usual, coughing up phlegm and expectorating onto the pile of faded sand. Wiz tries to ignore this.

'Reincarnation. You know. When you've had other lives before. And you keep having lives after you've died.'

'Fuck me,' followed by a belch, comes Bert's less than rewarding response.

'Look, I'll explain another time. I've got exams. I've got to go.' Gives George's matted head a pat and cycles off.

It was not a satisfactory meeting. Which ever way he looks at it. Not a single word of sense or wisdom can he extract from it, no matter how he tries to interpret it and twist it to his advantage.

Her dancing class morning. And wearing a leotard and tights beneath her raincoat, Liz cycles off into the rain on her old bike, with its basket attached to the handlebars. She has not driven since the accident. She waves to several people she knows on her way to the school, a converted and extended church in Jericho. Why Jericho? she has often wondered. She has come across several Gibraltars also, a Flanders and an Egypt. *Weird*, to coin her son's expression.

The prep school is in a long street of mostly red-brick Victorian buildings. A spindly line of saplings vainly struggles upwards, encased in dog-deterring wire meshing. A paper mill and factory rise above the melancholy terrace of uniform doors and windows and strung-out washing, and every so often the tumescent chimney funnel ejaculates smoke that covers the dismal architecture with a thin haze that makes her think of Whistler's London. And of the bedsit near Tower Bridge where she was living when she met Alastair. Those were the days of smog. And the plaintive horn of an invisible ship penetrating eerily through it. Smog and mad sex . . . But here, the canal runs alongside to lift the gloom, the barges providing a flash of relief with their splurges of colour. The school has established a good reputation, thanks to the efforts of its headmistress, with whom she has become quite friendly. Her group today are the infants. A motley bunch of four-to-five-year-olds; all girls, with the exception of one boy, Damien, who is apt to burst into tears at the least thing. The children are given the choice of dancing or gym. The other boys tease him, so she gathers, but he refuses to be put off. Baryshnikov, she calls him, explaining who he is. He takes the sobriquet very seriously. He has a natural sense of movement and is far and away the best pupil of either group that she has. Maybe one day he will be famous. And will he remember his first dancing class? One day, one day . . .

And meanwhile, on her way there, temporary traffic lights have been set up a couple of streets away and cones jut into the road while a terrace of dilapidated houses is being demolished to make way for a community centre. She stops at the lights along with two or three cars, and notices an old man hunched into a threadbare coat, standing on the pavement, gazing up at one of the cottages as the arm of a JCB lays into its upper storey. Instinctively she pulls over on her bike, sliding off the saddle and manoeuvring it, feet planted either side, in and out of the cones onto the pavement. She touches the man's shoulder, and he starts. She feels his whole body jerk. He is tiny. Sparrow-frail.

'I didn't mean to give you a fright,' she says. 'But are you all right? You shouldn't be standing here, you know. It's dangerous.'

'This was my home,' he tells her, still gazing upwards and shaking his head bemusedly. 'I used to live here. For close on forty years this was my home. Those curtains – you can still see them hanging – that was where my wife slept when she was ill. I nursed her in that room.'

Her eyes follow his pointed shaking finger to the ground floor window left of the front door. A net curtain is hanging there lopsidedly.

'I'm sorry. I'm so sorry,' she says.

He gives another shake of the head.

And round them: the cheerful voices, the rough laughter of the workmen intent on reducing the buildings to rubble as quickly as possible, without a thought for those individuals who have been displaced. Like children smacking their chubby hands down on a tower of coloured bricks. She has the impression the labourers are enjoying their job, the sense of power, the thrill of destruction.

'But you really shouldn't stand here.'

He finally looks at her with sagging, resigned eyes; the whites have a yellow, liverish tinge to them. 'It's memories, isn't it?' he says. 'That's all life is, isn't it?' Allowing her to lead him to a safer area. And she nods in sad agreement.

The image of him remains with her all the way to the school, as she gets off the bike and padlocks it to the lamppost, as she enters the building and the sounds of children's voices come from behind various doors; as she goes into the classroom and cries of, 'Mrs Miller! Mrs Miller!' 'Hello Mrs Miller,' greet her. She should have asked him where he lives now. It will plague her not knowing his fate. Oh the irony: a community centre traded for an old man's memories.

But now it is the turn of the very young. There are nine of them in this class. On Thursday afternoons she teaches an older group. They are all assembled, chattering and excited, prancing and preening, raising their arms in arcs and pointing their toes while Liz plugs in the hi-fi system and sorts out appropriate tapes. Once there had been a pianist, but she had also been the French teacher and the lessons had clashed. It's better this way. Liz used to feel guilty making the poor woman stop and start the whole time just as she was getting into the swing of things; could sense her frustration and was continually apologising. The machine had liberated her.

So – eight little girls of mixed shapes and colouring, all in sugar-pink leotards and tights, and Damien the little boy, in a t-shirt and black tights. She addresses each child individually, touching her – and him – on the head in a light caress. Damien is angelic-looking, with a platinum fringe and shadowed green eyes, and without exception the girls flirt outrageously with him and squabble over him. Whenever he cries they immediately form a possessive swarm round him.

The old man's image remains constant. I'll phone the council and find out where he's been moved to, she resolves.

The expectant, upturned faces take her back to her early dancing-class days. The only time she had been really happy as a child was when she was dancing . . . Transported into fantasy. You were rich or poor, ugly or beautiful; you had lost your most treasured object, had found it again. You mimed your way, danced your way through a rainbow of emotions with your pointed toes and extended fingers, your eyes intense, your heart full. You voyaged in a world of make-believe which was the only world that mattered. And when your name was called out, and you were singled out for the others to watch, how proud you were as you flexed your calves ever more tightly and pointed your toe so hard you could fit a rolling pin beneath the arch you made with your foot.

She puts her class through their exercise routine: the first three basic feet positions, then stretching and bending. Their sticky little hands squeak on the wooden bar, and their feet in the soft-soled pumps scrape on the pine floor with a charcoal-on-paper sound. She doesn't believe in patronising them by putting on 'baby' music or nursery rhymes. That's for playtime, she tells them. Dancing is proper, serious work. And at this their faces instantly become grave and important as they listen to her every word with rapt ears. So she plays Mozart or Wagner, or whatever is appropriate. Debussy this morning. Klaus's fan has given her an idea.

She holds it up for everyone to see, and they crowd round. 'It's so-o-o pretty . . .' 'It smells nice . . .' 'I like the dangly black bits . . .' 'I wish I had a fan like it . . .'

'Well in this mime-dance you do have a fan like it,' Liz tells them brightly. You have just been given it as a gift, and you pretend to take it sl-ow-ly from someone's hands and you gaze at it in utter joy. Then you must thank the person – using your hands and arms and positions of course, not talking, and you dance about very happily with it, making different movements with it. But a terrible thing happens next . . .' She gives an exaggerated intake of breath, clutching at her chest, and the children gasp with her, waiting with big, afraid eyes. She draws out the moment of suspense, biting on her lower lip and fixing her eyes sorrowfully on each of them in turn.

'What?' a small voice says into the anticipatory silence.

'The pretty fan breaks. All the little wooden sections come apart and scatter on the floor. You have to mime being very, very sad. And then you bend down and sl-ow-ly, very gr-ace-ful-ly pick up each piece . . .'

She switches on the tape. 'Ready?'

He kissed her after he gave it to her. And she had let him for a number of reasons. Because she wanted to feel sexual and womanly; because she did like him; because she was grateful to him for restoring – even slightly – a sense of pride in herself; because she was angry with Alastair for not understanding what she needed; because she wanted masculine reassurance; because she was so unhappy. She felt nothing. His tongue in her mouth, round her tongue, the firm, probing pressure of his lips, his hand cupping her chin – nothing moved her. She felt nothing whatsoever. It was not unpleasant; it was more as if it wasn't happening. But afterwards, reliving it, she began to think, maybe, maybe . . . And found herself looking forward to seeing him again. Then, that Sunday afternoon she had discovered the pressed rose, and she had been irritable with him. A repeated 'I love you', only drew a sarcastic response. Yet he hung around her the way a maltreated dog will stick by its owner.

Thinking about Klaus now, she feels mean. Tomorrow morning, Wednesday, she will be seeing him for a lesson and will explain to him. It is not in her nature to be unkind. How far would she have gone to prove her womanliness to herself? she wonders. Would she still go? Loving one man, wanting one man only. Ever. But frigid with him.

She and Alastair used to play a game called connections. On a walk together, or lying in bed after making love, one of them would say a word which would spark a sequence of associated words.

'Dark night.' 'Your dinner jacket.' 'Your green evening dress.' 'Emeralds.' 'Your drop earrings.' 'Falling stars.' 'Shells on the beach.' 'Cornet . . . Ice-cream.' 'Licking it from between your legs.' 'Wrapping them round your neck . . .'

Never would she have imagined she could become frigid.

The children are all at different stages in their mime. Some are still at the joyful stage, others are fanning themselves coquettishly, others are picking up pieces from the floor. A couple, Jack included, are lamenting the breakage. It is anarchy. An orchestra with no conductor or leader.

'Oh dear, oh dear,' she calls out, clapping her hands and switching off the machine. 'Perhaps we should take this a bit at a time.'

'Jack's crying,' says one five-year-old, whose plump tummy pushes out her belly-button visibly through the leotard. Predictably they cluster round Jack.

Liz goes up to him. 'Darling, it's not true. The fan's not really broken . . .'

But it is. Mysteriously, Klaus's fan is in segments on the table where she left it.

The girl, Megumi, has the usual problems with L's and R's, the same difficulties with the definite and indefinite article. She is pretty and exotic, like her name; light-voiced. Her hair, in a high ponytail, is the length Liz's used to be and hangs like a slick of black tar down her back. And she distracts Liz by doing exquisite doodles down the margin of her exercise book whilst managing to look at her with her beautiful expressionless eyes.

In perverse mood, for there is something she cannot pinpoint about the girl that arouses in her a rare sense of antagonism, Liz presents her with the *Complete Works of Edgar Allan Poe*. First she has to read the biographical notes, which she does in her slow, precise English, shaping her pink, soft lips carefully round the vowels and consonants; then they prepare to tackle 'The Tell-Tale Heart'.

'Make use of all the punctuation,' Liz says, while Megumi tranquilly draws unicorns on a blank sheet of her pad. 'Poe uses it very deliberately and cleverly. Note all the exclamation marks. It will help convey the sense. Read it slowly, just as you did the short biography. It may seem complicated but actually there are very few words you won't understand, though some of them are used in a different sense from how they would be today. "You fancy me mad", for instance, does not mean, "You are attracted to me" – and anyway it would be the adverb, "madly"; it means "I daresay you think I'm mad." The implication being, therefore, that he believes himself to be sane. Note the way the narrator confides in the reader. He is addressing his story to us and as such we are drawn into his mind.'

'"True!"' Megumi reads with just the right inflexion, '"Nervous – very, very dreadfully nervous I had been and am; but why *will* you say that I am mad? . . ."'

She remembers her 'Rs and 'Ls, flattening her tongue or holding it to the roof of her mouth accordingly, as Liz instructed; reading with sense and intelligence. Even humour. Liz is bewildered by her. The girl (girl? she must be in her mid to late twenties; it is hard to tell) is poised, utterly, dauntingly poised and distant. And the finely-drawn unicorns have manes of serpents' heads with protruding forked tongues.

She sits back. The short story had been Ben's favourite. He knew it backwards; used to quote from it, adopting a sinister voice. He would pounce on his parents, shrieking out, '"For your gold I have no desire. I think it is your *eye*! Yes . . . Your Evil Eye!"'

'". . . Plesently I heard a sright groan . . ."' the girl reads, stumbling for the first time.

'"P*r*esently I heard a s*l*ight groan",' Liz corrects her gently, smiling.

The girl smiles politely in acknowledgement and continues, tracing each line, each word with her childlike forefinger, frowning in concentration. The tiny frown makes barely a pucker in the smooth closed face.

'"Meantime the hellish tattoo of the heart increased. It grew quicker and *quicker*",' Ben hissed ghoulishly in her ear, coming up behind her while she was peeling vegetables and covering her eyes with his hands.

'And I shall tattoo you with my hellish wrath if you don't let me get on with this,' she replied, prising his hands from her eyes and lightly slapping them. And off he had danced. Laughing.

So many ways of loving, of missing, of grieving, of getting on with your life. The presence of one cherished son does not ease the absence of the other.

'Well read. Very well read,' she compliments Megumi, touching her arm briefly.

'I like the story. It is most interesting,' the girl says.

'It was my son's favourite story. His bedtime reading.'

'I think it would make me have very bad dreams.' She speaks very concisely, in her musical voice, smiling her hard little smile.

'Shall we discuss it a bit? What is your general impression?'

'It seems very modern, how it is written.'

'Yes, I agree. And what about it being written as though the narrator is talking to the reader? What is your opinion of this?'

'My opinion is that this is very clever device—'

'*A* very clever device. Or perhaps you could use the word, ploy, instead of device.'

'My opinion is that this is a very clever ploy,' Megumi repeats.

'Why?'

'Because the reader is committing the acts with the narrator. The reader is experiencing his bad desires and his fears.'

'Wicked or evil would be better than bad. Well done, Megumi. And would you say he is mad?'

For the first time the girl looks uncertain. But her answer is measured as always. 'I think that it is difficult for us to judge. I think he is very calculating. He is very afraid.'

'But his act of murder—'

'I do not like the old man either. Perhaps I would do the same,' she answers disconcertingly. And to that, Liz has no suitable reply. Megumi releases her hair from its ponytail, and it spills round her cameo-skinned face and round her shoulders.

They discuss the text for a while longer, and she is about to leave, when Alastair arrives back. How can Liz miss it, the way he stands in the doorway simply staring? She introduces them.

'Megumi has got on very well with the Edgar Allan Poe,' she says. 'You remember, the story Ben used to love—'

'Oh God yes.' She can tell he is trying hard not to stare at the girl. '"The Tell-Tale Heart". He used to drive us crazy with it.'

'For the next lesson I should prefer to read some D H Lawrence,' Megumi says calmly, running her tongue round her plump lips and looking at Alastair.

'A young lady who knows what she wants,' he jokes, after a startled pause.

'You're back early.' Liz feels dry-mouthed.

'My last patient cancelled. She had a double booking.'

'You are doctor?' Megumi's eyes widen.

'Dentist. I'm a dentist.'

She opens her mouth and taps her white teeth with her finger. 'I have trouble with my teeth. With my wise teeth.'

He laughs. 'Wisdom teeth.' He rifles about in his jacket pocket and pulling out a card, hands it to her. 'Come and see me. We'll get you sorted.'

'Thank you.'

Upstairs, Liz shows her student out.

'Your husband is very nice,' Megumi says. 'He is very charming man.'

8

The geese in Port Meadow beckon in the dawn with an extraordinary collective creaking noise, like a giant's door slowly opening on rusty hinges, that can be heard for miles. This morning Wiz's screaming in the early hours drowns out everything, sends shockwaves reverberating through the house. He is back there, entrapped helplessly once more in that scene of unexpurgated horror.

'Wiz – darling – it's all right.'

'I was there. I was back there.' Sweat-drenched; the sheet, the pillowcase, sodden.

'But you're not. You're all right. You're safe. In your room. I'm here . . . Dad's here.'

The blurry rumpled figure of his father haloed in the doorway. His mother's fingers circling on his forehead, smoothing his hair. He hoists himself up onto his elbows, befuddled. The red, coal embers of his nightmare flicker, and with each spark another image is released before it too dies away and all that is left is a residue of sadness. Reaching out instinctively, he links his arms round his mother's neck, forgetting in his moment of need and impulse, his recent ambivalence towards her. She envelops him, cradles his head, rocks him gently; and he clings to her.

'I thought you were dead too,' he mumbles against the cool silk of her dressing gown and the warm 'V' of exposed skin above it. 'I mean then. At the time . . . You know. I thought you were dead too.'

Then. At the time. He was spared nothing and can recall it in graphic, cinematic frames. His mother has a blank. The last thing she recollects is Ben's 'Shit, what's happening?' Whereas he saw everything. Everything. It cannot be eradicated; only fades like the pattern on his mother's dressing gown that has been washed a thousand times; but never completely.

Alastair creeps away. He is an outsider in all this, and, no, he can never know what it was like, only what it is like. The repercussions.

'Where's Schrödinger gone? I want Schrödinger,' he hears Wiz say plaintively, like a very young child.

A couple of weeks have elapsed – everybody is bemoaning the wet and cold. Oxford 'Greens' are I-told-you-so smug. The swallows have hatched, four out of five, into hideous bits of gnarled skin, like knotted elastic bands. The swan and her cygnets have installed themselves beneath the weeping ash and now come running towards Wiz when he appears, expectant of crusts; he is monitoring their development in a small notebook he has bought especially. Mr Singh's squabble with his neighbour has become all-out war: ruby nectarines are now on display outside his shop, and he polishes them one by one ostentatiously, lips stitched into a tight smug seam within his beard; his neighbour, meanwhile, is stocking blue writing paper, envelopes and roller-ball pens. Wiz has failed history but passed everything else, scraping through science: he is on his way to becoming a vet. College examinations, college disputes, and college balls . . . and the streets are thronged with tourists, the air discordant with a babble of tongues – the Japanese remind Wiz of bed springs twanging. Liz has phoned the council and traced the old man who lost his home. The Sunday Wiz and Alastair spent together in Symonds Yat seems a long time ago; dreams of buying a boat, intimate man-to-man chat, tentative shared confidences lost to the incomprehensible vagaries of adults' moods. Wiz has postponed giving his father Frederick's mother's number until he has inspected her first. Alastair's thoughts stray guilty-excitedly to a Japanese girl with a black bra visible beneath her tight white t-shirt; invoke her calculating, strawberry mouth and I-know-what-I-want eyes.

And Wiz has seen his mother and Klaus at the Phoenix cinema together.

Mid June, and on the smaller scale of things quite a lot has happened. There has been a subtle shifting of moods and motives, desires and doubts. Deception is in the air and the spurious starting to replace the real. It is as though a piece of solid ice were breaking up into pieces to float without form or direction across the limitless surface of black water.

Exams have taken up Wiz's time, and he has not seen Frederick. He has spoken to him on the telephone, however, and to his mother. She sounded friendly. I've heard so much about you, she said. I am looking forward to meeting you. This evening she will. He has finally devised a way and is going round there after school to watch a wildlife video with Frederick in which he has professed interest. Meanwhile, there has been a distinctly odd feel about his own home the last fortnight. His father alternates between being abstracted and irritable – it is as though he imagined their closeness that day in Symonds Yat, the sinewy arm paternal round his shoulder. His mother's eyes are worried, her scar is pink. She has bought a short white sundress and with her large feet and thin ankles sprouting beneath it, and little dark head above it, looks like a tired waif. Like that she makes him feel a rush of love for her that obliterates the incipient resentment pricking at him. As protector of her secrets, seeing her in that dress inspires him with fierce loyalty. He cannot know that his father is similarly moved.

The atmosphere at home crackles with isolation and mistrust – oh what is going on? – and the staccato of the rain. The rain, the wintry weather, doesn't let up. And over Liz's sundress goes a shapeless beige cardigan. What has happened to summer?

The cinema incident occurred two days ago, on Wednesday afternoon. They had had their last exam the previous day – RE, which nobody except Trevor Fox really counted – and the school was awash with relief. The general mood was one of relaxation. Wiz and Josh took advantage of it to skive off to the Phoenix.

The film was *Bullets Over Broadway*, directed by Woody Allen, and they arrived early, bought a large box of honeyed popcorn and settled noisily in their seats towards the back. Wiz consulted his new Swatch – blue, clear plastic strap, and the numerals glowed in the dark: 2.35. There were the usual adverts, the usual trailers during which Josh maintained a loud running commentary, using jargon gleaned from his producer father and uttered in the superior tones of one who knows his stuff. Someone behind him kicked his seat and hissed at him to be quiet, to which Josh reeled round.

'It's only a trailer for fuck's sake.'

Wiz slid down into his seat and dug his hand into the popcorn. He hated scenes. He was in the midst of cramming a fistful of popcorn into his mouth when the lights brightened and at that moment he saw them: making their way to two seats a couple of rows in front. Her head was slightly bent. His was forward in that rather jaunty way he had. He had a jaunty walk also. She seemed to trail behind him rather. They settled into their seats, and even from the back she was so distinguishable, with her neat round head and ballerina's back. He could see them clearly. Watched Klaus sliding his arm round her neck. Wiz writhed in his seat. The box of popcorn upset and the contents shot everywhere.

'Fuck. What d'you do that for?'

'I couldn't help it. I've just seen someone I know.'

'You can pay me my share.'

'I will.'

'What the fuck happened?'

'I told you. I saw someone I know.'

'Who?'

The lights dimming. The main film about to start. He had vowed to tell just one person. Josh had been away at the time, so he had told Frederick instead: I think my mother's having an affair. Now he wished he could tell Josh; but it seemed disloyal, telling his mother's secret to two people. On the other hand he knew all kinds of things about Josh: about his dyslexia; about what the baby-sitter did with him when he was twelve; what he did to a friend's male dog, who followed him about devotedly for the duration of his stay; that he cheated in the maths exam; that he had a fear of the dark and had to sleep with his door open and the landing light on. I can hear my parents making love, he told Wiz . . .

Right now Wiz could hardly breathe. Right now he was almost choking. It was as though he was being pumped full of concrete and his body was swelling to bursting point with it.

'My mother. I don't want her to see me. She'll go mad.'

He stumbled up from his seat as the credits started to roll. Popcorn clung to his anorak and jeans, some slid off and he crunched it beneath his feet. He could feel it in his hair.

'Sit down. Don't be an idiot.'

'Shut up will you,' from behind.

'Piss off.' Josh swivelled angrily, his goalie's shoulders threatening.

'No really. I've got to go. They go crazy about that sort of thing. My parents. Really. You stay.'

'You bet I will.'

'Listen, I'm sorry.' He hovered uncertainly. 'I mean it's not my fault.'

'No. OK. I'll tell you about it. If it's good I'll want to go a second time. You can come then. Don't forget you owe me the popcorn.'

That's what he liked about Josh. He never bore a grudge.

'If you don't be quiet I'll call the manager.'

'I'm going. I'm going.'

But not before making out the forms of his mother and Klaus. Klaus was leaning his head almost – though not quite – against hers. Wiz bolted from the cinema, knocking his legs against dark seats and irate feet, into the fluorescent-bright foyer, then the dismal rain and slate sky outside, his heart banging against his chest, seeming as though it might detonate. He leant against the royal-blue exterior of the building, to one side of the doorway, beneath all the film posters – Woody Allen sporting a trilby hat in his director's guise – tears he wasn't aware of slithering down his cheeks; gulping in air, gulping in the rain; shedding popcorn.

'Are you all right?' a voice, someone asked, faceless beneath an umbrella.

'I'm fine.' And elbowed past, ran for his bike, cycled home at top speed, his repressed sobbing coming as small noises like hiccoughs from the back of his throat.

'I will go to the cinema,' Klaus had said after their lesson.

'"Am going." You have already made the decision. What are you going to see?'

'This latest film which Woody Allen has been directing. The Bullet something.'

'Has directed. *Bullets Over Broadway*. I want to see that.'

'Come with me. I will take you.'

'I don't think that's a very good idea, Klaus.'

'Liz – *Liz*.' He gave a weary, exaggerated sigh. 'I am not proposing that we will go to bed, merely that we will go to the cinema. What harm is it to go to a film we are both wishing to see?'

That was how the day started this morning, Friday, with Wiz's unearthly screaming. Now he stands in chapel day-dreaming, grey-smudged grey eyes, pinched cheeks, watching the light bounce off the modern stained-glass windows. At least the rain has stopped. Mr Ferguson (Ferrr-gus, he's known as), the warden, is in particularly dry mood, his high Scottish voice nasal and scornful as he harps on about self-discipline. 'Self-discipline – not to be confused with discipline – seems to have been usurped by instant gratification . . .' Usurrupt, grratification, he says, in his daily, five-minute homily, curling his lip into a smile. The more scathing he becomes, the more he smiles. Ferrr-gus, the Smiling Assassin. He manages to link the theme of self-discipline to the strict uniform regulations he has imposed. 'I shall not name names, but it has come to my notice that several boys – how shall I *poot* it now? – have taken it upon themselves to adapt the rrregulations . . .' He lingers affectionately, for maximum impact, over the word. 'How many times must I reiterate that Doc Martens are not permitted in this school?' He pauses. 'Unless permission is sought on medical grounds.' His small attempt at humour eludes the younger pupils, who have never heard of Doc Martens in the orthopaedic sense. 'Those found disobeying the rules will have to stay behind and clear up the artroom as punishment.'

When all is said and done, he's a meek old goat really.

They finish with 'Onward Christian Soldiers', and file out, dispersing to their respective houses. Five hundred and seventy-five pupils and an appropriate ratio of teachers.

'You OK? You look like a ghost,' observes Josh in the classroom.

'Sort of . . . No, not really. I had a bad night. Bad dreams.' He has debated whether to say anything about his mother, but decided against it for the moment. And he's seeing Frederick later. He's already started with Frederick.

'You poor sod,' Josh comments sympathetically. His conversation is littered with expletives.

'I don't often have them now.'

'They'll go one day.'

Wiz looks sceptical.

'I had this crazy, warped dream last night,' Josh says.

'What about?'

'Well you know the Bobbit case? The American guy whose wife lopped off his dick? There was this picture of him in a magazine of my mother's; he's become some kind of icon in the States—'

'Was that the dream?'

'No, that was real. But I dreamed my sister was about to saw off my dick. We were in our swimming pool in our place in Portugal, and she comes at me with this saw as I'm lying on my back. God, it was awful, I can tell you.'

'Ugh. Ouch.' Wiz clutches at his crotch. 'What a thought.'

'*Exactly*. I tell you I could hardly look at her this morning.'

They both start laughing. Then Wiz falls silent. 'It's the sound of metal,' he says. 'It was awful. So loud. Like an explosion. I keep hearing it . . . I'm frightened of being in a car,' he confides for the first time.

'The best way to conquer fear is to do the thing you're scared of,' Josh says. 'Mum was terrified of flying, so she took flying lessons.'

'I'm too young to learn to drive.'

'I could teach you. There's this disused airstrip I've been to lots of times with Dad. I'm really experienced.'

'I don't know,' Wiz says doubtfully.

'In the holidays, before I go to Portugal.'

'What would I drive?'

'Your parents' car. I'd only take you round the small roads.'

'They'd never let me.'

'God, you're thick sometimes. You don't tell them, do you?'

He is already filled with dread thinking about it. He doesn't want to incur Josh's anger by going against him – he's lucky enough to have a friend like him; doesn't want to lose him. His only hope is that Josh might forget. But for now this has only added to his list of worries.

In break he wanders into RR1 – Recreation Room 1 – used by Shell and the fourth forms. Normally they'd be in the playground, but it's still partially flooded. Somebody is quietly strumming on a guitar. A group of boys is gossiping about Hugh Grant and the prostitute, Divine. 'She's much sexier-looking than Elizabeth Hurley,' someone says. 'Bullshit,' another boy contests. 'My father organised a tart for me for my thirteenth birthday,' throws out one fourteen-year-old blond Goliath nonchalantly. 'God, Sven, you're a fucking liar,' Josh says. Sven gives an unconcerned shrug. The fact is no one can be certain it isn't true: he's Swedish, after all.

At this point the conversation is curtailed and a sudden hush falls upon the room with the unexpected appearance of A Female: small, thin, dark hair in a twenties' bob, wearing a long black skirt and white cropped top. In the lower and upper sixth students wear 'mufti'. Nervous giggling and nudging accompanies her serene passage across the room, to where Wiz is sitting making notes from a school library book about the lesser horseshoe bat. He has been taking no part in the conversation and is only alerted to any change by the silence. When he realises she is making towards him, he could die. It's really embarrassing her coming into RR1. A girl. She's even from another house.

'Hello Wiz,' she says calmly, apparently oblivious to the nervous interest her entrance has provoked, the total suspension of all conversation.

'Oh hi,' he replies grimly into his chest, feeling his cheeks becoming suffused with red.

'I cut this out of the paper this morning to show you,' says Emma, bright, hazel eyes without all the black round them; small freckled nose. 'I thought you'd be interested after what you said that evening at the gallery.'

Everyone is listening. Dozens of thirteen- and fourteen-year-old ears are straining, and Wiz is only longing to melt into invisibility.

'What is it? What did I say?' He draws with his foot on the coir flooring, gives an apprehensive smile with a tinge of bravado.

'You said that your favourite bird was a golden eagle.'

He perks up a bit at this. 'Yes. I mean they're so magnificent.'

'Yes – hey guys,' she turns on the roomful of curious boys, taking them by surprise, spinning round on her heels aggressively, thrusting her hips forward and fastening a fist on either side. 'Haven't you ever seen a girl before? Don't be so *embryonic.*'

'Hark at her!' one boy jeers. Followed by laughter. But the tension is diffused and the normal talking starts again.

'I'm sorry,' Wiz apologises to her, for them, for himself, now the worst embarrassment is over; and he knows that although they'll no doubt rag him later, in reality he will have gone up a notch in their estimation. It is not even as though she's ugly. In fact she's quite cute in a thin way.

She's cool, too – the way she did that: put the boys sharply in their place.

She hands him the cutting. 'Mystery of golden eagle found shot in glen', the headline runs.

> Police are investigating the illegal shooting of a golden eagle found dead with thirty pellet wounds. One theory is that it may have been killed by people who believe that eagles are responsible for dwindling numbers of grouse. The adult bird, which has a six-foot wingspan, was shot at close range. Killing a golden eagle, a protected species, carries a maximum fine of £5,000. There are around 425 breeding pairs, all in the Highlands except for a pair in the Lake District . . .

'That's awful. That's so awful,' Wiz says. The redness of his cheeks gone, leaving him paler than ever. Nothing's going his way. Things are going from worse to worse. This has got to be some kind of bad portent, the eagle being killed.

'Oh dear, I shouldn't have told you! Listen, it wouldn't have known anything. Oh I wish I hadn't shown you now. It was brainless.' A concerned hand on his – and a snigger from close by. She glances up sharply. 'Infantile, infantile!' she chants to whoever it was, and the sniggering stops.

'I hope they catch whoever did it. I hope they kill them.'

'Well, I don't suppose they'll kill them, but they might well catch them,' she says pragmatically. Then, brightly, 'Hey, I've had an idea.'

Ben used to say that: Hey, I've had an idea! His eyes would gleam at the same time. And off he might go to fetch the telephone directory, to look up people with strange names and phone them up: Mr Sidebottom? This is your local councillor . . . Ve haff vays of straightening you out . . . Mr Smelly? Might I recommend our new spring-scented bath oil . . . Convulsed, he would hang-up and cavort round the room. 'Oh God, oh it's so *funny* . . .'

Makes Wiz smile, remembering. Yes, he misses Ben sometimes.

'What?' he asks Emma, still smiling.

'That's better. You've got a nice smile. I can't tell you. I've only just thought of it. It depends. It might not come to anything. I've got to discuss the idea with – with someone – first.'

'You'll tell me though?'

'If it comes to anything I will.'

And so it is with mixed feelings that he returns to the classroom. And despite the inevitable jibes, he knows they are all envious of him. Friendly with a *girl* from the lower sixth. And really not bad-looking at all. In fact there's a hint of Winona Ryder about her. The face shape and chiselled chin. And she'd said he had a nice smile. If he wasn't gummy he thinks he would have. His mother has the same: a short upper lip with a minute horizontal line above it when she smiles, then that bit of exposed gum. Even I can't do anything about that, his father says.

Liz has never before encountered anyone like Megumi. Over the years she has taught – what, a dozen? More? Japanese students. Mostly girls. Without exception they have been shy, sweet, giggling-behind-the-hand creatures; unsophisticated and meek; rarely venturing an opinion or instigating a conversation. Megumi is provocatively dressed, worldly, has been on the cover of a Japanese beauty magazine, has spent two months in America and seems fixed now on transferring shores permanently to Britain. She is no Butterfly, Liz reflects, and Alastair no Pinkerton. It is not the one but the other who is vulnerable. A kind of seduction role-reversal. Her name means Grace, or Blessing. She is twenty-five, and is reading philosophy at New College. Does Liz misinterpret the innuendo in the girl's conversation? Perhaps there is none after all. She is unfailingly polite. If she is cunning, then her cunning is larded with direct-eyed gazes that should imply honesty and evoke trust but instead disturb Liz even more, spilling out, so she believes, ruthlessness and challenge.

'How would you compare Oxford to Tokyo?' Liz asks her this Friday afternoon, after her lesson with Klaus (she could smile over the irony of her would-be suitor making way for Alastair's would-be . . . would-be what? These two students have suddenly assumed such importance in her life).

'I think England – Oxford – is nicer than Tokyo. It is very old beautiful city—'

'Don't forget the indefinite article, Megumi. *A* very old. City is a 'countable' noun. In fact you would put 'beautiful' first. Appearance adjectives tend to go first. So – *A* beautiful, very old city.'

'*A* beautiful, very old city. Tokyo was much bombed in the war and now it is reconstructed and it is very modern. There are very many buildings everywhere and a great many people. There is too much noise and traffic.'

'Fine. Good, Megumi. But I want you to start developing your vocabulary, be a bit more imaginative. English can be an extremely vivid and descriptive language.'

But Megumi has not finished, acknowledges Liz's comments with a small blink, and continues: 'The women are fortunate in England. Not only in Oxford, but everywhere in England. And America. I think in whole Europe, as matter of fact.'

'*The* whole *of* Europe, as *a* matter of fact . . . Why is that?'

'In Japan the men are not so good to women. Women must be in second place. They must be very quiet. Very polite. They must not ever complain. I do not like such behaviour. It is not modern. It is why I will live in England after my degree.'

'To meet a husband?'

'No. To be liberated.'

She is in every way a daunting young lady. And the picture expands by the minute.

'How are your wisdom teeth, Megumi?' Liz asks.

'Your husband is most kind. I have spoken with him yesterday and he had made appointment for me.'

This time the grammatical errors – the article, verb tenses – go uncorrected. Megumi unconcernedly drawing a design like a peacock's displayed tail in her exercise book. Liz, caught by surprise, a shock spasm running through her. Seeing again her husband standing in the kitchen doorway as his eyes alighted on Megumi: you could have knocked him down.

He has said nothing to her. Not yesterday evening. Not this morning. Oh by the way, Megumi rang me . . . No, nothing at all. There is a kind of inevitability in the pattern which is being formed. Perhaps in Megumi's enigmatic detachedness there is no studied calculation or ulterior motive. But Liz, in her fragility and with her sense of sexual inadequacy, feels as though she is drowning beneath a pile of gravel, suffocating as it pours on top of her, until her outstretched fingertips are submerged.

'Please tell me about the Morel household,' she says finally, heavily, into the cool waiting air in which Megumi's pencil scrapes gently, inexorably, against the page of her book.

And lets her thoughts drift; whilst in her clear, light, precise tones Megumi describes to her the events of the first chapter of *Sons and Lovers*.

Wiz rides along the cycle track that runs parallel to the Marston Ferry Road, playing his mouth organ as he cycles – no particular tune; but it feels good nonetheless. And the wind has changed, heralding better weather. It lifts his hair from his forehead, fans his curls, is brisk on his cheeks.

'Don't cycle back in the dark, darling.' His mother's lips on one side of his face. Himself tensing at the physical contact. He can't help it, she feels *dirty*, since seeing her at the cinema. Tacky-dirty. Doing-it-with-Klaus-dirty. Can't bear to think of her in that way. His mother and sex. Her body she's never hidden from him – walking about naked as she does, bathing with the door open: her shark's-fin spine, high ribcage and pointy breasts; and the dense black triangle between her legs. His *mother*. Why has it happened? Why is she doing it? She is betraying them all. Yet it is up to him to cover for her, be her silent conspirator, *balance the equation*. He has set himself up as guardian of the family, and he hates it. Hates her for doing this to them; but loves her fiercely.

Frederick's home in Mill Lane, Marston Village, is a pretty stone cottage attached to a larger house. A woman answers his knock on the door; there is no bell.

'So *you're* Wiz,' she says, letting him in.

'Yes. Hi. Thanks.'

He steps inside, finding himself immediately in a large open-plan room that combines a kitchen and living area. Everything is light and spacious and tidy. The few ornaments are in modern glass or ceramic, deliberately placed. It is so different from his own home with its untidy clutter and scant thought for deliberate positioning of *objets*.

'It's really cool – I mean nice,' he comments, looking round and finally letting his eyes rest for a moment on her: tall, big-boned, a great deal of curling fair hair; very direct blue eyes. Good-looking? Probably. How can he tell? She has big breasts though. He can't help noticing *those*. They jut out in front of her like a ledge, straining through her white t-shirt. God.

'Frederick's taking a shower. I'll call him . . . Frederick!' she calls up the wide spiral staircase. 'Wiz is here.'

'OK,' filters distantly down.

Viz. She has the faintest of accents he only then detected, and wonders where she is from; reckons this is a plus factor in her favour. Foreigners are always more interesting. He had not known Frederick was half foreign. He picks up a large smooth stone of gradated rose and umbers from a table and runs his hands round it; recalls beach holidays, floating on his tummy over lazy waves. Water polo with Ben. They have been away already this year, in spring, to Tuscany, where it rained nearly the whole time. They spent one entire day in the Uffizi, himself plugged into his Walkman. He could have screamed with boredom by the end.

'Sit down. Make yourself at home.'

'Thanks.' He puts down the stone carefully, yearning suddenly to be by the sea. Sinking into a giant deeply-cushioned sofa with a cream, textured fabric; imagining he is sinking into foamy surf. He doesn't know what to say. He would like to bring up her being foreign; at some point has to bring up the tennis thing.

'So you're the ornithologist,' she says.

'Well not a *real* ornithologist,' he answers seriously, tugging on some strands of his hair, winding them round his finger and then releasing them. 'I mean it takes years to become a proper ornithologist. And I'm – diversifying –' (a new word, he notes to himself in surprise) '– to other animals a bit more now as well. I want to train as a vet when I leave school.'

'That sounds very interesting.' Her eyes are smiling, warm. She has quite a large nose, and a wide face. From overhead comes thudding, presumably from Frederick: heavy footsteps back and forth.

'Frederick says you play tennis a lot.'

'You could say I'm an addict.' She gives an easy laugh and crosses her legs. She's wearing jeans, so he can't see what they're like, but imagines they're fatter than his mother's; and longer, as she is so much taller. She's bigger all over. Liz's opposite, in fact. Is that good or bad? Probably good, he thinks.

'My father's mad about tennis, too. In fact he's always looking for someone else to play with.'

'Me too. Tell him to ring me.'

Oh so easy. Sl-ip-ping so easily into place. Wiz feels tremors of excitement running through him, like tiny insects on his skin. And for a moment he feels almost gleeful, quite heady with a unique sense of power.

'OK, I will.'

Frederick appears: feet and long legs visible first, then the rest of him as he descends the winding, open-tread staircase. Tousled wet hair uncombed; face a livid pink; towel round his neck; eyes by contrast to his bright complexion, a pale aquamarine like his mother's, without his glasses.

'I'm trying out lenses,' he says, squinting at Wiz. 'Spots are bad enough without glasses.'

'They'll go in a year or so,' his mother says.

'Oh yeah. That's great consolation for the present. What do I do meanwhile? Put a pillowcase over my head?'

He sounds really down, really glum. Something must have happened since they last saw each other a fortnight ago.

'They're not that bad,' Wiz says.

'Well I daresay they'll go when I'm in Africa. It would be typical, wouldn't it? I won't care what I look like there. I'll be too busy . . . And there won't be a certain female I'm bothered about.'

'Oops, I'm in the way here.' His mother gets up and goes upstairs. A door closes and then there is the sound of the television. Clapping. A man's voice. Some sort of quiz show. 'And for two points, who can tell me the nationality of Desiderius Erasmus?'

'Dutch,' they hear Frederick's mother shout out.

'My mother's Dutch,' Frederick tells him.

'You never said.'

'Why should I? It's not a big deal.'

'Anyway, who's Desi-whatsit?'

'Desiderius Erasmus? Haven't you done him at school? He was a Renaissance scholar and theologian.'

'Oh I vaguely remember. I'm hopeless at history. I failed my history exam. I got thirty-two per cent.'

'Did they mind?'

'Who?'

'Your parents.'

'No. I passed everything else. Even science. I got sixty-one for it. Anyway, they're preoccupied. With other things. So what's up?'

'You're too young.'

'That's not fair.'

It's the first time Frederick has made any allusion to their age difference. Until now he has made Wiz feel they were equals, and he was proud because of it. 'My friend Frederick, who's eighteen . . .' he would let slip at school. Although even he knows that it is as much Frederick's ungainly awkwardness as their mutual interests which has drawn them together. He guesses Frederick does not really have a close friend; that he is a bit of a misfit, the sort others might poke fun at.

Nonetheless, he is hurt.

'I know about everything,' he says defensively, thrusting his chin forward. 'I've seen loads of videos that are '18', And magazines. I can show you my magazines if you like. I—'

No, better not say he stole them. Every time he thinks about taking them down from the top shelf and hiding them in his rucksack while Mr Singh was making them both tea in the back room, he feels terrible. He has abused his employer's trust. But how else was he to acquire them?

'What kind of magazines?'

'Girls. You know.' He gestures to his own thin chest and makes cups with his hands.

'OK. Well there was this girl I liked a lot. It's why I got the lenses. They cost me a fortune.' He blinks as he says it. His eyes are starting to go the colour of his face. 'I've got astigmatism, which meant soft lenses were out as they can't correct it, so these are hard . . . Or are they gas permeable? I can't remember. It's written down somewhere. But they're jolly uncomfortable if you want to know.'

'All because of this girl?'

'Yeah . . . She's reading zoology at Worcester. She's cracking-looking and I thought she liked me. You know – *fancied*. So I try and start something, don't I? And *she* said she only liked me in the platonic sense. She said she was sorry and all that but – oh, I know it's my acne. It puts everyone off. It would put *me* off. It's vile. If I didn't have these bloody spots and great blotches, I could get to screw a girl. I'd sell my soul to get rid of my acne, I really would.'

This is rather more than Wiz bargained for. He tries to sound as though he has this kind of conversation everyday. A phrase leaps to his mind – where he has read or heard it, he could not say: a man of Savoir Faire.

'Well, soon you will get to – to screw – a girl' (he has never used the word before, even with Josh). 'I mean it's bound to happen one day, isn't it? It does to all blokes. Not everyone cares about the way people look. And you're not ugly. There're loads of people you see married and things who are much uglier.'

Frederick's face breaks into a big grin. He sits back in his chair, plants his feet forward and starts laughing.

'Sometimes you can be so funny. It's unintentional, which makes it funnier.'

'What have I said?' Wiz begins laughing also, but looks bewildered at the same time.

'Nothing. It's all right. You want to see the video now?'

He had forgotten about the video. It had simply been the pretext for meeting Frederick's mother.

'Sure.'

'If we can hear it above Mum's quiz show upstairs. I think she thinks the louder she has the volume the more she'll be likely to understand the questions.' He has an odd way of getting to his feet, as though he is disentangling his limbs like a contortionist. He lopes over to the kitchen-end of the room, opens a cupboard there.

'Catch!' Throwing Wiz a packet of crisps; barbecue-flavoured. He pushes the film into the video machine and presses several buttons. The screen becomes a Madagascan forest, and a lemur springs into focus. The boys sit next to one another on the cream sofa, plunging their hands with automatic regularity into their crisp packets, dropping crumbs, while on the screen fluffy, huge-eyed creatures perform acrobatics.

'I saw my mother at the Phoenix with her lover two days ago,' Wiz remarks, gazing fixedly at the lemur.

'. . . The sifaka, a beautiful creature with a pure white fur, a little larger than the ring-tail, has become a specialist in jumping. Its legs are considerably longer than its arms and enable it to leap four or five metres from one tree to another . . .' David Attenborough's soft commentary drifts over. And from above: '. . . For three points: To what mountain range does Brocken belong? And for a bonus point – what is the legend attached to it?'

'Smart-ass!' shouts Erika.

'You don't mean it!' says Frederick.

'Dad, here's the number you wanted. You know. Frederick's mother, who's looking for someone to play tennis with. She's really good apparently.'

Alastair takes the scrap of paper from his son. Doodles of birds' beaks all round the edge.

'She's Dutch,' Wiz lets slip. 'Really nice.' Contemplates drawing the shape of a curvaceous woman's body in the air, and decides against it. He's gone back to being self-conscious with his father again. The man-to-man business wouldn't seem natural now.

'I'll give her a ring in the morning. We might be able to get a game in this weekend,' Alastair says, pocketing the piece of paper.

'Don't lose it.'

'Hark who's talking!'

But at the moment his mind is taken up with an appointment on Wednesday, five days away. He is a man of fourty-four and he is actually counting days. Even as he counts, guilt strikes him like the bell tolling for Mass. He was brought up as a Catholic and old habits die hard. Stifled by his upbringing, his recalcitrant thoughts do not sit naturally or comfortably within him, but struggle against each other. Eden's rosy apples dancing maniacally in his head.

9

'She's very nice,' Alastair says about Frederick's mother in reply to Wiz's question after his game of tennis this Sunday. 'And a superb player. Really strong.'

Wiz's spirits soar. They are in the kitchen. His mother is cooking lunch. She is not a brilliant cook, if the truth be known. A bit chaotic. Things usually get burned or are too underdone, and when she bothers with sauces they are usually lumpy. He wills her to be more interested in the discussion.

'And she's very good-looking, isn't she? I mean do you think she's beautiful?'

His mother actually does glance over at this point. Oven gloves on hands, poised with a baking tray containing something he cannot see in it, she stops mid-stream.

'Well I don't know about beautiful, but she's certainly a good-looking woman. Handsome might be a better word,' his father says.

How can a woman be handsome? Nonetheless, he is encouraged: they got on, she's a good tennis player, and *handsome* . . .

'It's really sad,' he perseveres. 'Her husband walked out on her and Frederick. She supported him all by herself. You know – school fees and everything. She does everything on her own. She had employment agencies which she started herself. You should see her cottage,' he enthuses. 'The way she's done it—'

'You sound as though you're doing a selling job on her,' Liz says dryly, putting the dish in the oven.

At last! A reaction. She sounded peeved didn't she? Really quite peeved. The foundations have been laid and now the first bricks put in place.

Then to cap it: 'I look forward to playing with her again during the week,' Alastair says.

The Larches, in Summertown, smells of stale skin and boiled food and memories of other incarnations. Silk flowers on a table in the hall look fusty and forgotten. The shiny, pale blue walls bear fire alarm instructions and general notices between the exposed meter box and Monet's *Water Lilies*. The linoleum is worn and marked from the constant wheels of chairs and prodding of zimmer frames. Sunny midday, Monday, and not a soul about. Her urge is to turn and run from this place – but she sees again the net curtain hanging bravely in a downstairs window: a last relic before the JCB swung its arm through a man's life; and the thin old man shivering beside her. Now there is a space like a comb with its teeth missing, where once the row of houses stood. So she walks purposefully along the dimly-lit passageway towards an open door – whence come the sounds of chinking crockery and the chirping of budgerigars.

About twenty-five old people, at individual tables, are having lunch. They are all wearing bibs, and not a word is being uttered by a single one of them as they routinely, uninterestedly, make the trembling journey with fork or spoon to mouths that seem so distant from their plates. In one corner a television is murmuring. By the window is a huge cage in which ten or so assorted budgies are preening themselves, swinging on perches, nibbling at millet branches and generally compensating for the hushed gloom with their exuberant chatter. In a fish tank, against another wall, exquisite tropical fish weave brightly, mysteriously in and out of their lush underwater world. A nurse stacking plates onto a trolley calls out absently, 'Eat up Mrs Brown . . . Manners, Mr Finney . . .'

It is so awful. So utterly dispiriting. So humiliating. From her half-concealed position just outside the entrance to the room, Liz observes in dismay the bent, grizzled heads intent on the task of getting food into their mouth – and sometimes one or the other of them might pause forgetfully or defeatedly, and the food slithers from the fork, and their hand will drop to the tray in front of them, and their eyes fasten vacantly on the television or the fish or the birds; or perhaps wistfully on the window, dreaming of what lies beyond; or on nothing at all, only on their own introspection: that the sum total of their lives, their childhood pranks and illicit loves, has amounted to nothing more than this. Amongst them, she spots him: *her* old man; neatly dressed, neatly brushed, eating tidily by himself. What does he mean to her? What is she doing here? The smell of boiled food and incontinence repel her.

'The way so many people end up . . . It's sad isn't it?' a voice says beside her; and she turns, startled. A blonde woman has joined her and is regarding them with mixed compassion and objectivity in her eyes.

'Have you come to see someone?'

'Sort of.'

'Mealtimes are such a zoo. I'm Monday's do-gooder. A voluntary worker.' Smiling. *Vorker,* she says. She has the slightest of accents, exaggerates her dipthongs. 'Who have you "sort of" come to visit, then?'

'A man called Charles Flegg.'

'He's a relative of yours?'

'No. I don't even know him. I saw him a couple of weeks or so ago, He was standing outside his cottage, watching it being demolished. I spoke to him. He was so pathetic. I phoned the council and was told he'd been moved here.'

'He is not worth your pity,' the woman says. Gives a small, dry laugh. 'Fascist Flegg, he's known as. Given half a chance he'll tell you about his marches with Oswald Mosley in the thirties and give you his best Nazi salute. He has some unusual scrapbooks, too. He regales the others with terrible stories, and one old woman here knew his wife very well and says he was physically and mentally abusive to her. She said that there were rumours he was a paedophile. A thoroughly nice human being in other words! Yes, that shrivelled little figure with his crumpled turtle's neck,' she says, pointing in the direction of Liz's disbelieving gaze.

'He looks so helpless and – benign.'

'They all do, don't they? But once they were all young and no doubt many of them were afflicted with hang-ups and prejudices and pettinesses, or were liars or selfish or drunk . . .'

'I suppose we do rather ascribe to old people virtues they might never have had. We say, "he's a dear old man," or "she's a sweet old woman," when in fact we know absolutely nothing about them or their pasts.'

'Exactly. We regard them in the same way we regard babies whose minds aren't formed yet. And Flegg is the very worst. The others won't speak to him – and I could tell you a thing or two about some of them, too. He's thoroughly evil. Fancy doing a spot of voluntary work for the next half hour or so?'

She copies the other woman. Helps feed the battling forgetful mouths, wipe dribbling chins; smells urine on several of them . . . 'I'm not hungry,' whines one. 'I need the lav,' moans another. 'You Lady Thatcher's daughter?' a woman with long silver plaits asks, curiously. 'They'll be coming to get me soon,' she adds. 'Who?' says Liz. 'Them. You know. *Them.*' She consults an imaginary wristwatch. 'They're late,' she informs Liz, nodding.

I want to get out. I have to go home. But instead she goes up to the old man. Charles Flegg. Fascist Flegg. Despite knowing what she now does about him, she goes up to him just like she has done all the others. He is the reason she is here, after all. He doesn't recognise her and she does not enlighten him. Every crumb of his food is finished. His knife and fork are neatly together. Only a speck of saliva is on his chin. And aware of this himself, he fumblingly brings out a handkerchief from a pocket and dabs at it. His eyes are watery-pale. She tries to imagine him as a robust young man, marching through the Jewish areas of London, brandishing fascist banners and handing out propaganda leaflets, returning home to abuse his wife. And one day did he regret his treatment of her and nurse her? Is his mouth perhaps a little cruel? Is there a trace of a sadistic gleam in his faded eyes?

'Nobody cares about me here,' he says plaintively, as she removes his plate. And she finds herself in danger of pitying him again. Still has a problem not seeing him just as 'a harmless old man'.

'My name's Erika,' the blonde woman says as Liz prepares to leave.

She forgets the name immediately, tries to forget the entire episode and escapes into the street. Reprieved.

Generally Oxford makes her feel old, filled as it is with students and so much ardour and energy. Now, riding her bicycle through a leafy avenue, slowing at each speed hump, now she feels positively young, wants to dance on the pavement with her youth, throw back her head with laughter. So relieved to be away from the place. Relieved to be reprieved . . . Giggles at the rhyme. But during the short journey home, her elation dissipates. She can not rid herself of the thought: Poor old things; poor old sweet, harmless nice old things. One day – she thinks – One day . . . There but for the grace of God go I.

She does not intend to tell anyone about today.

His mother is wearing her new white dress and a long amber necklace; when she sits down in the cramped lower circle the dress rides up her thighs. She has legs like a teenage girl. Next to her, Nita is all woman in figure-hugging black, her auburn hair skimming her shoulders in a thick curve. Christopher Wren did not have comfort in mind when he designed the Sheldonian Theatre, and the two men sit squashed together side by side. Wiz is sandwiched between his parents. The dividing line, he thinks, gazing up at the painted ceiling, at the massive organ pipes and row upon row of uncomfortable bench seating. Quite a few people, his parents included, have brought cushions with them. He came to a degree ceremony here once. It went on for ever, part of it in Latin. Name after name, until he thought he would go crazy with boredom. But first was a grand procession of the fellows and professors and dignitaries in their robes – all very serious and self-important. 'They all look so elitist-smug,' commented Ben, beside him, writing mathematical equations all over the programme. They sat high up and it was sweltering hot – just as it is now in the packed hall. And now, his eyes rove idly over the audience. And come to rest on Klaus. Klaus has seen him also, was just homing in on Liz, when his glance met her son's. He gives one of his little nods. He is obviously by himself. Should Wiz tell her? He doesn't need to. She has been looking around also and has noticed him for herself. The colour singes her cheeks and she lifts her hand in a tiny, hesitant wave. Was this planned?

'Who are you waving to?' Alastair asks.

'Klaus,' she says abruptly, closing her palm again, as though she were snapping shut a purse containing all her money, safely away from pickpockets.

Look at him, Wiz commands his father silently. He's your enemy. But Alastair doesn't so much as peep in Klaus's direction.

The orchestra comes in, closely followed by the leader, and lastly the conductor. When the clapping dies down he ushers in the opening notes of Brahms's First Symphony, a ferocious expression on his face. Wiz quite enjoys some classical music, but Brahms is too heavy for him. He shifts about, bored and hot, in his seat.

'Keep still, will you?' Alastair says.

Pouts and rivets his feet together. His jeans are shorter than they were, he notices. Perhaps he's grown a bit. Or perhaps they've shrunk. The conductor dancing – positively leaping – on his plinth, and not once does any member of the orchestra look at him, keeping their faces steadfast on their scores. One of the cellists is a girl. He plucks his mother's opera glasses that she always brings to concerts, from her lap; *pans in* – to use Josh's phrase – on her: quite pretty for a musician. Closes in on some of the others: the sweating trumpeter who keeps fluffing coming in; a violinist whose few strands of hair are combed in a band across his bald pate – what happens when the wind blows? Another violinist, a woman. She has beautiful, pale hands he can imagine stroking him, feeling him; and then he notices that her wedding finger has no ring but bears a deep, pale imprint as though she has only just removed it. He wonders about that for a bit. In the row just beneath him a couple are deep in a silent quarrel, scrawling notes to each other on the programme. Through the opera glasses Wiz can read the messages. 'You are, without exception, the most selfish man I've ever met, and I've met a few,' the girl has just written. What's the point in relationships? A few years, then everyone always ends up rowing or not speaking to each other? Turns the glasses towards Klaus, feeling himself camouflaged behind them: Klaus's eyes are like lasers on Liz's profile. He rests the glasses on his knee. His mother is hunched forward, enraptured, apparently oblivious to Klaus, her knees twitching as though she wants to dance. His aunt is on the verge of sleep, her head lolling. He can see her struggling to keep her eyes open. Like that she looks quite old, actually. He passes the remainder of the first half by imagining what bird everyone in the orchestra would be. The violinist with the strip of hair would be a moorhen, the woman with the beautiful hands, a skylark . . .

Klaus manages to corner Liz at the end of the concert, on the way out of the Sheldonian, when she and Wiz are slightly apart from the others.

'Brahms's music and your melancholic eyes were too much for my blood,' Wiz hears him whisper.

'Klaus, this is my husband,' Liz says brightly as Alastair approaches; and the two men shake hands.

Back home Nita says, 'I must confess an overdose of Brahms sends me to sleep. I read something once in a French magazine, written by a nineteenth-century critic: *"Quel mathématicien est cet homme, Brahms,"* it said. *"Mais quel compositeur dismal."'*

'What does that mean?' asks Wiz, picking at the lasagne topping from the serving dish on the kitchen table. ('Don't do that,' his father reproves.)

'It means, literally, my dearest boy: "What a mathematician this man Brahms is, but what a dismal composer," and I tend to agree.'

'Was he a mathematician then?'

'No darling,' his mother intercedes. 'But his music was very deliberately structured. Personally, I find it uplifting and not in the least dismal.'

'Nita slept for most of the time.'

'Telltale,' says his aunt.

'Dinner.' His mother seems quite calm, considering, he thinks. And the more he contemplates it, the more certain he is that she and Klaus arranged to see each other there. Come to think of it, when she said she was going to the loo, she was probably talking to him. An *assignation*. She is being *devious*, and it is so hard to trust her, to respect her when he knows all these bad things about her. And yet she goes about the place acting normally. A bit quieter, a bit more worried-looking; but however hard he looks for it he can find no guilt anywhere in the familiarity of her features, no falsity in her behaviour. It makes it worse – that she is such a consummate actress.

His aunt is on top form, having recovered from her tiredness; regales them with anecdotes – she is always a mine of scandalous stories and gossip: '. . . So to get her own back she fastened the handcuffs round the bed post and then to her partner – who just thought he was in for a bit of innocent bondage. And when the phone rang for him she said, "I'm afraid he's a bit tied up at the moment," and she left him there.'

His mother is laughing tears, but his father is grimacing in discomfort, glancing over at Wiz, then trying to catch his sister's eye as if to say 'Not in front of . . .' Her husband is used to her, is smiling benevolently and tapping his toes to something in his head.

'. . . And Toby hates garlic, so to punish him she cooks an entire meal with garlic . . .'

'Sit down Wiz darling.' He does so, next to his aunt, who immediately rests her hand on his knee. Does she do it deliberately? How can she not know the effect it has on him? He becomes all hot; tries to focus on eating his lasagne.

'. . . And my dears, in the midst of this terribly chic dinner, down comes the seventeen-year-old daughter, putting in an appearance high on pot . . .'

He doesn't really listen to each tale, more to the rise and fall of her rich voice with its undertone of wicked humour; fighting to disregard the hand clenching then relaxing on his knee according to what point she is making in her narration.

'. . . And those awful sandals and grey socks the Oxford bearded-wonders insist on wearing . . .' She's drinking wine as she talks, splutters slightly with laughter. '. . . Do you know what I call them? I call them Academic Footwear!'

Even her brother laughs at this. He's drinking quite heavily for him, Wiz notices. Fast. Gulping it down and quickly replenishing the glass. Somehow he and Nita get onto the past, their childhood, the do-you-remember bit.

'Do you remember how father used to carve chicken and turkey in wafer thin slices, and how we'd be itching with impatience because it took so long, and we had to wait for him before beginning? The food would be cold by then . . . And mother's long suffering expression . . .'

'God yes. And do you remember how he never got dressed on a Sunday until he'd done the crossword, and he'd saunter next door in his dressing gown for clues . . .'

'The man's surname was Russell—'

'And he couldn't say his "Rs"', Alastair interrupted, smiling, genial-faced, rather drunk. '"Wussell here," he'd answer the phone! Oh my God how I longed to take the mickey out of him but never had the nerve.'

'Grown-ups seemed so terrifying in those days,' Nita muses.

'Father *was* terrifying. I think mother was liberated when he died.'

'Until the glaucoma and arthritis. It's cruel. She's got nothing. Everything she loved – her music, playing the piano, her garden, painting, she can't enjoy. Sitting in that darkened room. It's cruel.'

'Yes, it's a bugger.'

Wiz looks at his father askance; he's never heard him use the word before. But alcohol has loosened Alastair's inhibitions and he is relaxed and good-humoured. So that when Nita says to Wiz, 'Do you find grown-ups terrifying, dearest boy?' he answers truthfully, facing his father square, 'I sometimes find Dad a bit.'

'There you are,' Nita cries. 'You see Alastair! History repeating itself. Your son is terrified of you. You should respect children, you know – not that Wiz is a child. Adults may have acquired knowledge, but young people have a keener intelligence.'

'But that's awful,' Alastair says, genuinely grieved. You're not really terrified of me, are you?'

'Well, only sometimes, and only a bit,' Wiz says, smiling to lighten the truth, pulling the back of his sweatshirt over his head, end-up, making a kind of balaclava out of it that almost hides his eyes.

His father puts his arm round him in Symonds Yat fashion. 'Sometimes is too often. I'm sorry for that. I get a bit grumpy. I can't help it. It's the way I am.'

You weren't with Ben. He so nearly says it – thinks for a suspended moment he actually did – but the words were in his head.

Says to his uncle instead, 'I really loved that sculpture you did. The one of the golden eagle. Actually I thought it was brilliant. It's my favourite bird.

'I'm glad you liked it,' Chris replies.

'Go on Chris, give it to the boy, it's only worth a couple of thousand,' Alastair, quite drunk now, arm anchored heavily round his son's neck, teases.

'My husband is the meanest man alive,' Nita comments. Is she joking? Is there a flash of resentment in her tone? 'If he were a ghost he wouldn't give you a fright.'

The conversation changes track after that; Nita speaks about her work, in particular a child undergoing chemotherapy for cancer.

'I remember as a little girl having my feet X-rayed in a shoe shop for the correct fitting.' This sudden remark from Liz is the first time she has said anything for some while, and they all turn towards her in surprise. 'I used to love seeing my green toes. It made me really happy.'

She never mentions her childhood; and Alastair removes his arm from round his son to reach across the table for his wife's hand. Somehow, for them all, this single happy memory is filled with poignancy and assumes disproportionate importance: a little girl, feet planted firmly together in a machine, gazing down at the green bones of her toes, and the rim of space between them and the shoes. Alastair's eyes exude boozy affection. And seeing them like that Wiz can, for those minutes (and how his heart fills), almost believe that nothing is wrong after all. Or if it was, then it might get better.

On the whole, he reflects later in his bed, listening to the creaking geese, waiting for the last train to rumble past, it has been a good evening.

In their bed, Alastair attempts to make love to Liz. But he is flaccid, cannot get an erection; rolls off her, disgruntled. 'I'm sorry. It's the drink.'

'It doesn't matter.' He has his appointment with Megumi tomorrow.

'No. It wouldn't, would it?' he mutters, his voice slurred but the innuendo clear nonetheless.

She lies beside him, still and tight as a mummy, arms

crossed protectively over her body. 'Why haven't you told me you're seeing Megumi tomorrow?' she says quietly.

But he is asleep. Noisily asleep – and she so fearfully isolated in her wakefulness. Her fears, her isolation, the past, skipping voices – these are begining to take her over. They are beginning to take the physical form of mocking gargoyles. Sometimes they descend from the balustrades to which they cling, and chase, like hideous dwarves, after her.

10 ʃ

'... Three, present. Four, occlusal. Five present. Six, present ...'

Alastair's voice carries clearly outside the door; a youthful tenor. Megumi is in the chair. Those are Megumi's little even white teeth he is examining. And his fingers of one hand are firmly clasping her perfect chin, while the others feel the softness of her lips and his eyes penetrate the moist depths of her mouth, then meet her dark eyes – submissive eyes as he prods about expertly, tenderly at her teeth; every action he makes significant and symbolic. And his power over her, his skill, are a combined seductive force.

What if she burst in now, and before he could say anything, were to fling herself at him and kiss him passionately then and there, in front of Megumi? and later, tonight, she would undress herself slowly, then him, and make love to him the way she had done when she first knew him, when he had been a shy, reserved, good Catholic young man, and she an amoral dancer. And for an instant, a flash of an instant, standing there outside her husband's surgery, Liz feels a spark of intense sexual desire for him.

At any moment now the nurse – who doubles as receptionist – having heard the bell, will come out and find her here, and tell Alastair. 'What are you doing here?' he would demand coldly, thwarted.

She creeps away. But still finds it in herself to hope: perhaps he simply forgot about seeing Megumi today until he looked in his appointment book. Resolves, if he mentions it then I'll make the first move in bed. Experiences again that odd little sexual spark. Hopes upon hope he will mention it. If he doesn't, if he doesn't . . .

'Your trousers are above your ankle bone. Old Ferrrgus will be on to you,' Josh remarks at school. That's the good news: his jeans haven't shrunk, like he wondered the other day; he has really grown an inch – moved into third smallest place from second. But that's about all that is good. Everything seems to be conspiring against him at present. And now look what's happened: his mother and Frederick's mother have become friends, and Alastair's tennis partner, a divorcé, is madly in love with Erika, and she with him. 'I've got you to thank, Wiz,' she told him. He can't believe it! He hadn't envisaged they would play doubles. And even more weird, it turns out his mother has met her already at an old people's home where she was visiting some old Nazi – the tale becomes more convoluted by the minute. Erika has been round at least half-a-dozen times during the last three weeks; they even have friends in common. He comes home from school, and there she is in the kitchen. He can hear their laughter from outside, trinkets of female conversation, then the muted tones of exchanged confidences. Sometimes Anna is there also – it transpires she was one of the mutual friends – and the three of them might be sitting by the canal dangling their feet in the water, his mother smoking her penultimate cigarette of the day, wearing another new sundress; she never used to be interested in clothes, and the reason she is now is obvious. Cups of tea and a plate of melting chocolate biscuits by them, and perhaps Anna's watercolours – they look as though they haven't a care in the world, when he comes upon them like that; and he begrudges them every decibel of their laughter. Feels it to be at his cost. And so munificent are they – 'Wiz, come and join us' – 'Wiz darling, how was your day?' – 'Wiz, how lovely to see you' – 'How's the twitcher then?' Secure female companionship forming ranks against him while embracing him with their bountiful suntanned warmth; plying him with biscuits and tea and questions.

Plan A has been ruined.

But when his mother is alone, that expression, as though she is being pursued, returns to her eyes. Her lips are pale without the vamp-red lipstick. And almost zealously she practises her ballet exercises, as though she is expurgating something from within her. He is studying *Macbeth* at school, is reminded of Lady Macbeth continually washing her hands, scrubbing away her sins. And *A Tale of Two Cities*: Madame Defarge knitting, knitting. Obsession and guilt so often go together, don't they? He is so confused towards his mother now. And her face tumbles, stricken, when he shrugs away her arm, wriggles out of an embrace. He wants to get at her for messing everything up, wants to hate her, tries to harden himself to this end. Yet he misses the contact he himself evades. He is punishing himself as much as her. He is still her protector. And that makes it worse: that she does not know he has cast himself in this role and cannot be grateful, therefore. One of his parents' friends is a barrister. How can you stand up in court and defend someone you know is guilty? Liz asked once. And that is what he feels like: a barrister defending his client although he knows in his heart the client is guilty.

Oddly, it is better with his father at the moment. His father seems to be behaving rather strangely nowadays: abstracted, always in a hurry – yet conversely less irritable (perhaps he took seriously Wiz's remark that time with Nita?). When he is around he is mostly closeted in his Lair, playing Scott Joplin on the piano, or moody French CDs on the hi-fi. Or, now that the swallows have left their nest, is busy with the Austin Healey, reinstated in the carport. He has just fitted a new walnut dashboard in it. It resembles a cockpit, the interior, with all its dials and knobs. If the car didn't have to move, could remain stationary, he could quite like it, like a docile pet . . .

'Josh, do you know any women on their own, widows or divorcées or something?' he asked the other day.

'Fancy an older woman then?' Josh leered at him.

'Not for *me*.' He coloured, swung his body round one way then the other, trying to effect a casual image. 'Someone – I know, that's all.'

'Shit, you are weird. You're so secretive sometimes. Ask Sven, why don't you? He's the one that's always bragging on.'

He cornered Sven a little later. 'My mother,' said Sven promptly. 'She's divorced from my father. But she says she's sick of men. Or is it for you?'

'Of course not.'

'That's a shame.' Sven winked knowingly. 'Actually I used to know somebody – rather well – but she's left the area. Older women!' And he blew a kiss into the air.

'He's such a fucking bullshitter,' was Josh's comment, when Wiz reported back the conversation.

Plan B fills his nights, his dreams and his wakefulness; his mind is constantly preoccupied with Plan B, which he has already put into action – and has made a list with ideas on it. It is costing him quite a bit of money, as a matter of fact, as he finds himself in shops making odd little purchases. And he has quite a collection of receipts, discovered from raiding bins; and a few from a really posh restaurant, where he actually went inside. 'I'm collecting receipts for a collage I'm making,' he said. And the Italian manager was most helpful, and also gave him a handful of round white peppermints, like pebbles. He ate three; the rest he will keep, along with his other acquisitions. She will be bound to wonder about the mints, won't she? Knows his father never eats sweets. He had not known he could be so devious, is quite proud of his cunning – and then remembers with a sobering jolt: these are real people. These are my parents. Me. Our lives. It is all up to me.

If Plan B succeeds it will put an end to her affair. She will come to her senses and give up Klaus. That the world of grown-ups might differ in actuality from his youthful concept of it, does not occur to him. That his cunning could have harmful consequences, does not enter his mind. His conscience is clear. It is other consciences about which he is troubled.

But his own is troubled on another front today.

'Got the spare car keys?' whispers Josh this morning.

'Yes.'

'You'll see. I'll cure you. I promise. I tell you, my mother's a new person since she learnt to fly.'

Before he can be cured there is the English lesson to get through, and eight verses of a poem to recite. Cecil Day-Lewis's 'My Mother's Sister'. Naturally, he immediately thought of his own aunt; and when he read the first verse could, at a stretch, relate it to her: the green eyes, maybe; and with a bit of imagination, the hair she could sit on. There any similarities ended. The author, recalling himself as a four-year-old and ultimately a fourteen-year-old, apparently felt only chaste love for this good, selfless woman. Is he warped that he has these erotic thoughts about his aunt? Do other kids get a hard on when their aunts hug them? Fantasise about them whilst doing it to themselves?

He has a real problem learning poetry. 'Maybe I'm

dyslexic,' he offered to his mother. 'I mean I have a problem with maps too. I can never remember where countries are, or names of places. That's supposed to be a sign of dyslexia.'

Dyslexia excuses Josh from all kinds of things. It's really useful.

'Your bird books don't seem to pose a problem darling.' Liz, in her light, dry mode; the old cryptic lift of the eyebrow.

So last night he spent more than an hour trying to learn the poem – pacing his room, gazing out of the window at primary-coloured barges, at distant sun-drunk ponies grazing the bleached grass (and only a few weeks ago how emerald-lush it had been; and before that, bleakly flooded); closer to home – and the swans dozing in the garden in the extended shadows of the weeping ash, serpent necks looped and heads buried under their wings. All this familiarity. He could love it. He could enjoy it. Schrödinger stretched out (he was surprisingly long, like that) on his sweat shirt on the bed. He read to the cat, throwing his chest out in thespian fashion, arms wide: '". . . I see her against the pearl sky of Dublin/Before the turn of the century, a young woman/with all those brothers and sisters, green eyes, hair/she could sit on; for high life, a meandering sermon . . ."' Where was the rhythm? He could find no rhythm. To the mirror, facing himself solemnly then, and without the text: '". . . I see her against the sky – the *pearl* sky – of Dublin," um – "Before the turn of the century – with all those –" no – "a young woman, with all those sisters . . ."' Lifting up the book again to consult it, stamping his feet in frustration. One boy in his class could glance at a ten-line verse and recite it perfectly by memory a moment later. It wasn't fair. It really wasn't.

Old Hutchinson, so jovial and patient at the ornithology club meetings and on twitching jaunts, can be a caustic bastard if he thinks you haven't done your English homework. He refuses to believe that Wiz's stumbling, feeble attempts at recitation are the result of an hour's toil. So Wiz has devised a solution to the problem (although how many more times he can resort to these tactics without Hutchinson wising up to it, is uncertain). When it is his turn to stand up, on cue Piers Lomax, the boy in front of him – so fat his flesh cascades over the back rungs of his chair – obligingly opens his desk lid on the pretext of searching for something within. There, stuck to the inside of the lid, will be the poem, clearly written for Wiz to read.

'Faultless performance,' Hutchinson says this morning, with his wolfish smile.

'Thank you Sir,' says Wiz, grinning in response.

'Oh not you Miller – (in ornithology he calls Wiz by his nickname. It is as though he is two different men). '– No, Miller, I was congratulating *Lomax*.'

'Me, Sir?' Piers lets the desk lid drop with a bang. His rolls of fat judder with the impact.

'Yes Lomax. A most riveting performance.'

A general, apprehensive titter accompanies this. Laughter at another pupil's discomfort. Relief not to be the target oneself.

'Perhaps I could be treated to a private viewing of the performance after class is over. In my study,' Hutchinson, who is actually not old and looks little more than a boy himself, says.

Lomax is dealt with first – a beached whale with pleading eyes – and summarily dismissed. Then it is Wiz's turn. He squirms uncomfortably, defensively, before the master.

'I didn't think you would cheat, Wiz,' he says, surprisingly gently, and reverting to the use of the sobriquet.

Wiz raises his chin from his chest indignantly at this, grasping the short end of his maroon-and-grey striped tie.

'I didn't cheat. I don't. I mean you refuse to believe I try and learn it. But I do. I spend bloody hours—' the words are coming out in a hot rage, overtaking him, '—doing my work, saying the lines over and over and *over*—' stamping his foot now, furious, frustrated, tears spring to his eyes, his cheeks burning and infused with red, '—and you just refuse to believe me. I can't learn it. It won't din in. It just won't. It's not my fault.'

'Hey chap, let's talk this through.' Leads Wiz to a chair and makes him sit down. Sits down himself a couple of feet away. 'This isn't just about Cecil Day-Lewis and poetry, is it?'

He shakes his head, unable to speak, fighting desperately against crying, telling himself, I will not, I will not, face contorted with the effort. The master's eyes exuding sympathy, his tilted head, his leaning body and outstretched hand all demonstrating his compassion for the boy's anguish.

'You're allowed to cry you know. Men can and do and should cry.'

Tries to smile, gritting his teeth against his pain, and still shaking his head.

'Tell you what – I'll make us some tea.'

PG Tips teabags. His mother likes Lapsang. Ref*een*ed tea or pleb tea? she asks guests. The sight of Hutchinson – average height, slouch-shouldered, sharp ferret-featured, dark-sand-coloured hair – bustling about being domestic, is quite comforting in a way. The agony in him subsides and the overpowering urge to howl lessens. He notes small details of the room: the divan bed (Hutchinson also sleeps in here), the Doisneau prints Wiz recognises from a MOMA exhibition, a photo of a pretty black girl, pens in an 'ugly-mug' on the chaotic desk, and books everywhere. Except for a tracksuit top, all clothes are out of sight. By the time the cup of tea is in his hands he is almost controlled once more. So long as Hutchinson isn't too nice. If he is too nice then Wiz will be in danger of blubbing once more. It isn't so much that he would be ashamed; it's that he has the feeling that once he starts he will never, ever be able to stop.

'Is it something you want to talk about?'

'No.' Uttered in a clenched tone. 'Thank you, Sir,' remembering his manners; and then blushes as he thinks of his outburst. What came over him, yelling like that at a master?

'I know it's a cliché, but sometimes it really does help to talk about things.'

'I can't . . . It'll sort out.'

'Will it?'

'Yes.' *He* will *make* it sort out.

Whenever he feels daunted by something, his mother says he should see it as a challenge as opposed to an obstacle. Meet it square, she encourages him. It does help to see matters in this light. His brow clears slightly. If he applied this principle to learning poetry or prose, he wonders, would it help? He wishes he could view the prospect of this afternoon as a challenge, but he can't. He is, quite simply, dreading it. It distracts him for a few seconds from the immediate situation.

Hutchinson brings him back to it. 'I'm not going to pry if you don't want to tell me. But if you change your mind, I want you to know that you can come to me at any time. Any secret will be safe with me, I assure you. It won't go beyond these four walls. And you'll find me pretty unshockable.'

'Thank you, Sir. I'm really sorry. About everything.'

'Forget it.'

'You won't say anything to my parents or to Ferr – Mr Fergus?'

'Four walls.' Hutchinson gestures round him. 'Oh, and by the way, I was going to save it for ornithology club tomorrow, but I'll tell you now to cheer you up. I'm planning a small trip for anybody who's interested at the end of the summer holidays.'

'Where?'

'The Lake District.'

Wiz gives a start. The tiniest seed of excitement begins to throb in his chest.

'To Haweswater,' the master says, looking levelly at him.

'You mean—'

'There's no guarantee you'll see one of course. You know there's just one breeding pair, and they have a twenty-five-mile territory.'

But Wiz ignores this – has bounded up from his chair. 'Oh God, I don't believe it. That's so great. It's brilliant. It's absolutely brilliant.' Suddenly everything else is inconsequential.

'Wiz, you mustn't set your hopes too high.'

'No, I know. I won't.' Nevertheless his face is transformed from a minute ago. Alive with excitement.

'Well that's what you must tell yourself – not to get your hopes up. I'd hate you to be disappointed. It'll be a fun trip, anyway. Try and see it that way.'

'I can always go to Scotland one day if we don't see one,' he says philosophically.

'That's the attitude.'

'One was shot a few weeks ago,' Wiz informs him shyly.

'I know. I read about it. Emma told me you were quite upset. The trip was her idea, actually. She wanted to tell you herself. And now I've spoiled her secret.'

Wiz is close to tears of a different kind now. God, what is happening to him? All these emotions curdling inside him, swinging from one extreme to the other.

'I could pretend I didn't know, couldn't I?' he suggests.

'That might be nice.' Hutchinson gets up. The interview

is over. Wiz is already up – has been revolving and flinging his arms about, and is quite drained now from such a gamut of emotion.

'Oh, and Wiz,' the master says at the door, showing him out, hand kindly on the small of his back. 'Try and see life as a challenge and not a hurdle.'

He stares at him in disbelief; then his face breaks into a wide smile. 'You should marry my mother, Sir.' And charges off down the passageway.

'And don't *run*, Miller,' comes the mock-stern voice after him.

The Golf is parked in its usual place, and behind it this afternoon, is the Healey, for some reason not in the carport. Stealthily, they slink up to it and unlock it with the spare keys.

'Maybe I'd better get it out for you,' Josh suggests. 'It's in quite a small space.'

'I don't know,' Wiz says unhappily, at the passenger door, fingers poised on handle. 'Suppose you bash it. Suppose you bash the Healey. Dad will go off his head.'

'Trust me, won't you, for fuck's sake?' Josh puts on his bored voice and Wiz shuts up. Where is his mother? Teaching? Tries to remember if it's ballet or English this afternoon, but can't focus on anything except the car and his dissolving bowels.

The Golf is a tip inside: magazines (what's his father doing with so many travel brochures?), envelopes, scrunched-up Kleenex, (sugarless) chewing-gum wrappers, biros, maps, wellingtons, tennis balls, tennis shoes, racket – apart from dog hairs, dead leaves, and a haze of dust over everything.

Josh starts the engine first time, shifts into reverse and manoeuvres the car out of the parking slot easily. Wiz is impressed.

'You see,' Josh gloats. 'I think I'll just go up the road a

bit and then you can take over.' Proceeds round the bend for a few metres.

'This bit's one way,' remarks Wiz. 'You're going the wrong way.'

'You might have told me. Now you tell me.'

'I forgot.'

'Oh shit. I'll have to do a three-point turn, and there are cars parked both sides.'

A car approaching them slowly, hooting; driver gesticulating. Wiz slithers down in his seat in case it's someone he knows.

'Fuck him,' Josh says, breathing hard, busy with the steering wheel and gear stick. 'He'll have to wait.'

Eventually they're facing the right way; have to pass his house again. Daring to peep through the gate: Lowry in the garden. And he aches to be there himself, safely the other side of the gate. Instead he is here, in the boiling hot, grubby little car, stopping now to pull into the kerb – and he is exchanging positions with his friend.

Josh is surprisingly patient and professional – goes through all the controls with him – which Wiz knows anyway – explaining how they work with the cool authority of an old hand, which in a way he is. Wiz hasn't seen this side of him before, had not taken seriously his ambition to be a racing driver one day. All kids want to be racing drivers, he said. But he has to admit Josh has what it takes. And so does his father. His father's rich enough to fund him while he indulges his whims. And maybe it is not such a far-fetched idea after all: Josh knows at least as much about cars as Wiz does birds, and whilst he is brilliant on the sportsfield, he is hopeless academically.

'Ve-ry sl-ow-ly,' Josh says. 'Now, don't try and steer – just keep the wheel steady. Keep your foot very lightly on the accelerator. Ease your left foot really gently off the clutch.' His passenger sun visor is down so he can look into the mirror, in true driving instructor fashion.

And so they accomplish their first limping, hesitant lap. Occasionally Josh takes the steering wheel from him or, ever alert, makes ready to use the handbrake when another car approaches. They do a complete circuit. Finally Josh parks the car for him neatly, facing the same way as before. They get out.

'Well done, well done,' he compliments Wiz, clapping him on the back.

'*You* were brilliant. It was brilliant. Really brilliant,' Wiz enthuses, sparkling-eyed, laughing in his relief. Weak-kneed, but happy. He did it. He's done it. He can drive a car. He slaps its side, like the flank of a horse, then boxes Josh in the same way Ben used to box him. It's not bad for one day is it? He can drive a car, he's grown an inch, and in September he's going golden-eagle spotting in the Lake District. It isn't all terrible.

Before locking the car, when Josh isn't watching, he places a lipstick beneath the road map on the passenger seat. He knows his parents are going out in the car this evening. His mother is unlikely to miss the lipstick, as she will have to remove the map before sitting down.

He shows Josh the swallows' nest before opening the gate. The birds have gone. Flown. But not far. A nearby telegraph wire offers a handy perch.

'One got nabbed,' he says. 'Before it had even begun to fly. There was no sign of it. It must have been a magpie or rook or something. A cat couldn't have got up there.'

They go inside the house. His mother is not in the kitchen, and he hangs the car keys back on the hook, under Lowry's choke-chain, while Josh pokes his finger through the cage at the parrot.

'Hi Mum,' he calls cheerfully, forgetful of his animosity.

She is not in, apparently. It isn't unusual that the doors

are all unlocked. It's that kind of road, where people leave notes on the front door, clear for intruders: 'Gone shopping. Back in half an hour.' Or, 'Key under mat.'

So he is not anxious. Besides, he is early. But – perhaps she is with Klaus at this moment. Feels the bitterness rise in him again, that callous little lump. She is probably in his arms.

'I'm just going to dump this in my room.' He swings his holdall at Josh, who's engrossed in conversation with the Archduke.

On his way upstairs to his room he passes Ben's. The door is wide open, and she is in there. Lying on her back on the bed. Asleep. Ben's ancient, sightless bear clasped in her hand across her chest.

11 5

'See you on the trip,' Emma said; eyes kohl-rimmed on this last day of school; glossy brown hair newly bobbed, forming wings on her narrow cheeks.

'Yes. Thanks. For fixing it with Hutchinson and everything.'

'All part of the service.'

Hesitated 'I like your hair.'

'Thank you.' Gives a little mock curtsey. 'And I like yours.'

'It's too curl—'

He didn't finish. There, just inside the school gates, in front of everyone, she kissed him goodbye. The lightest, briefest, most surprising, unselfconscious – on her part – contact of lips against his. They were the same height when they were close. Then without a backward glance, she darted away; everything she did was quick and assured. He watched her disappear from sight, willing her to turn round and wave. But she did not. Did it count? Was that a first kiss?

Nearly two months until the trip, until he gets the chance of seeing a golden eagle. And until he sees Emma again. In his head, on his RSPB calendar, in his diary, he is striking off the weeks, the days, calculating the hours, wondering how he'll get through them. Trying to recall the fleeting pressure of her lips on his, trying to remember, remember . . . Were her eyes shut? Is he in love?

Megumi has stopped coming to her.

'I think we have different ideas,' she said insouciantly across the scratched expanse of kitchen table, across the slanting blade of sunlight, the domestic clutter, symbols for which she had such scant regard.

'Yes Megumi, I think we have.' Careful to keep her tone even, not to fiddle with the teaspoon or pen or cotton reel, or show any surprise that might indicate she was not in control. Afterwards, threw in the rubbish bin *Sons and Lovers,* which she would never be able to look at again. Chain-smoked.

And that night moved out of the marital bed and into Ben's room.

'Why?' her husband said, with credible bewilderment.

He had the chance, didn't he, to tell her? Instead, simply, 'Why?'

'I'm sleeping badly,' she said.

If there was the comfort of doubt . . . But there isn't. She has found a lipstick in his car. Receipts and round white peppermints in his pocket. The smell of perfume on his shirt collar. Other pointers. Has resorted to that most basal of actions: riffling through his pockets and desk drawers. And in the wastepaper basket, a crunched up ball of navy and gold wrapping paper, and an empty box with the printed words 'a gift for you' on it. Sometimes the phone rings and is put down when she answers. Infatuation has made Alastair reckless, behave in the most atypical fashion. Does he really care so little about her to be so blatant?

They lie in their respective beds, she in the hollow made by her son; he with his leg flung across the mould of her body. Insomnia settles upon him now. Is this a crisis point in their marriage, he wonders? Or did crisis point arrive earlier and this is the acknowledgement? How should one tackle it? He has not been groomed for this. Nothing in his upbringing, in his nature, is compatible with this. Whilst on the one hand his mind roves – flies – with unsuppressed excitement to the possibilities on offer, on the other it is planted firmly in the juices of the past; begs, yearns for its return, cannot quite believe it is gone for good. Realises there is no one, but no one, in whom to confide.

Megumi, minus her wisdom teeth, uncomfortable and numb from the anaesthetic. And he shepherded her back to her flat, gripping her elbow. Lagged back several times to watch the tantalising sway of her bottom in its micro-skirt; legs long and olive-toned. Up two flights of stairs. The door closed behind them. And suddenly there he was, for the first time in nearly twenty years, alone with another woman in her apartment – this apartment patently not her taste with its drab beiges and browns. He had forgotten how to behave, how to react: longed to stay; longed to go, so that he could rehearse for this moment in the hope it would be repeated. She put on some music; chosen for him? *Enigma*. Pointedly erotic. I must lie down, she said, mumbling through her tortured mouth. Helped her onto the large sofa. Hovered awkwardly over her, toying with the petals of a large paper poppy in a square glass vase.

'What can I get you? Can I get you anything?' a piece of scarlet paper flower crumbled in his hand and fluttered to the floor.

'Possibly,' she said, peeping up coquettishly through downward lids. Hair a splurge of black around her, a waterfall over the arm of the sofa – wrenching his memory, catapulting it: Liz, a young dancer, dancing solo, naked, for *him* in his poky little room, then flinging herself face downward onto the bed, hair flowing forward; himself falling on top of her . . .

He did not know how to respond, thrown by the invasive memory. Had been envisaging this moment, and now foundered in its immensity; all the implications. Confounded by her interest in him. Why him?

Hovered for a moment longer, briefly touched the cascade of hair, withdrawing his hand as though burnt. 'I'll see myself out. I'll phone you tomorrow to check you're OK,' he said with that curtness which has always concealed his shyness and awkwardness.

He has met her for lunch in Gloucester Green once since then – nervous of seeing someone he knows, excuse ready on lips. Everything she says is measured and considered. She has strong, advanced views, uttered in that light voice. Her mind is modern, free thinking, Westernised, self-centred. Her vanity extreme. Her skirt barely covers her bottom, hair sweeps across one eye. The other gazes at him with unfathomable directness. She quotes Sartre – 'Being and Nothingness,' claims that emotion does not exist, is falsely manifested for convenience, has read all Anaïs Nin's volumes of erotica. They discussed safer subjects: Greek tragedy. Japanese politics. The role of Japan in the war. Japanese men's attitude to women. The cult sect, Aum. Natural disasters and their purpose in the world. She has no small talk, unless it is to flirt or fish for compliments, is fearsomely intelligent and self-possessed; and after two dental visits, the extraction of her wisdom teeth, the one luncheon and three further phone calls – two made by her – he is no closer to knowing her. Is not sure he likes her. But is hypnotically, irresistibly drawn to her and obsessed by her. Even a little afraid of her. He asks himself yet again (this early middle-aged average-looking man, as he sees himself), why me?

And now, lying alone in the marital bed, with its twin

troughs, and shreds of Liz's hair and blots of lipstick on the pillow, he feels a wave of grief coupled with a sense of failure; followed by a wave of triumph. She has given him the go ahead, hasn't she? Has shut him out, driven him away from her. He is fully excused any action he might commit; fully justified. The Catholic religion surely makes allowances for this sort of transgression: the hard-done-by husband. Excitement throttles him, sends needles through his limbs.

Does he dream of her, Liz wonders? Of oriental eyes? Imagining him in their bed, in his own private world. Since that extraordinary stray spark of sexual desire for her husband that day outside the surgery, Liz has had it several times. She is relieved at the signs of her return to normality, so relieved not to be forever entrapped in frigidity. Welcome back to womanhood. But laments the appalling timing. Or is that half, if not all of it? The fact that she has a rival. Her body asserting itself in protest and defiance. She will not test it on Alastair. Too frightened of rejection. And too frightened of acceptance – followed by rejection. No sweet words afterwards. No: I love you. No comforting: It's all right, you know. Everything's all right . . .

But the little nerve ends pluck at her with their resurrected needs. It was another reason for moving out. She did not want her body to betray her.

Switches on the lamp to read the paper. Ben's bear at the foot of the bed. Ben's scuffed trainers under the chair. All urges abruptly gone now with the snapping on of light and her first-born's domain illuminated. Sharon Stone watching her from the wardrobe. The yellow box holding his racket, skateboard and rugger ball; his old microscope on its stand. How would he have grown up? Bumptious and insufferable, for sure. But endearing and brilliant. His good humour would have made up for everything. His future partner would have needed huge resources of patience and tolerance, besides supreme intelligence and above average attractiveness. She will never know. Is forever responsible and penanced.

The paper runs a lonely hearts column on a Friday. She looks through it, intrigued. Some of the ads make her laugh to herself. One or two are blatant in their objective. One is clearly a married man: 'Weekday assignments wanted. Discretion assured.' The advertiser is well-built, fair, fit, 38, and extremely athletic . . .' Oi, oi, she thinks. Rent-a-bonk. Another makes her gasp out loud: 'Attractive, tall, 50-yr-old man would like to meet female leg amputee . . .' For God's sake. The man's sick. What a lot of creeps there are around. It's one thing to meet and then fancy an amputee under normal circumstances; but this shows some kind of sexual perversion she can only wonder at. Perhaps legs get in the way?

Turns to the announcements page; the Deaths columns. Stops at F: Farrell. Reads again. It must be her:

> On 21 July – after a long illness which she bore with utmost courage, Olivia Kathleen Farrell, a valued teacher to her students, and beloved friend and partner of Isabel. Funeral service at Tunbridge Wells Crematorium . . . Donations, if desired, to Parkinson's Disease Society.

Olivia Kathleen Farrell. Miss Farrell, she had only ever called her. Seen the Olivia K in signatures. How sad. But not all sad. From the small announcement it could be gleaned that she must have retired to where she had always longed to be, spoken of living one day: Tunbridge Wells; that she must ultimately have found love with a woman named Isabel. But she had died of Parkinson's. That was sad.

The meteor thud of memories, and Liz can see her clearly as she was then – a tall, angular forty-five-year-old woman with chin-length hair, short nose and freckled complexion and arms. Skin that blushed easily and burned in the sun. A nervous laugh like a prefix and suffix at the beginning and end of each sentence. A mellifluous voice that could captivate Liz when she listened to her reciting poetry or reading from plays. She remembered one of her favourites as being Rattigan's *The Deep Blue Sea*. She remembered, too, how the teacher's nondescript beige eyes would mist over when she listened to Brahms. She will forever associate her with Brahms. Her love of Brahms is through Olivia Kathleen Farrell. Her love of all culture. Remembers how she used to get the log fire going with an old leather pair of bellows. They sounded like an old man's laboured wheezing. And then the fire would catch and the small flames fan out before bursting into life; and the teacher would stand back looking at it with an expression of satisfaction. Never did she mention her fumblings to Liz. They remained consigned to the night, a beneath-the-covers secret. She would come into the room where Liz slept and, respectably clad in a Viyella nightdress, would slip next to her under the blankets. They never saw each other naked, except once, the beginning of it all. Liz was in the bath and Miss Farrell had come in – accidentally, to judge by her startled reaction. And then gazed as though mesmerised . . .

Liz can look back and recall only warmth and closeness and the ambiguity of the night. And large, cooked breakfasts the next morning – bacon, or softly boiled eggs and fingers of toast – to the cheerful accompaniment of Radio 2. Did she dream what happened?

Recollects, too, the little social gatherings held in her home: soirées, she liked to refer to them. And at these occasions she was in her element, transformed into the gracious hostess, brimming with scintillating conversation, a bright spot on either cheek, pouring out drinks while Liz handed round plates of deep-fried cheese puffs and tiny onion tarts to the assorted crowd of *artistes*. Liz had the impression, young though she was, that they were all takers. A struggling bunch with never-to-be-realised aspirations and flamboyant egos, descending upon her for free booze, free food and the chance to have a gathering and gossip under one roof. In return they offered her themselves, a glimpse of the other side, a risqué existence, wit, outrageousness. How sad. How sad.

Then after a year and a half, when she was seventeen, Liz holidayed with a friend and went to bed with her brother. Awkwardly she explained to Miss Farrell she had fallen in love, although this was untrue. I understand, I understand, the teacher said, dignified, and continued to take in the girl but ceased the visitations.

She had been tearful the day Liz had left school. Perhaps a little fearful too. Guilty in the stark light of their separating ways. 'I shall never forget you,' she said; and Liz reiterated. 'You won't –' Left it floating there. What? Tell anyone what happened? 'No,' said Liz.

And this Isabel. How long had they been together? She wishes she could write to her, meet her. Go to the funeral. But Tunbridge Wells was out of the question. She wishes she had remained in contact with Olivia Kathleen Farrell.

Lying here, her thoughts leaping about like summer-crazed fleas. Remembers reading about an earthquake – Greece? Korea? America? – and from under the rubble a man of ninety was found alive, and beside him the broken body of a four-year-old child. Where was the justice in that? She can hear the small boy's mother screaming wildly. Why? Why should this old man live and my baby die? Sleepily, she spins a story around it: The man had to live for he had a tale to tell, wisdom to impart, a lesson to teach. The child had to die, for he would have grown up wicked.

Herself. Once she was brave, stood up to people, didn't

care what they thought, laughed. Risked. Drove a car. It is so limiting not driving. She could go to the funeral in Tunbridge Wells if she could drive. Propelled into terrified wakefulness then from her drowsy rambling thoughts, at the prospect of driving, her chest in spasm. Pictures her father and stepmother plummeting into the ravine from the mountain road; and then her half-sister and brother were orphans. He has become a tree surgeon in Canada, and has four children of his own and three stepchildren. She never imagined he would grow up like that. His wife is eight years older than him, a tall, capable woman with Sioux blood in her. Liz, Alastair, Ben and Wiz visited them seven years ago. Her sister is another matter. 'We've had our differences,' she wrote after Ben died. 'But David (her banker husband) and I very much hope you'll come and visit us sometime soon in Esher.'

Didn't bother to reply. Recalls her as a little girl biting her arm and drawing blood; years later her nastiness over their father's trust fund, bringing lawyers into it when there was no need.

Macabre images: the dreadful one which keeps returning to her. A picture in the paper of a brown bear in China in a cage like a capsule, scarcely bigger than its own body. Injected with a syringe regularly and some substance drawn from its blood, believed to be an aphrodisiac . . . And she has heard about the appalling treatment in Indonesia to monkeys, served up live for food in restaurants . . .

The images, in a grotesque conveyor belt, trample on her tiredness and then settle to become more abstract, milder; skeins of colour rippling before her eyes, and stray sentences or words; the occasional clear picture: a cat basking in sunlight; a strange spiritual, transluscent-skinned face; books on a bowed shelf with undecipherable titles on tatty spines. Her father's thick eyebrows, wiry body and tanned hands. Her husband's curved nose and sensuous lips. I love you. I told you to check the tyres.

From one extreme to the other. Britain is engulfed by a heatwave. Yellow-ochre summer, and the dust thrown up by wheels, by feet. Melting tar, like black oil paint squeezed from an artist's tube onto the palette. Pavement trees wilting, and dogs too lethargic to raise their leg at them. Girls with lissom tanned limbs. Criss-cross streaks left in the blue sky by aeroplanes. Street musicians. Punts sliding by on the river and bodies littering the river banks, the parks. Crowded pubs. Concerts in Merton College Chapel and wine outside in the interval. Muted cries. The absence of birdsong. The scent of dry air, and of beer, and pollen. Impressions darting in and out like the dragonflies, like the wasps.

At the Trout a team from Radio Oxford was conducting an interview about the wasp epidemic. One of them approached Wiz and Frederick. Frederick was carefully trapping a buzzing creature in his glass, then turning the glass upside down. The wasp sounded like sizzling fat.

'Bingo,' said Frederick.

What did he think about the epidemic? the man asked Wiz.

'It's not their fault they're wasps,' said Wiz seriously.

'Hah. Good one. Like it. I'll use that,' the reporter said.

'Believe in God,' shouts the vagrant who patrols St Ebbes daily with his sandwich board.

Normality. But the secret undercurrent pulling ever stronger. And Wiz has found his mother's t-shirt that she sleeps in, on Ben's bed. It can only mean one thing.

Wiz picks up the second batch of papers from Mr Singh. Mr

Singh is unsmiling; one of his eyes is puffed up like a purple jellyfish. 'It is like being back in Punjab,' he says, pressing cotton wool doused with witch hazel to it. His neighbour sports a bruised and swollen lip. Each is threatening to sue the other for assault.

Bert's grey flesh reeks of sweat, his mouth of decay and indigestion and alcohol. His night's pickings lie in the dust about him in the form of peelings and bottles, cigarette stubs and paper bags; he forages bins as much for something to do as to assuage hunger. He was dozing when Wiz came upon him this morning, flicking at an invisible fly intruding upon who knows what dream. His mood now is as foul as his breath.

'You can't trust bleedin' no one nowadays,' he grumbles.

He has lost his mouth organ and therefore, he claims, his means of livelihood. 'A bloke tries to earn an honest crust and some toff goes off and nicks his property,' he tells Wiz. His leg is bound beneath his ragged trousers and Wiz is treated to the spectacular sight beneath the filthy bandage: a huge boil the size of a bottle top. Wiz can't bring himself to look at it.

'Get that,' Bert says proudly, forcing Wiz's head down with his hand. 'That's a proper good 'un that is.'

'Does it hurt?' He feels nauseous, wishes Bert would cover it up.

'Course it fuckin' hurts. What d'you think? Bloody toffs. All the same,' he says, going off at a tangent. 'Got it comin'. Shit . . .' Glares at Wiz. Resites his bandage and pulls down his trouser leg again, much to Wiz's relief.

He takes a swig from a brown strong-smelling bottle, then wipes a hand over his mouth. Lying across his good leg, the husky looks uninterestedly about him. The pile of sand beneath them has diminished and become absorbed into the ground. Bert's tattered coat is now their mat.

'I could take George for a walk by the river,' Wiz offers.

'Nah. He goes nowhere without me.'

'You could come too.'

'Nah . . . Bloody toffs.'

Wiz is not certain to whom he's alluding and feels discomfited. Does he come into the 'toff' bracket? Bert's piggy eyes have malice in them. This thing with him is leading nowhere, Wiz is beginning to feel. A few days ago his hopes were raised when Bert made quite a profound remark: that the kingdom of God was within you. But his mother told him that actually it was from St Luke's, chapter seventeen. How on earth did she know that, he asked? his mother being so irreligious – she used to tease his father for being 'pious'. 'Don't you remember?' she said. 'We chose it for Ben's funeral.'

However, he still harbours a faint optimism that one day Bert will reveal himself in his real light. This is my chosen route, he will proclaim; I can hide behind my grimy veneer and observe you all, laugh at you all, while all the time you think you're sneering at me. But this moment of revelation is starting to seem increasingly unlikely. Unless Bert is testing him deliberately.

'I'm really sorry about your mouth organ,' he says. 'Maybe it'll turn up though.'

'Nah. Someone nicked it while I were napping. Can't even take a fuckin' nap in peace nowadays.'

Wiz hesitates. He's been having some problems getting a decent sound out of his own mouth organ and the novelty of it has been starting to wear rather thin. After a bit his lips become sore. He fishes it out of his trouser pocket. If anything is likely to, surely this act of generosity he is about to make will prompt Bert to throw aside his cloak?

'You could have mine,' he proffers, with slight regret as he sees the greedy light in Bert's eyes. The instrument itself is an attractive thing to possess, like a chrome Mars bar. It made him feel important holding it, in much the same way as he likes the feel of his binoculars and camera hanging round his neck, and to know that his compass is in his pocket. These are somehow emblems of independence.

Bert has pounced, wrenching the harmonica from his grip. ''ere, that's mine.'

'It's not. It's mine. You know it is. You showed me tunes on it.'

'Maybe,' grunts Bert, clutching it for all it's worth. 'Maybe not. How do I know?'

'But you do know. You know I wouldn't take yours. And—' he's just remembered '– yours had a star stamped into it. Mine's got a circle. And it's not scratched.'

'Can't see. My eyes is bad,' the tramp retorts, squinting, pocketing the mouth organ for safety.

The ballet classes have finished for the summer, but his mother has two French boys and a German girl who she is teaching. The Japanese girl, Peg or Mug, or something like that, has left. But there is still Klaus of course. How does she – do they – manage to maintain the masquerade, pretending he is actually coming to her to improve his English? And what a *poser* he is anyway. This morning, after the Bert episode, Wiz goes to Dixons to look at their telescopes in stock and find out some prices. Ends up spending a couple of hours there. For the last half hour or so of that he is glued to a huge television screen showing a Dracula video. An Asian girl is also immersed in it. And for thirty minutes they stand there together staring up at the screen without speaking, and then part company.

Cycles home to find Klaus in his father's Lair playing the piano: Liszt, he announces to Wiz, when he sees him in the doorway, scowling. Granted, it sounds rather good, but to Wiz this is the grossest kind of disloyalty. This is his father's special place. And his mother standing close to the piano stool with a stupid smile.

'How could you let him play it?' he challenges her when Klaus has drifted off, after protracted goodbyes.

'What *are* you talking about?' She looks mystified. He hates the way she is always acting so innocent.

'That's Dad's room.'

'So? The piano happens to be in there.' Puzzled eyebrows still folded into her nose. 'It was a bit heavy to move into the kitchen.' A quirk of the old humour.

'Oh forget it.'

'Come on, give me a hug,' she pleads, opening her arms, a let's-be-friends smile on her face.

Not long ago he would have gone into their sanctuary. Now he doesn't make a move, feet planted sulkily there, in the light-splattered hallway. He can hear the echoing strains of Liszt. Sees Klaus's fingers streaking up and down the keyboard; Liz's wrapt expression.

'Has something upset you? You've been gone a long time.'

'I went to Dixons to look around.'

'See anything that interested you?'

'Sort of . . . Some telescopes and camcorders,' he says grudging her the conversation.

'And what about Bert? How was Bert this morning?' She struggles on, trying to draw him out, perplexed by his mood.

'Ok . . . I gave him my mouth organ.' So used to telling her things. Can't quite lose the habit.

'But you loved that harmonica. And I thought he had his own.'

'He lost it. I gave him mine. He thought I stole his.'

He's ended up talking to her as usual. He didn't intend to. He intended to punish her for Klaus playing the piano. For everything.'

'Oh no. Why would he think that?'

'Because he's crazy.'

'I thought you liked him,' Liz says gently, keeping the surprise from her voice.

'Well I don't now. He's just a loony old tramp.' As he says it he realises it's true. Disillusion bites into him. 'And he stinks.' He pulls a disgusted expression.

So this is what is wrong with him, she thinks. It's not her, after all. He's disappointed about Bert. In the same way as when he learnt Father Christmas was a hoax. 'Why tell it in the beginning, if it isn't true?' he wept, aged six and a half. Why, indeed, she wondered? To prepare the child for later lies?

'Shall we do something together this afternoon?' she suggests, longing suddenly to be alone with him, to establish their old rapport. 'We could go to the Pitt Rivers museum, or Ashmolean . . . Or take Lowry to the Parks. We could take a picnic somewhere, if you like. Oh, let's do something.'

She sounds like a girl, urgent, enthusiastic, her hand grabbing his impulsively. And when he does not respond, the light in her eyes deadens.

'I'm going to do my golden eagle project. I want to do that.'

'I thought you were doing one on otters.'

'I am also.'

'Well at least sit in the garden and do it. You look so pale.'

'I don't want to be disturbed.'

'I won't disturb you,' she says, sounding hurt, her hurt piercing him. And she turns away from him to go downstairs into the kitchen, calling out over her shoulder. 'I might even go out myself somewhere.'

Sits this afternoon under the weeping ash – the swans are nowhere to be seen – baseball cap low over his curls, shading his eyes; writing, glancing up occasionally at a small moored motor launch and the white-haired occupant sitting with his feet dangling over the edge of his boat, eating sandwiches.

'Writing your memoirs?' the man says.

He smiles. Doesn't reply. Why do grown-ups always feel the need to pass some comment? Goes back to what he is writing.

> The GOLDEN EAGLE. Scientific name: AQUILA CHRYSAETOS. Order: (Raptor) ACCIPITRIFORMES. Family: ACCITRIDAE. Length: 75–85 cms. 2-metre wing span. Britain's largest bird of prey. Females larger than male; lay eggs April. Incubation 6 weeks. At 11 weeks nest vacated.
>
> The pair in Haweswater – aged about 10 years – have had no success with breeding for 3 years. Golden eagles can live up to 20 yrs. They are 6 before they reach maturity. Contrary to belief golden eagles rarely kill sheep. They have no need, as in the mountainous regions which they inhabit there is plenty of carrion: sheep which have fallen from ledges or died naturally, similarly red deer, besides ptarmigan, hare, pigeon – just about anything, in fact!
>
> From a distance, in flight, a buzzard is often mistaken for a golden eagle, as both soar on wings raised in a shallow 'V'. Therefore it is important to note that the eagle's head is more protruding and its wings are often 'pinched-in' at the body.

He stops writing. The man has finished his sandwiches. Unties the boat from its mooring. Steps down behind the steering wheel and starts the engine. A deep gargling, throbbing noise emits, and a jet of smoke clouds the water. 'Cheerio then,' he calls. 'Happy writing.'

'Yes. Bye,' he says back this time.

Everybody is away or going away. Josh in Portugal, Sven in Sweden, Frederick about to depart for Zaire. Emma in Minorca. He pictures her in a bikini on a beach, surrounded by boys. Acting really cool, the way she does. He feels a small stab of jealousy. He picks up a stick and trails it around the dusty patch around him. Swan muck everywhere. His mother yells at Lowry for eating it. 'Dogs are so *gross*,' she comments. 'And your father lets him lick his face.'

A sharp-needle pain as a splinter from the stick embeds itself deep in his thumb. Wiz stands up, about to find his mother; she is brilliant at getting out splinters. Then remembers: he is supposed to be being aloof towards her. Can't just go running to her the way he did. Sits down again. He squeezes his finger until it becomes purple. The splinter becomes more entrenched. 'Blast,' he shouts out loud. Fishes out his penknife from his jeans pocket and selects a suitable blade; digs round a bit. It's really painful. Yet there is something soothing, something positive about the pain. He squeezes again, drawing blood but no splinter.

. . . There is an art to extracting a splinter, his mother said. You have to go at it laterally . . .

He has made a real mess of it, can no longer even see the splinter for all the mess, the inflamed, frayed skin and blobs of blood; but he can feel it is still there. Spits on it and rubs it a bit. There it is, buried as deep as ever, like a black comma, with all the flesh around it discoloured and lacerated after his probing about. He'll be lucky if it doesn't become septic. His whole finger might go septic. He might have to have it off. The poison could go all the way up his hand, even his arm.

He deliberates a few minutes, then he gets up and goes in search of his mother.

12

His parents are barely speaking to one another. Coolly civil, that's about all. There is no effort to do things together, no 'jolly-family' trips. Mealtimes are strained: the clink of cutlery against china, the sounds of masticating like the sounds of cymbals in a library; until the tension makes his throat ache and he finds it hard to swallow, and the urge to laugh wildly overtakes him. What is going on? It is worse than he imagined. His mother has moved properly into Ben's room – her dressing gown on the hook of the door; t-shirt nightdress on the pillow; brush on the desk; books and magazines on the bedside table. And the alarm clock. She makes no secret of it. Gave the excuse, Daddy snores.

And has she said anything to him yet, confronted him about the lipsticks, the receipts from restaurants, the other clues he has scattered about? He phones from call boxes on weekends, hangs up when she answers (his thudding heart, galloping pulse). And still Klaus turns up for his lessons. Swaggers in, hound-eyed. Wiz could end up as one of those tug-of-love kids you read about, pawns in their parents' war zone. With Klaus as a stepfather. Inconceivable. Can't wait to get away.

And meanwhile, each morning, after the paper rounds (avoids Bert assiduously, begrudges him the gleaming mouth organ; is contemplating buying another), he goes and sits in the Golf, puts the key in the ignition, starts it up. The swallows are nesting for a second time in the carport, so the Healey is always in front of him. But sometimes there is a space behind, if old Hatchet-face next door has gone off somewhere in her car early, and behind him will be empty. He's not entirely happy about moving the car in a confined area. It tends to leap about alarmingly, lunging forward with a cough. So usually he'll just sit in the driver's seat, engine running, head back, dreaming of where he could go if he wasn't stuck here, dependent. He'd like to drive to the Stokenchurch area, where red kites have been successfully reintroduced. To Didcot power station, where he has heard there are a pair of peregrines. To the sea – and camping out on the beach, listening to the sucking in and spitting out, the rolling in and out of the waves on the shore; standing at the water's edge, letting it skirt round his ankles. And thinking of the beach leads him to recall Ben showing him a granule of sand under the microscope. It looked like crystal. So beautiful. 'You see a whole new world under the lens of a microscope,' said Ben. He said it with wonderment, with reverence. Imagines fetching Emma from her home, escorting her suavely round to the passenger side of the Golf, opening the door for her, and driving off nonchalantly. He is friends now with the car. But still hates his father's driving, the way they seem to hurtle towards the vehicle in front.

A banging at his window. Wrenching open of the door. His mother's face zooming in close to his own, mouth in a rictus of horror, eyes huge and panicked, all great black irises.

'Wiz, what are you doing? What on *earth* are you doing?'

'Nothing.'

'But you are. The engine's running for heaven's sake.'

She leans over and switches it off, pulls the key out

of the ignition; tugs at Wiz's arm. He shakes it off and sits firm, jutting-lipped, gazing straight ahead through the windscreen (Mrs Gerald's whiskery mongrel squatting to shit on their mutual neighbour's path, beneath the festooned windows).

'Get out this minute, will you.'

He can hear the fright through the anger in her voice; doesn't respond, doesn't move. There will be a quarrel, inevitably. He can count on one hand the number of times they have quarrelled in fourteen years. There is even a spare finger for this time. Close as they are – were – their natures in harmony with one another, there never seems to have been reason or occasion. But of course, she does not know *he* knows about her secret, and therefore, he realises, she is uncomprehending about the change in him. Perhaps one day she will be grateful to him. And so, he sits on stubbornly, steadfastly, stoking his resentment with images of Klaus at his father's piano, Klaus leaning his head towards her at the cinema, Klaus's patronising attitude towards him. Gazes fixedly ahead – the little grey dog now kicking out its back feet before trotting off merrily down the road, curly tail wagging.

'Right. Out. Marching orders. I said *out.*' His mother's face a pale buff, except for the pink scar. White-lipped. Standing back now with hands on hips, washerwoman style.

For a moment he contemplates slamming the door, locking himself in and her out. Would she just remain there? If she didn't, he could sneak out and disappear until she calmed down. Unsure what to do, how to perpetuate what he has begun. Unused to this kind of situation, or to conflict, inclined as he is by nature to be acquiescent; accustomed to seeking the shelter of his mother rather than inciting her wrath. He is starting to wish he had simply got out of the car with dignity in the first place. To do so now would look weak.

While he is deliberating she reaches forward and yanks at his hair, wrenching his head back and sideways towards herself and the door.

'That hurts,' he shouts. 'You're hurting me.'

'That's the intention, pal. Out.'

'Bitch. Stupid bitch.'

'What did you say?' Her grip tightening, fastening round the roots of his hair. He tries to relax into her grasp, leaning towards her, clenching his jaw against the pain. Unable to see the incredulity in her eyes, the ugly contorted lines of her mouth. Mutters, 'You heard.'

A sharp stinging across his right cheek, catching his ear. His mother's hand. The shock. The sorrow. But she has released his hair, is standing back with an appalled expression on her gaunt face, lips drawn in. Looks skeletal in that instant. And he takes advantage of the situation to make a dash for it. Blunders up from the driving seat, barging past her and helter-skelter through the gate – not stopping to shut it behind him – inside the house and upstairs to his bathroom, where he drives the bolt home.

But there is no need. Liz doesn't move from where she is standing, is bent double as though in agony, her legs, her feet as though they are merged to become the trunk and roots of a tree growing from the ground. And she is shrinking and rising, shrinking and rising from her spot. What is happening all around her? Who is this unrecognisable teenager? Where has her little boy gone? And her husband running around with a Japanese siren. Everything is collapsing. She is collapsing.

And Wiz, realising his mother is not coming after him, parts the net curtain at the bathroom window which overlooks the street, sees her still by the car, folded over like a parcel, arms nutcracker tight about herself. He has a sweeping sense of very great shame for what he has done. Yet it is *she* who is wrong, he reminds himself; she who is at fault; she who has put him in this impossible predicament. Nevertheless, he is filled with a profound sense of loss. Feels directionless. The old rules and values and guidelines no longer apply. He is on his own with the anarchy of his confusion. Not used to having no one to run to, to counsel him.

They avoid each other for the rest of the day.

Days of seamless, mind-numbing sun. In the humid evenings, Alastair thrashes out the dregs of his Catholicism on the tennis court, whilst across the net his partner pants out details of his affair with Erika. Ecstatically in love, as though nobody has ever loved before. Alastair's own secrets tickling his tongue. A day has been arranged. He has set aside an entire afternoon. Meanwhile he and his wife flit politely past one another. He cannot avoid noticing her pallor when everyone else is suntanned. Her thinness. She has taken to wearing make-up: lipstick and dark stuff round the eyes. Is back smoking as much as before. Bakes cakes and biscuits which go stale, exercises obsessively, spends hours in the bath reading books he read as a student: Kafka, Hesse, Proust; picks flowers which she forgets to change so that the petals shed and the water becomes fetid. And sometimes his heart keens towards her. He cannot comprehend how they of all couples have got to this stage. Sees it written in the third person: The estranged couple . . . And from the bathroom cupboard the KY jelly and massage oil have gone. He presumes she has thrown them away. Was it on an impulse? He tries to imagine what were her thoughts as she did it. How very final and symbolic this seems to him.

At nights his thoughts are jumbled. Remembers: Ben shinning down the apple tree; skinned knees. And then himself as a boy, drinking Coca-Cola from a wasp-waisted bottle in the street – a forbidden thing; common, his mother said – and thus punishable. Wistful smile as he can see himself dancing (badly) to the Beatles. Has the urge to take up sailing again. And why not? Why shouldn't he? Is he not entitled to some happiness in this life? At nights: and the bedroom door is ajar. In hope Liz might come in? Making it easy for her? But Lowry comes in instead, springs onto the bed then lays very still, waiting to be turfed off. But he is not. Alastair strokes his silky osseous head, thinking that he is nervous about tomorrow, wishing Liz would manifest herself so he could cancel the whole thing . . . whilst at the same time his mind projects itself, propelled by excitement, and his hand stroking Lowry moves away from the dog's head to himself.

'Dear Mr Forest,' Wiz writes to the county recorder listed in *Bird Watching* magazine.

> I was at Shotover this morning and suddenly a goshawk passed overhead. At first I thought I must be wrong as I know there aren't any usually round here, but it was much bigger than a sparrowhawk and didn't have the distinctive striped belly, but was white and brown underneath it. Also, I could see through my binoculars that it had the white stripe going from above its eye to its nape, so that was what made me SURE. So I would like this to be made an official sighting, please, and for you to put it in the magazine, with my name. By the way I am aged 14 and greatly enjoy your magazine, which I get regularly.
>
> Yours, Oscar Miller.

Frederick and himself saying goodbye outside the Trout. Himself surprisingly sad. Frederick has forsaken his lenses for his glasses again.

'AIDS is rampant in Zaire,' he says. 'So that's it for a year, isn't it? Destined still not to have it for another year. "Zaire – land of the great apes and not so great AIDS." He gives a rueful laugh. 'Not to forget ebola,' he adds.

But his skin is a bit better. Less like a ploughed field. The sun seems to have done it some good. Wiz mentions this.

'Do you think so? I was wondering. Thought it was my imagination. You know, you see the same face every day. Not that I ever look at mine except to shave. And that's quite hard when you've got skin like mine. Oh well, that's something, if it's improved. At least that's something. And you've grown, by the way.'

'I know. Two and a half inches in three months.'

'All the worry, I suppose,' Frederick teases, not realising how close he is to home truths. Wiz has ceased to talk about his mother. The problem has gone beyond talking about. Especially as Erica and she are friends now. It could all get back. So he shoulders his cumbrous secrets alone.

'My mother's getting engaged you know,' Frederick says on cue. 'I've never seen her so happy. She deserves it. It's thanks to you, indirectly.'

Oh the irony,

'It's as well I'm going really,' Frederick confides. 'Everything's happened so quickly. I'm a bit jealous, in all honesty. It's strange not having her to myself. We've been just the two of us for so many years. This way, by my going away, I'll have time to adjust to the idea when I come home. I'll have lived away. I'll be able to adapt better. I'll probably want to have my own place and rent something. I want her to be happy. Of course I do. I mustn't begrudge it and be selfish. It's just it's hard to accept that's all. So anyway, my going will give us both some space.'

Wiz suddenly recognises what a truly nice guy Frederick is, and how he has come to rely upon seeing him.

'I'll miss coming here.' Shuffling his new trainers about

in the dusty ground, deliberately trying to coat them so they don't look so spanking new. His feet have grown also. 'I'll miss talking and going to the movies and things.'

'Maybe I'll write. You're a good-value kid.'

'I'll be fifteen when I next see you.' The same age Ben had been. It could happen to him on his fifteenth birthday. For a moment—

'Really old.' Frederick cutting short the wayward train of his thoughts.

'Well, anyway . . . I mean I hope you have a great time.'

'Yeah. And don't worry. You know. About your mother. Maybe you're wrong. Look, she's not said anything to *my* mother. I'd know if she has, as my mother tells me everything. So – I hope you find your golden eagles in the Lake District.'

'Yes.'

Stands awkwardly. Both of them awkward. Neither sure how to say goodbye. In the end they shake hands formally.

Wiz goes off. Frederick returns to clearing away the glasses for the last time. Looks up at Wiz's disappearing slump-shouldered back view. Calls out, 'I *will* write.'

Wiz turns round at that; rare, winsome grin illuminating his face. 'I will too.' Feels brighter. Already looking forward to a year of letters.

When he arrives back his mother is in the kitchen cooking, her apron over her shorts. She looks really comical like that.

'Hello darling,' she says brightly. False brightness. After their quarrel things have been forced; nothing mentioned by either of them about it.

'Hi.'

Until recently he would have kissed her and been embraced back by her, would have remained for a few moments in the enclave of her arms. They would have discussed their respective days. What are you cooking? he'd have asked. But doesn't this time. She volunteers the information instead: a chocolate cake. He guessed that anyway. The open page of the cookery book is covered with chocolate from other sessions.

'Want a clean-out?'

About to refuse – but why cut off his nose? 'OK.' Takes the plastic spatula from her and scrapes it round the earthenware bowl. The mouth-melting sweetness of cake mixture.

'Good?'

He nods without saying anything, wiping round the bowl with his index finger now, until only pale beige traces remain.

'I don't know why I bother to bake it. Everyone prefers the mixture,' she jokes conversationally.

He gives a polite, tight smile. Who is the cake for, he wonders? Is anyone coming round? Doesn't ask, as it would mean expressing interest. Doesn't volunteer any help with the pile of washing up, something he often used to do, liking the sense of homeliness and of companionship it gave him. He trails out of the kitchen, dragging his toes in order to age his trainers. Pursued by his mother's bleeding eyes.

Megumi's flat. Her rented room. Megumi's sagging, rented bed. Her own silk, Japanese print spread covering it. A two-foot-high Japanese puppet prancing overhead, swinging gently with the faint breeze coming through the open window. And outside, the sounds of Oxford normality drowning the middle-aged metronome of Alastair's heart. Everything else in the room – the green plant, more paper poppies in a vase, books, baskets with bright contents – goes unobserved by him. The bed, Megumi herself, even, briefly, a third-person image of himself, monopolise his vision's circumference. And in this small unprepossessing room above a French patisserie, with its view across St Giles to the Lamb, they fall voraciously upon each other. When did he last experience this almost excruciating, bursting sense of urgency, obliterating every other emotion? Her mouth, her tongue, her skin are fresh, soft, moist, female, responsive; young. His hands run frenziedly over her body – relishing its texture, its femininity – under her skirt, down the front of her dress and bra to the little perspiring cleft of her breasts; cupping his fingers round, massaging their smooth pertness and tiny protruding nipples – Megumi's head thrown back; throat pale, arced. Downwards again, to the surprising fullness of her thighs, lingering there, then sliding his hand under the elastic of her lacy knickers, making ripe, wet contact there – can't get enough of touching and feeling her invisible parts through the erotic flimsy barrier of her dress. Lips following the passage of his hands, then back to her mouth again. Mouth glued to mouth, tongue hooking round tongue. Her hand finally unzipping his trousers and finding its way: expert, small and firm. He emits a groan. She makes not a sound. One of her legs is wrapped round his, so that they fall onto the bed. He hardly knows what he is doing. Driven crazy. Pulls off his shoes, socks, trousers and pants, then wrenches her dress over her head. She shakes her long black hair free. And there she is, sprawled out for him: legs parted, back arched, skin an olive tincture. Small, rounded, perfect.

And something else. Her eyes seem to be laughing. Tough, unloving, greedy, knowing eyes in the deceptive sweet triangle of her face. Her seductress's hair falling forward from a centre parting. Pink tongue just visible through plum lips. She is utterly in control of herself as well as of him.

This glimpse of her unnerves him and in that enlightening

moment, with extraordinary abruptness, jolts him from one frame of mind to another, so that a complete reversal takes place within him. In a matter of seconds all his sexual urgency dissipates, shrivels like a burned piece of Cellophane; as he, more literally, shrivels.

The days and weeks of fantasising, the delicious night-time imagery and conjuring-up, the tantalising waiting; the grappling with Catholic guilt and marriage vows and the meaning of sin; the ghost of the old Liz reproaching him; the final knowledge that it was going to happen and the wonderful, agonising longing for it; being in a permanent state of erection like a twenty-year-old: all nullified. For weeks he has lived in a euphoric, rampant haze, as though drunk. Now he feels like a cored apple.

So, here he is in her room. No longer rampant. No longer demented with desire. Horribly sober and detached and chilled. And of course, impotent. He would be, is, will be, impotent. Has absolutely no desire for her whatsoever. Covers the embarrassing evidence of his deflated body and mind. Swings his legs quickly over so that he is sitting on the edge of the bed, hunching over himself. Ectomorphic type. Lean. No spare flesh on him except a bit of a tub-shape round the middle. What now? What must she be thinking, lying there motionless. Doesn't glance at her to see what her expression might be. What should he say? His first transgression – and he cannot go through with it. What is wrong with him that he cannot have sex with a beautiful, ready-for-him girl simply because she looks at him without love?

'I can't,' he says.

She misinterprets his meaning. Sits up and sidles close to him. 'I will help you. You will see. There will not be problem. Let me—'

'No. I didn't mean that I wasn't *able* to. I meant that I actually don't want to.'

'I don't understand.'

'No. I don't expect you to.'

'You are strange. Very strange man.'

'Yes, I daresay.'

'You do not think I am pretty?'

'You're very pretty.' He smiles at that, at her piqued vanity, pouting selfish mouth. So young and self-important. Used to getting her own way.

'Come here. I can make you want me again.'

The occasional cute lapses of language. The Japanese dropping of consonants. If he were another kind of man it is at this point he might wish to prove himself, show his prowess; and Alastair has considerable prowess. But he is not another kind of man. He gets off the bed, starts gathering up his clothes, strewn like bunting the day after the celebrations, bends to put his socks on.

She is sitting up now, arms propping up her head and neck, watching him lazily; sphinx expression.

'My American friend at college says to me that a man who puts socks on first, he is not trustworthy.'

'I've done it that way all my life.'

'However, she is correct, don't you think? You are here with me and you are married man.'

'But you—'

'It is not my responsibility if the man wish to go away from wife. It is his decision. He have ultimate command over his senses.'

'And that is precisely what I have just exercised,' he says, beginning to become angry, tugging on pants then trousers, tucking in his shirt as hurriedly as he can. Humiliated by her lecturing, disliking her; and himself for having allowed himself to become embroiled in this.

'I am disappointed in you,' she tells him calmly, sitting cross-legged now, unashamed by the displaying of her wares. 'I thought to myself, he is older, he will be different.

He will know what I want, not like stupid boys. I sense – I am clever with sensing such matters – I sense your marriage have problems, and so I think that this is man for me. But I am wrong. You are the same as others. You are stupid. You are weak. I am sorry for your wife.'

He strides from the room with no further words exchanged between them, leaves her sitting there in the lotus position on the silk spread, the might-have-been scene of passion.

Decides to walk in the Parks to clear his head. Still smarting. Chastened. Ears ringing. So where does he go from here? What is there for him at home? His marriage is clearly shot to bits. Is he destined to remain celibate? Cannot contemplate this as an option. Then what is the answer, if Megumi and her charms cannot provide it? Talk with Liz? Listen – we have to talk. Her porcupine manner, the separate sleeping arrangements, the disappearance of the KY jelly and massage oil, preclude it. Yes he is a coward. Yes, maybe he is weak. Yes, he has been proven untrustworthy. So then, will he muddle along? Others do. Alastair: very English and inhibited and afraid. A twenty-something Japanese girl has taught him a few salutary lessons.

It is back to the travel brochures.

13

Liz has a dream. She is in a huge multistorey car park, in the Renault in which they had the accident. There are a thousand exit signs, all pointing different ways. And she drives round and round and round, increasingly frantic, claustrophobia rising in her chest, in her throat, filling her eyes. An eternal quest to get out. Wakes up gasping. On fire with panic. Rolls over and immediately fumbles for the lamp – knocking over the glass of water beside it in her urgency. Ben's red sphere spills friendly pop-art warmth. The panic does not abate, so she gets up from the bed to switch on the main light. Goes then to the window; pushes it wide open, opens the curtains fully. Breathes in fresh end-of-the-heatwave rain; fresh cool; glistening pavements and road reflecting from the street lamps; the dull swishing of tyres from the main road; rustling trees soaking up the beneficent rain; night-time silence, night-time sounds; yellow ochre irradiation from the poet's room on the third floor of the house across the street. She should feel comforted, but doesn't. She is not a part of any of it. It is all outside of her and beyond her. The exit arrows, the terrible sense of being trapped, of isolation and panic that she felt in the car park as she drove round and round for ever, cling thickly to her, coating her tongue with fear and hopelessness. She is unable to rouse from this nightmare with the gulping, thankful relief others might feel. She only exchanges one nightmare for another.

Bitch. Stupid bitch.

I told you to check the tyres.

Shit. What's happening?

Your husband is very nice. He is very charming man.

I love you. Liz? Liz – why must you always to laugh at me?

Ben, with his appetite for life. And she had snuffed it out. Borne him and killed him. Her first baby. God, why didn't I die instead of him? Does she speak it out loud? Returns slowly, pensively, to bed, leaving the room illuminated. Draws up her son's duvet to her chin and lies there, calm now. Eyes wide and focused on the ceiling light, which is like a moon. Song to the Moon, from Dvořák's *Rusalka*. She danced on the school stage to that; a nine-year-old sprite, while another, older girl sang. Her grandmother clapping in the front row of the audience.

Thinking: divergent thoughts suddenly converging in a direction they have never taken her before. Thinking, thinking.

Hutchinson arrives in a matt maroon 'V' registered Saab with a silver wheel arch awaiting respray. He stands in their doorway in the drizzle, wearing cords and a green country-style waterproof jacket. Ferret-sharp face in relaxed holiday-mode geniality.

'Just our luck, the weather breaking,' he remarks to Liz. Puts his hand on Wiz's shoulder.

'It's a shame. Really it is.' She turns, about to hug her son goodbye, but he is off, running towards the car.

'Wiz – hey, aren't you going to say goodbye to your mother?' the teacher calls.

'We have done already,' she fibs. 'Inside.'

She watches him hoisting the holdall into the boot. It's obvious he can't wait to get away from her. Calls out, 'Bye *again* darling,' emphasising the 'again' for Hutchinson's benefit. Wiz lifts his hand in a semblance of a brief wave then opens the passenger door and disappears into the dark blur of the interior. Did he seem to hesitate beforehand? When he waved, was there an expression on his face as though he wanted to run to her? His girlish fair curls and shadowed grey eyes. She can make out the outline of his head in the back of the car – at least he is in the back – as well as two other figures. And a boy in the front reading something.

'Are you all right?' Hutchinson asks Liz, touching her arm. 'You seem distressed.'

'No, I'm fine. I worry, that's all. You will drive carefully, won't you?'

'I promise.'

'Have you – have you checked the tyres?'

He smiles. 'And the oil. And the water.'

'I'm sorry.'

'Don't apologise. It's natural to worry.'

She waves the car off. But cannot see anyone waving in return. It rounds the bend, out of sight, and Liz goes back indoors.

'You've grown,' Emma tells Wiz as he settles next to her. Burnished cheekbones. Freckled nose. Eye-whites, whipped albumen-white.

He is so pleased to see her. But his mother's urchin forlornness meets the corner of his vision and snags at his pleasure. Finds it hard not to pull open the door and immediately rush back to her, be hugged by her. Be pals with her again. The only way he can desist is by not looking at her. He can still smell her marzipan shampoo in his nostrils.

The other two boys are about to go into the upper fifth in the coming term. Harry, in the front, is bulky, studious, red-haired; chin falling into neck without definition. He is a bit of a know-it-all, can be pompous and belligerent, but nothing too bad. He poses no threat. Tom, on the other side of Emma, is another matter. He has laughing green eyes and black hair, is half Irish, half Italian, speaks fluent Italian, clowns about, and is the sort who laughs at you within earshot. He makes Wiz feel uncomfortable, that if he doesn't watch his step he will find himself the butt of Tom's malicious humour. He can't really understand why Tom bothers about the ornithology club, let alone should want to come on a trip like this. Until Tom elucidates: 'It's mainly for the photography,' he explains. 'I've got a new camcorder. I want to do an amateur documentary about Mardale.'

'Mardale? What's Mardale?'

'You're kidding, Miller—' Harry, swivelling round in the front. 'Haven't you heard of Mardale?'

'No.' The heat of inadequacy rising within him, staining his cheeks.

'And neither have I,' says Emma staunchly. Her arm slung casually across the back of the seat so that it is behind Wiz's neck, which prickles as though tiny electrodes are attached to it. She is all in black: black jeans, black polo neck, black anorak. Glossy hair and skin. She looks so svelte, so stylish and so way beyond his reach. He must be out of his mind to think she might fancy him. Girls of her age – seventeen – go for boys at least the same, if not older. And his voice hasn't even broken. One thing is for sure: she's replaced his aunt in his affections. His aunt came over the other evening, and he felt nothing; was rather ashamed to think he had ever fancied her.

The back of Hutchinson's dark-sand head. His steady pale hands with gingerish hairs, on the wheel. On the ring road now, heading for the M40. 'Mardale,' he cuts in quickly, before Harry can have the gratification, 'was a seven hundred-year-old village at the head of Haweswater. It was, so one gathers, one of the most picturesque of all lakes, in an unspoiled valley bounded by a wonderful variety of trees. The lake was just two and a half miles long. And then, in the late thirties, Manchester Water Corporation decided to make it into a reservoir. This meant building a massive dam. It also meant extending the lake another two and a half miles. The only slight problem was Mardale. It was in the way. So what did these far-visioned jokers do? They did the obvious thing, didn't they? They demolished the seven-hundred-year-old village. Flattened it.'

'That's unbelievable.' Emma, outraged, slams her fist into her palm.

'You mean, hanging wouldn't have been good enough. I agree. So – what do you think has happened this exceptionally dry summer?'

Catches Wiz's eye in the mirror. Wiz racks his brain for an apposite answer; fails. Hates the way this is becoming like a lesson.

'The lake—' Harry begins.

'We know you know, Harry,' Hutchinson says.

'Well it's been on the national news. Everyone should know.' Disgruntled.

'I've been away,' Emma tells him.

And Wiz never watches the news. Finds it incredibly boring. Doesn't say it.

'Well the water level—' Emma starts.

'Would go down,' Wiz almost shouts jubilantly, happy to be able to appear at least half intelligent.

'Correct. And this is exactly what has happened. And also happened in 1984. And as a result of the reservoir drying, the ruins of Mardale have been exposed a second time.'

'Spoo-k-y.' Emma leans backs and shuts her eyes. Sooty lids.

'What about all the people who lived there at the time?' Wiz asks.

'Now aren't you a kind boy?' – Hutchinson, indicating, straining his neck towards the window to assess the traffic either side of him, and turning onto the motorway. A coach hangs back to let him into the middle lane. The traffic at this hour, nine o'clock, is fairly heavy. 'They were rehoused,' he answers Wiz. 'And for some of them it was like winning the lottery. Their cottages may have looked cutsie on the outside, but they had no electricity or water or inside loo, and were probably cold and damp. They were only too glad to be moved into a bungalow nearby with all mod cons. But, of course, that's not the point.'

'Anyway, I'm going to film it and try and interview some of the locals,' Tom says. 'And I'll try and make the eagles symbolic in some way.'

They are an odd little group, in the car. And it becomes obvious, as the journey wears on, that Tom fancies Emma and is trying to impress her. In a way he reminds Wiz of Ben, in showing-off mode, but without Ben's quick wit and intellect. Wiz discusses camcorders with him for a while to try and get on the right side of him, and is just beginning to feel safe when Tom says, 'So, you're moving out of baby-class this coming term then. It's Bye bye Shell. God, I remember going up from Shell into the fourth; it seems forever ago. Well, it is really.'

Wiz's confidence is demolished. A short-lived, false sense of security. But he knows this is just another attempt to score with Emma, by putting him down.

It does not have the desired effect.

'Some shells contain a pearl,' Emma remarks. 'Others are conspicuously empty.'

'What do you mean by that, then?' Tom leans towards her, face close to hers. Very firmly she cups her palm round his chin and pushes his head away.

'Work it out for yourself, you're such a big shot.'

Oh so cool. So marvellously cool, rising above it all; the only girl among four males. Almost regal. He loves her. Yes he does. He really thinks he loves her. Tom, the other side of Emma, sulking, humiliated. Fixed profile. And in front, the amused pink rims of Hutchinson's ears. Outside, heavy slanting rain, the interminable squeaking of the windscreen wipers. The interminable crawling traffic as they approach Birmingham. The weather forecast on the radio news, dismal for the next three days. And a combined groan greets this announcement.

'I want to wee,' Emma says, pulling a pained expression.

'I can't stop here,' Hutchinson tells her, looking at her in his mirror. 'Why didn't you go before we left?'

'I did. I want to go again. Girls have weaker bladders than blokes.'

'Is that a fact? Well who am I, a mere male, to challenge you?'

He pulls off at the next junction, searches for a pub and waits while she dashes inside. Tom smirking in the back of the car, nudging Wiz now, as though he is an ally. The feebleness of women unites them.

'The pub was closed,' she says, upon her return. 'The man opened up specially for me.

She has that effect on people, Wiz has noticed. People do things for her, take her seriously.

'Move up,' she prods him gently with her elbow.

'Aren't you coming back in the middle?' Tom sounds almost plaintive.

'I don't think so . . .' And then, more kindly. 'It saves clambering over.'

There is another three-mile tailback on the M6 near Warrington; signs warning of delays due to road repairs.

'Typical,' shouts Hutchinson, throwing his arms up in frustration. 'And do you see anyone working? Oh no, that would be too much to expect, wouldn't it? We'll just lay out two nice tidy little lines of cones for a bit of fun, then go home and watch *Neighbours*. Honestly, I'd bring back death by firing squad, I really would.'

'We've had hanging so far, now firing squad,' Emma says. 'What's next?'

'The electric chair?' Hutchinson takes up the bait joyfully. 'Or would you say dismembering?'

He swings onto the hard shoulder, hazard lights flashing. Cruises past the stationary traffic.

'Gosh that's brilliant,' Wiz remarks.

'I've got no choice. The old car overheats in jams for some reason no one's discovered. Don't worry. I have my story off pat if the police stop me. But keep a watch out anyway. And *don't* draw attention to us, for chrissake,' he tells Tom, who is waving brightly at the cars and their fuming drivers as they glide past them.

'Everyone should do it,' Harry says.

'Fortunately they don't,' Hutchinson replies, avoiding a patch of broken glass. 'Else it would be back to square one, with the hard shoulder blocked also.'

Lunch at a Granada Services. Upstairs – past the burger bar (Wiz had already been planning his: a double, plastered with ketchup *and* mustard, and a separate helping of French fries), past the buzzing entertainment machines and yelping crop-haired youths, to the self-service restaurant – where the food bears a passing resemblance to what it sets out to be. So comments Hutchinson – whose plate, by the time he has finished gesturing to the chef in charge, is stacked with steak and kidney pie, roast potatoes, new potatoes, three veg and a sausage for good measure. On a side plate is a roll and butter, and in a bowl a sponge pudding. 'We can all share if I don't have room.'

They all peer and offer vociferous opinion.

'I'll worry it off in no time with responsibility for you lot,' he says. 'And as for you,' he observes to Emma, whose yogurt pot, fruit salad and glass of apple juice are placed neatly in the centre of her tray, 'you'll become anorexic if you're not careful.'

'No way. I'm over seven stone.'

'Obese.'

'Well I'm only five foot three. That's not skinny. Kate Moss—'

'I don't want to hear about it, I really don't.' Hutchinson wags a warning finger. 'These blasted skeletal models should be—'

'Electric chair?'

'No.' He smiles, pulls a 'so there' expression. 'I was *going* to say they should be ashamed of themselves for the example they set to young girls.'

'I'll eat tonight,' she promises him. 'I always have a big dinner.'

'I shall be standing over you. If you don't, I'll pin your feet to the ground and force feed you like a Périgord goose.'

They find two tables next to each other. Hutchinson is on good form; treats them as adults. Tells them how as a student he returned to his digs unusually early one day to find his landlady pouring baby oil over her lover. Lets them recover from laughing (Wiz faintly embarrassed; slightly shocked) then poses them a question.

'If someone were to offer you the choice of great fame and a life of luxury in your lifetime, then total obscurity after your death; or a life of hardship and no recognition but posthumous fame and glory for centuries to come – oh and by the way, you would know about this in advance – which would you choose? I was prompted to think of this when I visited the Hayward Gallery in London recently, where there was an exhibition of the Impressionists alongside their forgotten contemporaries, the "Salon" artists. Now, in their lifetimes the Impressionists were reviled and impecunious, whereas the Salon artists were fêted. Then look what happened.'

He makes them put their answers on different pieces of paper. Doesn't want anyone to be influenced by anyone else, he explains. He means Emma, Wiz realises. Hutchinson knows they would all copy Emma. Wiz doesn't care about fame. Or luxury. But the idea of his name being talked about for years after his death – it is immortality in a way, isn't it?

They pass Hutchinson their folded bits of paper. He has filled in one also. 'Like a polling station,' he says, unravelling them. Harry, Tom and Hutchinson himself have opted for fame in their lifetime. Emma and Wiz posthumously.

Across the Formica surface of the table she reaches out for his hand. 'Shake on it, pardner,' she says in a Western accent. And he shakes her hand seriously, mute, eyes blatant with his infatuation.

Back on the road. But not for long. Suddenly there is an explosive bang and a burst of smoke from the exhaust, and the engine cuts. Hutchinson freewheels over to the hard shoulder, hazard lights blinking again. Legitimately.

'Holy Mary and blast, and everything else a thousand times worse, but not in front of the children,' Hutchinson says. Stomps out of the car and opens the bonnet.

'I can't bear it,' Wiz moans. 'We're not going to get there, I know it. Everything's going wrong. Even the weather's changed. It's too much to expect this to go right.' He is despairing.

'Shush,' says Emma. And takes his hand. Massages his palm.

Tom leers at them. Chants the 'Wedding March'.

'Oh go back to the womb,' Emma tells him.

'It's electrical,' Harry says from the front, head buried in an ordnance survey map. 'Probably just the plugs or points or something.'

'It's only one of the points,' calls out Hutchinson from under the bonnet lid. 'The contact spring is bust. I'll have to get hold of the AA. They guarantee service within the hour.'

'Told you,' Harry gloats, as Hutchinson sprints, collar up against the rain, towards the emergency phone a hundred yards away.

'You see? It'll be all right. You're such a pessimist,' Emma consoles Wiz, giving his hand a final stroke before removing her own. He is ecstatic. For a moment he almost doesn't care about getting to the lakes, even about seeing an eagle, he is so ecstatic. Imagines being marooned here all night, under cover of darkness. Her and him asleep in each other's arms.

Just under an hour later, the welcome – as far as the others are concerned – sight of the AA's mustard-coloured vehicle. Cheerful driver with ripe northern bur. 'We'll have this fixed in a flash. You'll be on your way again in no time,' he says, disregarding the rain running down his neck. He is true to his word. And this time they really are back on the road. No hold-ups. Past Lancaster. Past the sign that says, Cumbria – and their spirits lift – and another pointing to Kendal, and the southern lakes. Then at junction 39 they leave the motorway and follow the sign for Shap, which reveals itself to be a dismal grey town straddling the A6; a mile of grim terraced houses and shops, made grimmer by the thick sky and the unremitting rain.

'Nearly there,' Hutchinson says. 'Don't worry.' He senses their anxiety about the surroundings by the sudden silence in the car. 'It improves.'

They turn off for Bampton, and in the space of a moment, a matter of a few hundred yards, are ferried a world away from the disheartening one they have just left. The winding lane narrows. To one side is a dry-stone wall, the other, high unruly hedgerow abundant with ripening blackberries. The broad expanse of the dales is dotted with Swaledale sheep; and looming as a backcloth is the sweep of the fells, patchy with bracken. And then something happens to the sky. A tiny fissure appears in it, becoming a chink of extraordinary brightness, the dense charcoal blanket ruptures and rents in two and a flood of yellow spreads rapidly across, casting gilded patterns on the fells, suffusing one half of the valley with light while the other remains plunged in darkness.

'Koos-ahtac,' murmurs Tom softly, whistling.

'I've never seen anything like it.' Emma.

Wiz is silent. *He* has. In a children's bible he once possessed: Jacob's ladder stretching up to the heavens, and the sun pouring out dazzling light onto God's messengers up the various rungs. For years it was his favourite picture. It filled him with unconscious wellbeing. Now this is like it; has the same effect on him. And for a few seconds he closes his eyes. Believes in impossible things.

'It's quite normal for round here,' Harry comments.

But Harry's prosaicism does not destroy the magic. Excited chatter breaks out.

'By the way Tom,' Hutchinson asks. 'What does Koo-achtac mean?'

'It's Arabic, sir,' Tom says evasively.

'I didn't ask what language it was. I asked what it meant?'

'I can't tell you. It's – er – rather – er – rude.'

'Oh go on Tom. We're all friends,' Hutchinson presses him.

'Well,' Tom says, sliding low in his seat. 'It means my sister's you-know-what.'

'Cunt, you mean,' finishes Emma equably.

At just past quarter to four they alight outside Field House in Bampton Grange, which is little more than a hamlet, comprising a few cottages and houses, a farm, post-office stores, church and a couple of pubs. The countryside is softly pretty. As they arrive a farmer is driving his herd of cattle over the old stone bridge. A sheepdog darts back and forth at the rear. Leggy calves that look no more than a couple of weeks' old press close to their mothers. The pattering sound of their hooves on the road surface; anxious lowing. Wiz makes a grab for his camera from the boot, Tom for his camcorder.

Field House is a converted barn. The landlady is small, bird-like, and from the East End of London. Cockney-chatty. Emma has a room to herself. Wiz is sharing with Hutchinson. Glad he isn't sharing with either of the other two boys.

'You can have the bed by the window,' Hutchinson says, patting the candlewick bedspread.

'Are you sure?'

'Absolutely. I'll be first out in a fire.'

Wiz goes over to the window, which is sited low. Has to stoop to see through it: a greenhouse full of pots; marmalade cat aloft the roof; chickens scratching about in the garden of weeds and gravel; then – farmland and sheep. The sun's warmth beats through the Velux window in the room's sloping ceiling.

'Do you snore?' He turns back to Hutchinson. 'I mean, my father snores.'

'You shouldn't give away trade secrets, Wiz. However, I don't think I snore. I believe I whistle though.'

'Whistle?' Wiz laughing; taking his compass out of his pocket and throwing it in the air and catching it.

'Yes. Like a kettle.' Imitates the sound. Wiz tries to copy him. The pair of them laughing, blowing through closed teeth idiotically.

They bundle back in the car again and drive towards Haweswater, a couple of miles away – time is of the essence, Hutchinson tells them – park at Burbanks in a dead-end lane of painted bungalows and cheerful gardens of gnomes and windmills, geraniums and petunias. A face appears between the brown curtains of one home. Disappears quickly when Wiz waves at it. There are a couple of other cars parked besides theirs. Nobody else is about.

'Right. We're going to follow the western side of the lake as far as Measand Beck.' Hutchinson strides in front, telescope folded and slung over one shoulder, map in hand.

They take a small lane between the bank of houses and bungalows which peters out into a public right of way: wild raspberries straggling from the hedgerows, and the pungent odour of wild garlic wafting from the woods on the left. The rain starts up spasmodically again, even though the sun is still shining. They come to a gate with a sign on it: 'Blue-green algae are present in this area. They may produce a toxic scum. If you see a scum you should avoid contact with it.'

Wiz stops to photograph the sign.

'You photograph the oddest things,' Tom says.

Emma shoots him one of her piercing looks. 'Scum, sighted,' she says.

'Anyway, it's significant,' Wiz defends himself. 'It shows about the environment and everything.'

'*What* does it show about the environment?' Harry, blinking in superior interest. The pouches of his cheeks already mottled from the fresh air. 'Expand.'

Wiz feels an increasing sense of resentment towards both the fifth formers, that he has had about all he can take of them. 'Why the hell should I?'

He runs ahead angrily, in front of Hutchinson, holding his camera and binoculars away from himself to stop them banging against his chest. Emma catches up with him as he slows to a furious walk. He is taller than her now. A couple of inches. He says tightly, 'They're so bloody supercilious. They think they're so wonderful. All the fifth formers do. Why are they all like that?'

'Because *they* were given a bad time when they were younger and they're getting their own back. And because sixteen is a bloody awful age for boys. They are even more pathetic at fifteen and sixteen than they are ordinarily.'

'Well I won't be like it.'

'No. I don't expect you will. You're sweet.'

Does he want to be sweet? It sounds distinctly unmasculine and little-boyish.

'What is "sweet?" Like a child you mean?'

'No, not like a child. Nice. Just nice.'

He stops in his tracks. Stands and faces her with one of his beatific smiles, holds his blown hair back from his forehead. 'Really? You mean it?'

'Yes. I don't say things I don't mean.'

He stares at her, uncertain. She stares back. He can't read her eyes. The sharp breeze blows her fringe away from her tanned forehead. He wishes he was older. Eighteen, maybe. Besotted-in-love. Knows for sure he's in love. A terrifying, wonderful, overwhelming feeling. He blurts out – hears his own voice blurting out: 'I wish I were older.'

'You will be one day.'

'Yes, but I wish now.' Out-pacing her, pretending to lark about, grabbing at an overhanging branch.

'Why?'

And the exquisite relief coupled with anguish as he answers – simultaneously speeding away from her – 'So you might let me kiss you.'

Bit by bit the sky seals up again. The blue is devoured.

Batwing shadows brush the fells. The track narrows and shingle peters out, to become a natural trodden path. The bittersweet, autumnal, damp-humus smells drenching the air. Yellowing trees; red bracken; and round, spiky, gorse bushes in flower. Small mountain ash in orange berry. Uncurious, glassy-eyed sheep. And a raven slowly lumbers its way between two crags. A squawking comes from the dark conifers.

A jay, thinks Wiz. He can still hear his own declaration in his head. What gave him the nerve? But he doesn't regret it. The rain becomes heavier; soft and exhilarating on his face. Then suddenly he has a glimpse of the lake, darkly glinting behind the screed of pines; and in abrupt reversal the sky parts again, the cloud shifts and the lake shimmers silver. The fells are neon-lit. He cannot get over it: the constantly changing sky. Then he sees it, marring everything: the dam at the north end. A monstrous scar extending the breadth of the lake. And from here the shore path is bounded by high, wire fencing resembling a frontier barrier. Yellow signs shriek out warning: Danger – Fast flowing water – High voltage – Deep chambers – Moving machinery – Dangerous chemicals. There is a bleakness, a sense of the futuristic, about this man-desecrated region of beauty.

Emma quietly rejoins him. 'It's such a shame.'

The entire reservoir is laid out before them. The jutting tongue of Riggindale. The water level is so low that the silt flanks of its basin are exposed, and rubble and slate form ugly mounds. Even in the bright sun there is a sense of desolation.

He can hear the water lapping on the stones. 'How could they?' he says to Emma.

The voices of the other behind them, all commenting now, loudly exclaiming and protesting. They can see figures over at Mardale Head walking across the basin, across the debris, over a small, intact bridge. Wiz raises his camera,

Tom his camcorder. Speaks quietly into it. For a while they all keep more or less together. The fencing has come down in places and it is possible to walk by the lake itself. But nobody is tempted. The beach looks unwelcoming.

'That great pile there was the old school, and the one next to it, a farm,' Hutchinson informs them, consulting the book he has just bought.

They come to a ford, Wiz is once more in front. Alone. Keeps lifting his binoculars to look at far-off shapes which are revealed as a sheep, or a shrub, or a cairn on a knoll. From somewhere comes the rushing of water; and he clambers higher to investigate, sure-footed and nimble. Tom is next, followed by Hutchinson and Emma. Lastly Harry. Panting, unfit. A waterfall cascades down smooth, worn boulders and jagged rocks; the path forms a natural bridge over it where the water goes underground.

'These are Measand Falls.' Hutchinson sets down his telescope. 'We haven't any time to go further.'

From here, in the sunlight, with the dam hidden from view, the lake looks more attractive. Wiz imagines it when the water level is high, concealing the rubble of Mardale, and the silt fascia of the lake basin. On the other side the countryside is mapped out, bounded into geometric shapes by dry-stone walls. Some hikers pass them, resembling camels with the humps of their equipment on their backs protected by green waterproofing.

'It's sit-down-and-wait time, folks,' says Hutchinson.

The string of tension uniting them. Wiz's hands clenched on his knees. Emma glancing at him. The minutes pass. An hour goes by. They stand about restlessly or sit, bored, on a boulder. The rain starts. Stops. Nothing flies overhead except a gull. The whole place seems empty of birdlife. There has been the raven, the squawking of the invisible jay, now the gull, but nothing else. It adds to the isolated feel of the place. Even the sheep seem motionless.

Down comes the rain again, too heavy this time to hang around. The fells, Mardale Head, the Rigg, are obscured. Hutchinson packs up his telescope in its case. Wiz shields his binoculars and camera beneath his jacket. Fights down his disappointment. There is still time, he tells himself. They retrace their steps briskly to the car.

At the Royal Oak that evening a drunken Glaswegian loudly holds fort, propping himself up against the cream vinyl wall. A group of visitors talk in raised voices. Birmingham accents. The elderly man is clearly deaf, and one of the women, her hair a lacquered platinum, has to keep repeating everything she says. In a corner two shrivelled, old, local men roll cigarettes in fingers stained the colour of hide. Behind the teak-veneered bar, the eccentric, middle-aged landlord takes orders in a camp, exaggeratedly pukka, accent. He has on a brocade waistcoat and a bow tie. He is completely misplaced in a pub like this, a village like this. It turns out he went to Trinity, Cambridge; Hutchinson to Trinity, Oxford. That he also read English. The pair spend the evening comparing notes. Chaucer bridges their differences.

Tom eating his sausages while playing darts against a youth with a shaven head and earring. Harry writing in his diary in miniscule writing. And one of the old men moves from his corner seat to come and sit by Emma and Wiz; regales them with stories. Of how, when the village was demolished all the graves had to be dug up and the bodies transported to Shap. And did you know, he says, in full flow now, that two hundred years ago, because Mardale had no rights of burial, the dead had to be taken to Shap then also, but there was no road. The coffin would be strapped to a pack horse which was led 1,600 feet up over the fells across Mardale Common. And once the horse broke away – galloped off with the coffin on its back and wasn't found until the next day, grazing in a spinney with the coffin still strapped to it. He, himself, could recall Mardale as clear as his own hand, he says, holding out his lined palm. He had attended the school there – all of a dozen pupils it could hold; had sat behind Bartholemew Parker – you could see the lice moving around his hair – whose parents had fought tooth and nail to hang onto their house; and he, Bartholemew, had gone on to be a director of the Manchester Water Authority . . . And did you also know, he told them between mouthfuls of beer, that the stone and windows of the draw-off tower built by the corporation came from the old church?

'God wouldn't have wanted that,' he says, wiping his mouth on his sleeve, stubbing out his cigarette. 'He creates a beautiful lake, and *them* destroys it. Destroys a whole village, a *church*, then shoves it in their flipping water tower. Nothing short of blasphemy that was.' Gets up, heads off towards the gents, already unbuttoning his flies.

'One up on Tom.' Wiz looks gleefully in his direction. He is losing to the boy with the shaven head. 'He'll go crazy when he hears he's missed out on a local story.'

'Just make sure you tell him. I will if you don't.' Emma is sipping wine with her fried haddock. Wiz pinching her chips. They're rather dry. He opens one of the packs of ketchup and pours it on the side of her plate without asking, and dips them in. Has finished his own chicken pie and jacket potato.

'What a dump this is,' she says.

The platinum-haired woman from the next table taps Emma's arm. 'Excuse me love, we came to see the Mardale remains – not that there's much to see – and someone said there are eagles around here. Is it true, do you know?'

'Yes, there are.'

'What time do they appear?'

Wiz listens in astonishment. Can't believe his ears. A

little drunk from his two glasses of cider; at having Emma to himself. Rather hyped-up-euphoric. He leans across her, suddenly impish: 'Ten past four,' he tells the woman, nodding for emphasis, earnest-expressioned. 'Every afternoon at ten past four by the bridge.'

'Thank you dear.'

She sits back again. 'Ten past four, Dad,' she shouts to the deaf old man beside her. 'He says they appear at ten past four.'

They smother their laughter. Their eyes are tear-filled with it. They bury their heads almost in their plates to hide their faces. He gets up and goes to the loo. Weird place, he thinks. He can hear the ranting Scotsman even in here. In the smeary mirror he catches sight of himself: out-of-control curls, flushed cheeks, glinting eyes. Mouth still laughing. His gums. He tries to stop laughing, but can't. His mouth tugs against his will. The laughter bubbles and brims. Feels really good. He pulls a face at himself.

Back at Field House – and Hutchinson in his boxer shorts, cleaning his teeth at the pink basin. He is narrow-shouldered; very white-skinned. And next to his alarm clock, beside the bed, is the same photo of the pretty young black woman that Wiz noticed in his study that day. Wiz, already in bed. He got into his pyjamas in the bathroom, embarrassed to strip in front of the teacher.

'I can't imagine getting het up about Chaucer,' he says.

'You would if you understood him. When you become familiar with the language it's a joy to read him. He's very humorous, and a great philosopher, a brilliant observer.'

'Mum likes Chaucer.' Blast. Why did he say that? He's always saying things then wishing he hadn't. Now old Hutchinson will start asking about his mother. He could kick himself sometimes, he really could. Doesn't want to think about his mother. Liz, forlorn-shouldered, forlorn-eyed in the doorway of their house. Bye again darling, he heard her call. And didn't acknowledge it.

But: 'A woman of discernment,' is all Hutchinson says.

And Wiz suddenly feels flat. Misses her. Actually, this is the first time he has been away on his own, other than to stay the odd night with a friend. He has always refused to go on trips before which have meant staying away. Been too shy. A Mummy's Boy, Ben used to taunt him. Ben, who was always independent. His mother seems – is – a long way away. He wishes he had said goodbye properly. Now he is parted from her his anger towards her diminishes and need for her grows. Klaus's face fades; hers is sharply manifested. Every feature, every contour, tiny line, her scar, the way her hair grows from her forehead: reproduced in his mind's vision. He longs, now, to talk about her to Hutchinson and have her come to life. But Hutchinson is in his bed, has switched off the overhead light and is deep in Wainwright's *Coast to Coast Walk*.

Wiz rolls over on his side. Sheet and blankets. He's used to a duvet. Cold. Hutchinson turns off his lamp. 'I can read by torch,' he says. 'I don't want to keep you awake.'

The moon shines straight through the Velux window, which has no blind. 'Shan't need to set the alarm. The light will stream through early,' Hutchinson says.

Wiz is quiet, thinking of his mother. He has a photo of them together in his wallet. And the girl next to Hutchinson's bed?

'Is she your girlfriend?'

'Who?' The teacher's voice, gentle in the darkness, across the space between their beds. Funny to be sleeping in the same room as old Hutchinson.

'The girl in your photo.'

'Yes.' Slight defensiveness in the terse answer.

'She looks nice.'

'She is. Very. She's a lawyer.' His pride is apparent in this voluntary morsel of information.

'She must be clever.'

'Yes.' Wiz can almost hear Hutchinson smiling. 'She's very clever. It hasn't been easy for her.'

'Why? Because she's black?'

'Mostly. Also because she's a woman.'

'It shouldn't matter though.'

'No it shouldn't. But try telling that to your average pea-brained client.'

The silence between them deepens. Hutchinson switches on his torch to read Wainwright. Wiz's breathing deepens. He drifts towards sleep. He is half happy because of Emma, half sad because of his mother. A chiaroscuro. The one seems to merge into the other. The happiness, the unhappiness blur and become indistinct, one from the other. He is conscious, as he falls asleep, of an incompleteness. Of questions without answers. Of space. A hole in which he is floating. He is cold.

'. . . Here are the sad remains of Riggindale farm, victim of the transformation of Haweswater into a reservoir . . .' wrote Wainwright. Hutchinson pauses in his reading, frowns. Sounds are coming from Wiz's bed. Whimpering. Small, animal-distressed whimpers. The moon picks out his huddled shape beneath the blankets. Hutchinson shines his torch on the half submerged head, and the arm flung out. Wiz is certainly asleep. Hutchinson turns off the torch. Then the moon retreats, and the room is infused with blackness. The extraordinary chameleon sky outside. And following the moon's disappearance there comes the intermittent, light tapping of rain on the Velux window, like scampering mice. Wiz's whimpering stops.

For several minutes he makes no further sound. Then: 'No,' he says clearly. Followed by a peal of Puck-like laughter. 'I'm chasing eagles.'

14

The French boy has thick glasses to correct astigmatism, distorting the shape of his eyes, and a stammer, which makes teaching him painful and difficult, involving trying to keep her gaze steady on him while he fumbles agonisingly to spit out a word or sentence. His face becomes twisted with the effort. She can hardly bring herself to correct him at the end of all that. They are not getting anywhere, this student and her. His parents are paying her for nothing. Her humour has deserted her, her lightness of spirit, and without these how can she teach young people, especially one like this?

When he is gone she does some ironing: a skirt of her own, a t-shirt of Wiz's, a couple of Alastair's shirts. Thoughtful, as the iron slicks back and forth over the flippers of the sleeves; can see Alastair buttoning up his shirt, easing his neck round the collar, knotting his tie whilst on the move. His long, tennis-strong legs beneath the tails of his shirt; his feet in black woollen socks. He only ever wears black woollen socks, which he puts on first, before anything. She used to tease him for that. He had looked hurt. It had been a couple of years before he got used to her caustic humour, her cryptic, dry remarks.

A pink mark on the collar of the shirt she is ironing – and the iron slips in her hand and scores the flesh of her wrist. Oh the cliché of a lipstick-on-your-collar stain. But anguish knows no clichés. There is no ointment for her anguish as there is for the burn on her wrist. She resumes her ironing; and as she irons the pink stain deeper into the collar she goes into the routine of her leg exercises, raising her left leg until it is at a right angle to her body; holds it quivering there.

She has to get ready for lunch at Erika's. There will be five of them. A girls' lunch, Erika said. I have something to tell you all. And Liz knows what that is. Putting on make-up to face her friend's happiness. Ready to bare her teeth in a glad smile through the crab soufflé Erika has told her she is making. She wishes she could cancel. Wishes she could take a train somewhere; sit in a train and rock obliviously with its motion, let it just take her wherever it will go. And there she will make her destination, wherever she has been set down.

The phone rings, but the caller hangs up when she answers. This has happened a lot lately. And this morning, in Alastair's navy blazer inside pocket – she has taken to ransacking his pockets – she found a crumpled drawing. Recognised one of Megumi's birds.

Three things this morning: the drawing, the lipstick, and now the phone call.

He puts down the phone. He had intended talking to her this time, unlike those other calls when he immediately replaces the receiver to make it seem suspicious. He really wanted to talk to her, tell her he loved her and missed her. Weary of being her protector. An impossible role to play. He wants to go back to being her son, wants her biting-sharp tongue and lift of the eyebrow, her gentle counsel; her gummy grin like his own and her sinewy dancer's arms cobra-like around him. But Harry wrenches the kiosk door open – 'We're all waiting for you' – and he hears her voice just as he hangs up: the first few digits of his own phone number. His mother's faraway voice. When he gets home he will make it right between them.

He emerges from the kiosk to confront Harry's irritable moon-face. Harry and Tom are not speaking. Harry has accused Tom of having dandruff, Tom, Harry of having BO.

'This is absurd,' Hutchinson finally says. 'We're supposed to be having fun. And for the record, everyone gets dandruff or BO at some stage, and halitosis, to boot. So let's get on with the day as equals, shall we?'

This morning they took the car to Swindale Common, turning off at Naddle Gate, driving over cattle grids, through heathland. They parked by a farm and walked down the track which led through scrubby grass to Swindale Beck. The fells alternately disappearing behind cloud then bursting into light; the clear-water, fast-flowing brook; thorny yellow gorse, teazle, thistle; and the steady munching of sheep. Between them they spotted a wheatear, three jackdaws and a meadow pipit. They had their picnic sitting on the car bonnet or on their anoraks on the ground: thermoses of milky-sweet tea provided by their landlady, KitKats, fruit, pasties, crisps. Not really hungry after the Goliath breakfast of Cumberland sausages and bacon. The smell of cooking had filtered upstairs from the kitchen directly below Wiz and Hutchinson's room. The smoky, mouthwatering odours had woken Wiz. Hutchinson was already up, dressed; reading in the chair. 'Good eh?' he remarked.

They are now at Burbanks again, where Hutchinson has arranged, as a surprise for them, to meet the RSPB eagle warden who will show them the eagles' sites. Iain is a huge, young, hairy Scotsman of immense height and breadth. Sirloin hands. Gets into the front with all his gear, his head brushing the roof. Harry has to squeeze in the back. Wiz and Emma are pushed closer together. She ends up half on his lap, half Tom's. Is the same thing happening to Tom's physiognomy as his own, he wonders?

'This is illegal,' Harry informs them all. 'You're only supposed to have five maximum in a car.'

'It's only for a couple of miles,' says Iain in his quiet, thick-accented basso.

They park at Mardale Head and pile out in relief, cramp-limbed. The sky is split open, gaping blue. Iain hoists his equipment across one huge shoulder and strides ahead. He looks like a Viking, Wiz thinks. His walking boots must be at least size thirteen.

Before them stretches the rubble of the village, spread over the dried-out lake bed. The old roads and walls are still intact, and the quaint hump of Chapel bridge. On Wood Howe, a small island normally submerged except for trees, a figure is standing immobile. The fells sweep into a wall round the basin. A lunar landscape, exuding a sense of surrealism. And a general mood of sombreness presides as they make their descent from the road, clambering over the rough ground and the stones. Nobody among the group speaks – they follow Iain in silence, who calls out odd bits of information: 'This whole area is the Riggindale valley. It's a classic U-shaped valley, as you can see . . . We're actually making for the Rigg itself . . . That's Kidsty Howes. Kidsty Pike. The one with the ridge is Twopenny Crag . . .'

Iain pauses to let them get their breath. They stop to look around them, absorb what he says and follow his pointing finger. Low, flimsy cloud now drifting towards the tops and obscuring them. Tom videoing madly, then letting his camera linger on Iain, who somehow blends with the landscape. Hutchinson looks dwarfed beside him; Emma, tiny and feminine. Wiz glances down at his trainers in satisfaction: they look as though he has had them all his life.

'A howe is a hill,' Harry addresses them, puffing. 'And a pike is a peak. I looked it up.'

'Well done, Harry,' says Hutchinson.

Wiz can never be sure when he is being sarcastic. He can feel the excitement rising up inside him, is striving to keep it at bay and not to let it overtake it. So afraid he will be disappointed. He must, Hutchinson told him, keep the thing in perspective. There will be other opportunities. Nevertheless, deep down, he knows how he will be if an eagle doesn't appear.

They continue walking. Over people's homes. Seven hundred years of history destroyed by a short-visioned body of beaurocrats, Hutchinson says angrily. Old Hutch, as Wiz now refers to him, has turned out to be a decent room companion, he tells Emma, who has fallen back, complaining of sore soles of her feet.

'I can't imagine seeing him at school again. You know, as an English teacher. I've seen him in another light, if you know what I mean. And his girlfriend's black. A lawyer. He says it's been really hard for her . . . What do you want to do when you leave school?'

He has almost lost his shyness with her, can talk quite naturally to her. The first girl he's ever really known or spoken to in any depth. His admission of yesterday, that he would like to kiss her, is as if the words had never been uttered. She probably thought he was joking, anyway; would never take such a remark seriously from someone like him.

'Go into a nunnery,' Emma says, deadpan. The others ahead of them now, picking their way over grey and umber heaps. For a moment he believes her. Then she bursts out laughing. 'Your expression. Oh Wiz, you really believed me.'

'Well you sounded so serious.' He looks wounded. Feels stupid, tricked; the familiar withering of confidence.

'Aw . . . Don't be upset now.' Links her arm through his. 'No, I want to go to art college. Study furniture design.'

'That sounds great.' Conscious of the sensation of her arm through his. Ticking energy. Tingling nerves.

'And you?'

'A vet.' The more often he says it, the more he is starting to mean it. A goal. Something to aim for outside all the uncertainties of his home life. He knows he will not waver from this decision. It is up to him to make it happen. He is not dependent on anyone else apart from himself for the outcome.

'Goodness.' Is there a light of respect in her eyes accompanying the small exclamation? Then she tilts her tanned face upwards towards the sky. 'It's going to rain again.' Pulls him onward. And he lets her tug him, before taking control and pulling her – laughing and protesting – 'ow, my feet' – across Mardale's pulverised remains.

They arrive at the Rigg, where the hide has been dismantled for the winter: an old sheepfold. And down comes the rain, just as Iain is about to set up the tripod and telescope. They all bury themselves in their anoraks and hoods. Water streams from the branches of the spruce and larch trees.

'This is hopeless,' Iain comments. 'You can't see a darn thing. And the eagles don't like rain.'

Optimism head-butted out of the way – and pessimism creeping in, in its place; and Wiz falls into a private mood of gloom comparable to the dour sky. The rain inveigles its way inside his trainers.

Iain occupies them with more information: 'As a rule eagles fly at a height of at least 1,000 feet,' he says, glancing round at them all as he speaks, voice muffled against the ferocious rattling rain. 'They are actually very shy creatures and avoid humans. If disturbed, they'll fly away, whereas a buzzard will attack. He pauses, continues, 'And quite often when an eagle is in flight you'll see it's surrounded by other birds – ravens, crows, buzzards – who form a mob as their means of defence. In fact, in spring a buzzard might occasionally even try and attack an eagle. This happened last April, and the eagle turned round and caught it and ate it! Retribution, eh?'

Wiz has plucked his biro from his pocket and is scribbling awkwardly within the cave of his anorak, taking notes. Tom grumbling because he can't use his camcorder, stamping his feet in frustration.

'. . . We had a hide at Whelter Knotts, near one of the perches – there are ten in all – and I was just sitting there when suddenly one of the eagles flew low right over me. I tell you, I got the fright of my life.'

'Oh God, that must have been great,' says Wiz, with envy in his tone.

'It was. Awe inspiring.'

For more than twenty minutes the rain doesn't abate. The sheepfold provides scant protection, and the rain drips from their hoods, their anorak collars, down their necks, inside their socks. Ian does his best to keep them entertained. Explains how virtually the whole of the year in an eagle's life is orientated towards breeding and incubation; how the male and female take an equal role, and are openly demonstrative towards one another, indulging in 'talon grappling' mid-air. Pair-bonding, he calls it.

The rain lessening and mist lifting, the clouds thinning and suddenly clearing – and miraculously the fells are exposed once more. Out comes the equipment. No time to lose. Iain fixes together his powerful tripod and telescope, Hutchinson his smaller one. Iain positions it for him, training it, like his own, on the granite face of Long Crag. Emma – ladies first, says Iain – is the first to look through the larger telescope. He is endlessly patient, endlessly informative. Seems genuinely to want to convey his passion to them, and for them to share his enthusiasm and knowledge. It's a whole way of life for me, he tells them. Not just a job. In the evenings he researches, and is working on a book. His seven-month contract here has just come to an end. It's pack-up time. Off to Bempton Cliffs, North Humberside, in the new year, and the thousands of sea birds there.

Wiz's gaze fixes enviously on him. He envies everything about him: his freedom, his job, his life; his virile, masculine appearance.

He guides Emma's vision step by step: 'There is a very thin, pale vertical strip – actually it's a pale stone – you should be able to see. Either side of that are well-defined dark lines which are where the rain water has run down . . .'

His huge hand on Emma's back. Surely she must feel attracted to him, this immense Scotsman with his quiet authority and knowledge, and his air of a philosopher. Wiz can imagine her falling in love with someone like that. Could not blame her. Hurts, nonetheless.

'. . . Above is a kind of V-shaped cleft and the nest is wedged in there. It's a huge bundle of sticks. They've used it two years running now.'

'I've got it,' says Emma, with controlled excitement.

'OK. So, they alternate between this eyrie and another. The one you're looking at now is a mile from here. It's about four foot deep by eight foot wide. There were just two eggs this year, laid on March twenty-second, and neither hatched.'

'Why do you reckon that was?' Hutchinson asks.

'Could simply be their age,' the warden answers. 'The male's at least twenty-three years old, and the female at least eighteen.'

Wiz, writing furiously now. Forgetting his jealousy and concentrating on facts. Adrenalin flowing. Tom's camcorder latched onto Iain's features, homing in on his caveman hair waving about in the wind.

Wiz is last in turn on the telescope. He accustoms his eye to the contours of the rock face and finds the eyrie almost immediately; is then directed by Iain to a couple of perches. He has nicknamed them both. The one to the left of a crag, he calls pimple, because of its shape. Another, immediately below Kidsty Pike, is a small lone bush he has named Kate.

'Kate?' Wiz queries.

'Yep. Kate Bush.'

The sun is suddenly incendiary. Off come the anoraks. And all they can do is sit and wait, intermittently glancing through binoculars or telescopes. Eyes strained constantly on the various sites or towards the sky. Silence between them now. Hoping. Even praying. But no eagle responds. Once they are fooled.

'Look,' yells Tom.

But Wiz knows, the second he sees it overhead: a buzzard. It's a buzzard. Half the size of an eagle and lacking the majesty. Only a buzzard. Although under normal circumstances seeing a buzzard would have been enough in itself; would have sent him cavorting with joy. Now he could kill Tom for getting it wrong.

The afternoon wears on. Iain tells them about the eagles' hunting habits. The weather changes again and again, and Wiz is worn out from his fluctuating emotions. And if they don't see anything with the warden, who knows all the haunts, what are the chances of doing so on their own? In a way he wishes they'd never come at all. And the day after tomorrow they go back home. And a few days after that: school.

He tries so hard to think about the good, the positive: his burgeoning friendship with Emma; the fact that he's coped with his first trip away from home; having grown two and a half inches in three months. And maybe he can return here in the breeding season when he can be almost assured of seeing the eagles . . . Or maybe go to Scotland one year. He takes a grip on the possibilities. Tries his utmost not to dwell on the dark: the vagaries of his parents, the dread they might divorce, Ben's phantom. One day he will be an adult and the crap will all be over with.

They pack up. Back over the rubble, which is slippery now from all the rain. 'Careful,' calls out Hutchinson. 'We had a hundred visitors a day to the RSPB post during the breeding season,' Wiz hears Iain telling him. They seem to have struck up a friendship. Hutchinson's head is tipped forward attentively. The men's muted voices reach Wiz's ears as he outpaces them. He needs to be by himself, to adjust to his disappointment. Conducts a little sermon in his head: Well I can come back . . . It was fun anyway . . . I've learnt a lot.

Beads of rain on the vivid orange rowan berries. Hanging oakweed. He comes to a protrusion of land where the skeletal black roots from severed trees sprawl like monstrous tarantulas waiting to pounce. They make him shudder. In fact the whole place does. He glances behind him to see how far they have walked, then upwards, and notices a mass of reddish shapes way up Lower Kidsty. Quickly takes the binoculars from their case: Deer. A herd of forty or fifty deer.

'Emma,' he shouts excitedly – and shows her through his own binoculars. Tom comes running also, followed by Harry, who slips, nearly falls, then saves himself in a spectacular balletic movement that has everyone laughing.

At Iain's home, provided by the RSPB, they sit at the small table in the dining area of the kitchen among the clutter of impermanence, the boxes and suitcases that herald his departure in a week's time. Wiz unscrews his thermos flask and is about to pour cold tea into the plastic cup, when Iain stops him.

'Don't be daft. You need something hot in you. I'm going to make some fresh.' He opens a packet of crumpets to toast. 'My pleasure,' he insists, when Hutchinson protests.

'Really, I've enjoyed myself with you all. I'm only sorry the kids haven't seen an eagle. But it's like that I'm afraid. You can't predict these things.' Unwraps chipped plates and saucers, bent knives from one of the packing cases, and puts them on the table.

'There'll be other times,' Hutchinson observes. Looks directly at Wiz as he says it. Who smiles bravely.

Smelling crumpets, and butter and jam; and the wood crackling in the grate.

One day he will do this. Before becoming a vet. In his gap year he will be a warden on a bird reserve. He can't wait for it.

And with the crystallising of his future, bites into his piping hot crumpet.

15

Alastair is standing over the bed – Liz we have to talk this evening. Does she dream it? Drowning sensation that transmits all the way down to her toes. Legs still sleep-numbed. The front door shutting: the finality of her husband's exit. Wind rattling the window like spilling beads. Grey light in Ben's room. The sponge of her head. She lies there, still half immersed in night's Henri Rousseau shapes and colours; recalls an incident from her childhood: taking the night ferry back to England. Waking up to the cliffs of Dover falling into the sea, she marvelled that behind the sheer chalk fascia hid the whole of England. And all you saw was a wall of teeth. An entire country inhabited by millions, all with their individual lives, lay behind there.

Liz we have to talk . . .

She is impaled by dread. Cannot face what he has to say.

The morning yawns in front of her. Klaus has changed his lesson to the afternoon. And how will she spend the hours in between? From downstairs comes the Archduke's squawking, changing to his ringing telephone. They have always assumed the Archduke is a 'he'. Funny if after all these years he was a 'she'.

Go for it, Ben used to say. And what is 'it'? The alternatives: she could stay in bed all morning; could see a friend; could go to the exhibition of Peruvian art at the

Museum of Modern Art; join the ebbing tide of tourists and browse the shops and sights; go to Browns and toy with a cappuccino and cheesecake, and eavesdrop on other people's conversations from behind the anonymity of dark glasses – for a few moments this thought is enticing. She could attempt to overcome her phobia and drive off in the car somewhere – and it comes to her suddenly: was that what Wiz was doing the day of their quarrel; trying to tackle an inner fear he had never discussed with her? She could walk in the Parks, sit by the river. Be. Once she was good at that, just 'Being'. Alastair had commented on it, envied her ability. He always needed to fill space with doing something: reading, making notes, playing computer chess. She has forgotten how to Be.

A few months ago she had been aware of a nascence of a tentative strength – like a subtle tickle – within her. It manifested itself in a renewed interest in her appearance, the things around her, the culling of her smoking; culminated in her mistimed sexual desire towards her husband. And then was aborted before it had time to develop. An energy curtailed. Remembers: her father's jet-stream criticism, his peremptory tone mashing her enthusiasm; her half-sister's demanding shrill voice; her stepmother's uninterested, patronising, 'Oh *really*?' – followed by her shrivelled little laugh – in truth saying: who *is* this child?' Liz's energy sapped. Sucked into their combined force.

School, her friends, books, dancing were her replenishment. And in the holidays, her grandmother preparing Welsh rarebit with freckled hands and carefully manicured pale pink nails, doing her best with treks to London on the Green Line bus, to the important museums and exhibitions; taking her shopping to Dickens and Jones for clothes a size too large, for her to 'grow into', but by the time she did they were out of date. Was always dressed either a year too old or a year too young for her age. Later, her grandmother's wrapped knees and plaintive lament: 'My poor child, my poor child.' And when she was gone, Olivia Kathleen Farrell took over.

Go for it Ma. For what? That rogue thought coasting along on the switchback of her other thoughts. Always present now. Sometimes muted; sometimes taking the form of a goading troll. Liz considers the morning's possibilities and realises: she has become frightened to go out. The alternatives are whittled away.

Habit, and Lowry's arrival in her room – muzzle pressed whining to her hand – drag her up. She envisages herself bustling around the kitchen with the radio on. *Desert Island Discs*. She will bake. She finds it soothing. It gives her a sense of homeliness. And so: she will fill the freezer with goodies, ready for Wiz's return, ready for the bad tidings her husband will break to her, of which she is already cognisant. Fill the house with wholesome TV-commercials-nuclear-family odours, and pretend that is how it is.

Oh how she yearns and pines.

The weather slightly more settled than yesterday. Disconnected blue atolls in a sea of dove grey. Hutchinson is particularly jocular over breakfast, chatting to the landlady, trying to motivate the silent group at the table (seersucker striped cloth; plastic cruets like at school), to make them glance up just once from their plates of Cumberland sausages, bacon, tomato and egg, chivy them out of their aimlessness.

There is no real plan for the day, so they walk to the Lowther Estate a mile or two away.

'I believe there's a birds of prey sanctuary round here,' Hutchinson says. Then: 'God, what a load of miseries you are.'

Scattered houses nestling within the cleavage of hills and clambering up two diverging lanes. Ancient elms and oaks shading the meadows which slope down to the beck, whose transparent water whistles over polished stones. On the other side of the stream, the fells sweeping away from the valley where native black ponies graze alongside long-tailed sheep.

Wiz lies by the stream. The beauty of the place deeply affects him; cuts him to the quick. He tries to ignore Harry's presence beside him. The others have gone to investigate the raptor sanctuary. Wiz is not interested. It's not the same seeing them in captivity. He doesn't really approve. Harry has remained behind to paint the view – preoccupied with measuring perspective at this moment, holding his pencil to his narrowed eye, then away. The soft dragging of pencil lead on paper. The brush whirling delicately around in the little jar of water. Actually Harry isn't too bad, once you get to know him. For all his belligerence, at least he doesn't jeer like Tom. In a way Wiz feels slightly sorry for him. He is old already. He will never change. He's already like a middle-aged man.

For half an hour the pair of them scarcely exchange a word. Wiz spots a kingfisher and duly records it in his notebook. From time to time peers through his binoculars into the far reaches of the sky, in case . . . Most of the time he lies back enjoying the sun edging its way through the pores of his face, letting the tranquility seep into him. Feels drowsy.

'What do you think?'

Harry's elbow in his ribs. Wiz, startled, irritated by the disruption of his peace.

'You woke me.'

'You weren't asleep. Your eyes were open.'

'I nearly was.'

'Anyway, what do you *think*? I've not finished it yet, of course.'

His small beige eyes are eager and intense. He thrusts the watercolour under Wiz's nostrils. It's surprisingly good. He has certainly captured the feel of the place. Looking at this picture would make Wiz want to come here – if he wasn't here already. Tells Harry this.

'So you *really* like it then?'

'Yes. It's great. It looks like a proper artist has done it.'

Pleasure shines from Harry's eyes. 'I'm doing art A-level.' This statement comes out in a burst, rather as though Harry is confiding a secret.

'Great,' says Wiz again. 'So will you be an artist?'

'No. I have to go into my father's business.' Said heavily; with resignation. And Wiz is given an insight into Harry's mind. He sees another aspect of him. A boy who, after all, does have his own longings but must cast them aside to comply with his father's wishes. It seems wrong, somehow. Wrong of the father to expect it. And what is also a revelation, is that Harry, who is so bossy, is under his father's thumb.

He is unsure what comment to make, but wants to offer some sort of consolation. 'Well I think you're really good . . . Maybe you could do both things. Do the business thing with your father *and* be an artist.'

'It's not that simple . . . Look, let's leave it.'

And the revealing moment is lost, as Harry bends to rattle his brush in the water then wipe it across a small green square in his box.

The others return: 'No eagles,' announces Tom. Emma takes her shoes off. Paddles barefoot up and down in the stream.

'Harry's picture's fantastic,' Wiz says, wanting the others to admire his work, to give the other boy a moment of glory. Harry is taken aback as they press round him, praise gushing forth. A new, modest Harry emerging. Wiz detects a moistness in his eyes.

'There's another birds of prey centre at Leighton Hall,' Hutchinson tells them as they walk back to Field House. 'They've got eagles there apparently. It's quite a drive, but it'll give us something to do our last afternoon.'

'Count me out,' Emma says.

'And me.' Wiz.

'It's better than nothing I suppose.' Tom has given up on Emma; on the whole trip; his mood has switched from one of cockiness to one of extreme, studied boredom.

Harry also opts to go.

'So me and Emma will stay behind,' says Wiz.

'Emma and *I*, Wiz. Emma and *I*.'

'What is wrong, Liz? There are tears in your eyes.'

It is as though her system has finally given up. The tally of disappointments, of grief, has acquired a notch too many. She is weary of giving; of missing; of emptiness; of flitting past with no contact. All the reserves of strength she had summoned up in order to cope with each sorrow as it occurred – gone. Her carapace has cracked and she seems to have collapsed. There isn't a part of her – mind, body, head, heart, every muscle in her back and shoulders, every facial muscle, that does not hurt. Her childhood keeps asserting itself to mingle with the present. The accident recurs and recurs. The seconds before it. The instant of impact. Waking up in hospital. Alastair's expression revealing what the doctor iterated – for Alastair was mute. Recurs and recurs. And she is worn out with it all, yet cannot sleep.

Nobody needs her. Not her husband, whose glance snags her throat with its hypocritical false concern. Nor any longer her second son. Once she felt guilty because in her heart she loved him more than her first. No, maybe that is inaccurate: differently; more easily. And now he flinches when she touches him, cannot bring himself to look at her, and when he does it is with torture and recrimination in his expression. What has she done to make him change towards her? He is distant from her at this moment, both literally – lying in wait who knows where for an eagle – and metaphorically. She has lost not one son but two. There is nobody in whom to confide. She has always been the confidante to her friends, never the confider. Too private. The ground is shifting from beneath her.

'No one needs me.' Head in hands. Curled forward over the kitchen table and open books. Small wilting neck and cropped black head like a seal, above a bulky cream cable-knit sweater.

Klaus depresses the button to stop the tape recorder. Enfolds his arm round her slight, woollen-clad frame, presses his lips to her hair.

'I need you, Liz.'

The warmth, the comfort of his cupped hand with its repeated stroking motion. Like warm cocoa. She relaxes into the caressing, sits up a little, leans back a little, her head towards his body. Schrödinger lying elongated on top of the folded towel drying on the Rayburn. The Archduke on his perch above the cage, busily plucking out tiny sprouting chest feathers. Lowry gnawing on a stolen bone beneath the table. A train hurling itself past. Sporadic rain. Mercury lines down the window. Memories. Voices like scattered gravel.

'Liz. You are so attractive, so interesting and unusual.'

Klaus turns his chair and straddles it like a horse. Tilts her chin gently, forcing her to look into his round brown eyes. Girl's eyelashes.

'No, Klaus.' As he lays his lips flat on hers.

He moves his face away slightly. 'I will do only what you are wanting.'

'What you *want*.' Tries to smile. 'Have I taught you nothing in the past months?'

'I make the errors deliberately in order that I can see you smile . . . Dearest Liz, don't you like me a little? I believe sometimes you do.'

'Of course I like you,' she shouts, shaking her head in exasperation. Angry with him because he can't understand what she is feeling; and because he is available to receive her anger.

'When I was a very small boy my mother told me a story about a mouse. Do you want I will tell it to you?'

Impervious to her anger; seems to take it as his due. He is inherently good natured. She relaxes again and rests her head tiredly against him. He is wearing a striped shirt over a thin navy polo neck; neatly creased jeans; expensive belt. His hair forms a thick line above his collar. His neck is muscular. What's wrong with her? For whom is she saving herself? Not her husband, that's for sure. She recalls youthful promiscuous days. Out of one bed into another. Rebelling against Olivia Kathleen Farrell, perhaps? Substituting sex for love.

'Yes. Tell me.'

And he tells her, whilst cradling her head and occasionally bending to kiss her forehead, of an orphaned mouse who lived at the base of a mountain and every evening heard a family of other mice singing at the top of the mountain. 'The mountain top was always bathed in sunlight,' he says. 'And the songs which they were singing were happy, beautiful songs. Like magic. The mouse at the bottom of the mountain was wishing very much that he can join them. He had no family, you see, and had the fantasy how it must be among them. So he decided he will somehow find a way to climb this high mountain to the very top . . .'

Liz, distracted by the charming story; lulled by his quaint English, by the hand round her head, by his masculine smell. Her eyes close – and she can feel the slight stubble on his chin as he nuzzles it against her cheeks; has no energy to resist him. Needy of being needed, of being wanted, of being a woman. Needy of love. His hand is down her pullover, beneath the V of her Indian cotton summer dress; warm on her breasts. She can feel her nipples standing out. It is as though she is someone else. This is not her house, her kitchen. She is not Liz. She is pure sensation, pure need. Pure, keening, painful emotion.

'. . . And the mouse sees the leaf floating towards him and he has an idea . . .'

He is a kind man.

'Klaus – come upstairs.'

Wiz and Emma making their way to Measand on their own. The temperature summer warm – and they tie their jumpers round their waists. Emma's arms bare and brown and skinny. Small breasts poking embarrassingly through her t-shirt. He tries not to notice, not to think of her in that way. Though in private he has been practising how to kiss, on his own hand: making a fist then pressing his lips into the soft part where his index finger is curled inside his thumb. Digging his tongue in there.

They climb to a cairn on the middle path and sit down on the damp grass, avoiding all the sheep droppings.

'It's quite a lot like Vermont here,' she says.

'Vermont? America, you mean?'

'Yes. My grandparents have a home there.'

'How come?'

'My mother's American. I'm half American.'

'Oh.'

Just when he thinks he knows her, he doesn't at all, and she slips away again, beyond reach.

'I've got Indian blood in me. Cherokee. Look.'

She drills his eyes with her own. The irises are yellow-flecked, and he starts to sink in them. Fails to see the Cherokee.

'Yes,' he says to extricate himself. She is so wordly compared to him. He doesn't have a chance. Not–A–Chance.

'They live in Boston, but they've got a holiday place by Sunapee lake. It's beautiful there. Woods all around. And deer. Chipmunks. The fall is wonderful. Paintbox-coloured leaves thick underfoot . . . The house is white clapboard – you know. With stencilling on the entire wall of the hallway. And they've got a sail boat. It's very small with a red sail. I go with my grandfather on it. Just him and me. I tell you Grandad makes the best ever pancakes. The American kind, not the English. They're smaller and fatter and you douse them with maple syrup so that the pancake sits in a pond of it. Then you put whipped butter on top. Mmm!' Chews on her lips.

What has he done, compared to her? She talks about Boston and Vermont so casually. He goes around with his eyes closed, he realises, forever timid. Boring.

'You're so lucky.'

'Me? Why?' She laughs. 'Wi-i-iz. You've got your "troubled" expression. What is it?' Slashes her hand crossways in the air, pretending to slap him.

'Nothing. Well, you've done so many things.'

'No I haven't. And anyway, so what?'

'Oh I don't know. Yes I do. It makes you interesting.' Shrugs moodily, picks at the coarse grass. Minute insects scurrying amongst it. Do they have feelings? imagination?

'OK, I'll confide something to you.'

He glances up at this.

'You know what I most hate about myself?'

Rolls closer towards her, smiling now. 'What?'

'Well apart from my many bad character traits—'

'What are they?'

'Not telling you now. Apart from *them, physically* what I most hate about myself is my birthmark. I've got a strawberry mark on the right part of my ribcage. I won't wear a bikini. I feel repulsive. I cry over it.'

'I bet it hardly shows.'

'Oh yes it does. It's huge. Like a red traffic light. It's five inches by three and three-quarters. I've measured it. It's gross.' Momentarily she looks genuinely stricken. 'I told you so you'd know that not everything's great for me. You see me as one thing, but nobody's really as you see them. Not inside themselves.'

He digests this.

'I hate my hair. And my gums showing when I smile,' he says.

'I like your smile. I told you that before. And your hair. You've got lovely hair.'

Reaches out to touch it.

Liz, lying shivering on the marital bed. Klaus leaning over her, tenderly examining her body.

'You have a body like a young girl . . .' He moves his hands lightly over her. 'There is only a tiny, tiny puckering of the flesh around your navel. It is like – it is like –' his hand pausing on her belly as he searches for the correct word. 'On a child's dress you have where the fabric it is sewn very close.'

'Smocking.'

'So.' Kisses the spot, lips lingering there. 'Liz, you are cold. You are thin, that is the problem. I shall warm you.' He clasps her tighter, murmuring endearments in German.

She cannot stop shivering. It is not her on the bed. Not her, absently running her fingers through this man's brown hair, down the solidness of his back – her hand does not venture anywhere else. She cannot bring herself even to look at him. He positions his body to cover hers. Everything he does, says, is tinged with consideration for her. Yes he loves her, there is no doubt of that. She cannot take his love.

Alastair.

Megumi's birds pecking in her skull.

'Oh Liz.' As Klaus enters her.

And the silent procession of tears down her nose, which he does not see with his eyes closed in bliss.

'It's really interesting how male birds don't have proper external sexual organs,' says Emma, breath coming in bursts, just behind Wiz as they climb towards the upper path, where the ground flattens out.

He is glad she cannot see his expression.

'It must be really awkward for them to mate, especially mid-flight,' she continues, on a level with him now. 'That's the sort of thing which makes me believe in God, you know. It's all so – intricate.'

Klaus stirring round inside her.

'If you knew how I was dreaming of this time.'

And a cracking-branch noise in her ears. The snapping back to reality. My God what am I doing? What am I *doing*? Trying to push him aside. Off her. Struggling to free her head, her lips from under the suction of his, disconnect their tongues. She is suffocating.

'Liz, what is—'

'I can't. I *can't*,' she screams, trying to breathe. 'Come out of me. Get off. Klaus get *off* me.'

Escaping from him, almost falling off the bed . . . and lurching into the bathroom. She locks the door and sits on the closed loo, bending forward so that her head is between her knees; seizes at wedges of hair – tugging and releasing it. Oh my God, oh my God, oh my God. Her teeth are like a cocktail shaker. Her shoulders, seismic-struck.

They stand by the Old Boundary Stone, just above the upper path. Ribbons of thin white cloud skim the tops of the fells. Wiz perches on the hump of a knoll, swinging his arms around him like a windmill. From this point only a sliver of the reservoir is visible and the cars on the opposite side appear as toys. The wind is stronger up here, whipping colour to their cheeks and making their eyes water. Emma unties her jumper and pulls it over her head, and Wiz catches a glimpse of her thin waist as her t-shirt rides up.

'We're five hundred and thirty metres high up here,' he informs her, having familiarised himself with the map.

'Does that mean above sea level?' It makes a change for her to be asking him something.

Checks the key. 'Yes. It says to the nearest metre above sea level.'

They lapse into comfortable silence, listening to their own breathing and the wind in the grass.

Klaus departs: 'I understand . . . Yes, really I do . . .'

Remarkable for his devotion, under any circumstances. She almost shuts the door in his troubled face.

For a few moments she is a creature possessed; charged with adrenalin and fury, hauling off the bedclothes, flinging them into the washing machine – thinking: at least he didn't come in me – re-making the bed with the striped duvet cover and pillowcases ready for Alastair's lone slumber. Remembers: Liz, we have to talk. Fear a vortex, and herself at its centre. The adrenalin spent, and exhaustion flooding her. Her head feels too large, too heavy for her body. She lies down on the bed; smelling clean linen and defeat.

'You never talk about your brother,' Wiz says.

'You never talk about yours.'

'My brother's dead.'

'I know. All the more reason. Mine's alive. There's nothing to say. Sometimes he's quite obnoxious, sometimes he's great. A typical alive brother, in other words.'

He ponders for a minute. 'Ben was the same, I suppose. He could be awful or quite bearable. He was the opposite to how I am. He was always larking about . . . you know . . . always cracking jokes. Maybe you wouldn't have liked him. He had a pretty high opinion of himself. But he was brilliant. Everyone said so. He was passionate about science. I mean, that was his thing. He used to rag me a lot. I hated that. But sometimes he could be fine. He was getting much better actually. Then he died.'

'Do you miss him?'

He thinks about this honestly. Misses how life was before Ben. How they were as a family. Misses the good bits about Ben himself. His staunch support when it mattered. As Emma said: a typical alive brother. Thinking about it from this premise changes everything. She has, as usual, rendered the complicated, simple.

Realises: 'Yes, I do.'

'How did he die?'

'In a car crash. My mother was driving. I was in the car too.'

'How terrible!'

'It was. Terrible.'

Liz, getting out of bed like an automaton. Her somnambulic passage to the bathroom, where she opens the mirror-fronted cabinet doors. Searches in there. Increasingly frantic. Finds what she is seeking right at the back, behind the milk of magnesia. Fingers curling round the brown bottle and tightening. Propelled onwards by the rogue thought, rogue voice. Her ruptured heart, and the two halves loudly chasing each other. Galloping hooves on tarmac. Her face in the mirror unearthly yellow. The pink, itching, throbbing scar. How could Klaus have loved her? She is hideous. And her body nothing but bones. Aching, aching bones.

The clouds thickening and gathering pace with the strengthening wind. The sun disappearing, and a chill spiking the air . . .

'It's going to belt down and we haven't brought our anoraks,' says Emma, staring towards Mardale Head, obliterated by a sheet of grey. 'I think we – Wiz?'

His head is swivelled in the opposite direction, his binoculars raised to his eyes. 'Emma,' he says, with quiet urgency in his tone, touching her arm with his free hand, 'Get your binoculars. *Quickly.*'

From a distance of perhaps two hundred yards away two huge birds are rapidly approaching. And this time there is no mistaking them as they draw closer: a pair of golden eagles in perfect parallel flight, regally soaring, their immense wings stretched wide and long heads like spears, as they bat their way southerly from the direction of the dam.

Wiz is almost sick with excitement, his whole body thrilling towards them, binoculars glued to his face. He can barely contain the urge to yell out; his tongue tethered, mouth parted in a silent, exultant whooping. And now they are almost directly overhead – oh God, he can all but hear the singing of their wings in the air – can decipher the paler, greyish patches on the underside of the flight and tail feathers, can make out the formidable hooked beaks, the raised fingers of the wings. Never has he seen anything like this. Never has he felt anything like this – and surely he never will again. His soul is on fire.

A barking 'Kaah' emits from of the birds, and it is as though this is a signal, for the larger of the two – the female – suddenly plunges into a dive, its wings partially closed, before soaring again spectacularly, then diving; repeating this several times while her partner circles high overhead, becoming enveloped in thin swirling cloud. Another 'Kaah' from the female; and this is surely a code between them – a love-cry? – as the next moment her mate is diving headlong towards her. He catches up with her; and there, in mid-air, above Wiz and Emma – transfixed, speechless, pressed against each other – the two eagles talon-grapple as Ian had described. Trembling fingered, Wiz exchanges the binoculars for his camera and begins taking photographs.

The display continues for several minutes; then, with another, a final, cry, comes abruptly to an end. The pair soar upwards once more, seemingly ever higher, disappearing in sedate unison towards Mardale Head.

And now Wiz wrenches off the binoculars and camera from round his neck, tosses them on the grass and breaks into a run along the flat path. Faster. Giving chase. Faster, faster, extending his arms wide. Flapping them. Planing. Launching himself. And he is flying, yes he is flying. Shrieking and laughing and *flying* . . . Comes eventually to a standstill, his shoulders lifting and falling from exertion.

The eagles are dots in the distance. And then there are only clouds. He stands gazing after them, chest full, breath trapped in his lungs. Turns back to where he has run from, to the far-off figure of Emma. She is smiling indulgently.

His moment. *His* moment. It is as though the entire performance had been for him. Him and Emma – as though it were intended they should be together to share it.

'Emma,' he calls. *'Emma.'*

The enormity of it all overwhelms him and he wants to break down and howl with it. He flops onto the ground. Lies sprawled on his back – careless of the damp, of the sheep droppings – spasms of elated laughter rippling through him, interspersed with the release of sobs of joy. It is as though his whole life has meaning.

At the precise moment hers has none. The bottle contains twenty-three Temazepam tablets – left over from when Ben had died. And she downs them all.

Emma appears with his binoculars and camera. 'You left these behind.'

He bounds up, grabs her arms and dances round with her.

'Fool.' She ruffles his hair.

And he pulls her to him without thinking and, forgetting his practice sessions, kisses her – a brief, reckless, daring kiss – before releasing her. Grinning afterwards, triumphantly; eyes alight. 'I've done it, I've done it!' Leaping around.

'What was all that about?' she says mildly, smiling back.

'Can I do it again? Properly.'

She falters, looks suddenly serious and vulnerable. 'I don't know Wiz. I really like you, but—'

'I'm too young, I know,' he says, instantly sober. But he can cope with her rejection. Right now he can cope with it.

'A bit. But you're cute. I really *do* like you. A lot. I sort of do fancy you. I just don't want your feelings to be hurt. You're so sensitive. And, well, we can't really go *out* together. Not yet. And in a year I'll be leaving school—'

'Do you have a boyfriend?'

'No.'

'If I promise I won't get hurt and everything, can I kiss you properly?'

'You really are *sweet*.'

That word again. And she sees his expression and, with a tender smile, takes his face in her hands and guides his lips onto her own.

Drowning in happiness. Is this what is meant by drowning in happiness?

And afterwards, upon his insistence, she shows him her birthmark.

'It's beautiful. I think it's beautiful,' he says, touching the pink stain. 'It's like a heart.'

The sun slews across the sky and everything goes black.

'Mr Hutchinson – sir – we saw the eagles. We saw—'

'Wiz, I'm afraid I've got some bad news.'

16

'Why, Liz?'

Because she wanted to die. Three days later is glad she did not.

She tells him: what she knows and does not know. Understands and does not understand. They slot in slices of the conundrum for one another. Taking a mallet to deceit. But sometimes the unpalatable truths are best left barricaded – for the time being at least; inconsequential shreds from a greater and more significant entirety. Then there are the answers Alastair cannot provide simply because he is unable to. What receipts? he says, bewildered. What phone calls? What lipstick in his car? Megumi never went in his car.

Liz's hollow cheeks and sunken eyes. Alastair's tears that keep brimming and flowing. His frightened hand a tight binding round the thinness of her lower arm. Avoiding the tubes and bags attached to her. Flowers – freesias and roses – in a hospital vase. Alastair's legs knotted round the metal legs of the chair beside the bed. The green curtained screen of privacy blocking out the sighs, the eyes of the other women in the ward: the moaning of one – the plaintive crying of a middle-aged woman for her mother long gone.

He returned home early to talk – Liz we have to talk this evening. But it was to try and make sense of what was happening to them, he explains. To put a stop to the spiralling deterioration. . . . 'I thought,' she says. 'I thought . . .' 'How did it all happen? Go so far?' he asks. 'We were the perfect couple.' He puts his tormented face between his hands and breaks down and quietly sobs.

Her fingers tenderly stroke his hair, the curve of his nose. 'Everything will be all right,' she soothes him, leaning over the pillow.

'It will, won't it?' he beseeches her, looking up imploringly. 'I love you so much. God I love you so much . . . When I saw you and I thought . . . Oh God . . .'

She has never seen him weep like this, even after Ben. Continues to stroke his hair. Her heart full. Eyes full.

She takes off her wedding ring, which has become loose round her finger, and hands it to him. He stares at her appalled.

'What—'

'Put it on my finger again. Please. Say the vows.'

Smiling now. His gaze not leaving her face. Sites the ring gently on her finger and holds it there. Captures her hand.

'With this ring, I thee wed . . . With this ring I pledge thee my troth . . . Is that right? I'm never sure of the order.'

'It'll do.'

He had set his heart on a camcorder, but it can wait. And perhaps he'd rather save for a telescope anyway. And Mr Singh has upped his wage fifty pence a round. Mr Singh: whose war with his neighbour had given him a purpose in life, oddly subdued now that his adversary has just exchanged contracts with an Italian who plans to turn it into a delicatessen. But already he is beginning to prime himself in readiness for future battles: 'Mark my words,'

he observes to Wiz. 'There will be hammering all day long for the next year while they do the alterations. It will drive me *crazy*, I tell you. I will be polite, of course, as I always am when I complain, but you know how the Italians are . . .'

This Saturday morning Wiz parks his bike down a side road and goes into the old jam factory, opposite the station. He doesn't quite know where to start looking, although he does have a vague idea in his head: something personal. It must be something personal. There is so much glass and porcelain – glittering stalls of decanters and dishes, inkstands, plates with buccolic scenes painted on them, vases, figurines, cups and saucers, *objets* whose usage or identity he cannot guess at, small boxes . . . And here he lingers for a few minutes over a round enamel box with a portrait of a beautiful young woman in the centre of its pink and gold lid.

'May I see that, please,' he asks the woman sitting knitting in the corner of her stall. The swift clacking of her needles. Thick, soft, charcoal wool.

'What dear?'

'There's a round box in the display cabinet here.'

'It's enchanting isn't it?' She stops knitting to assess him with kindly blue eyes behind spectacles. Her cheeks are maternal-fleshy. 'But it might be a little on the pricey side.'

'How much is it?'

'£1,250. It's South Staffordshire. Seventeen seventy, dear. It's a ladies' patch box.'

'Oh.'

She would have liked it so much. That such a small object could cost so much astounds him. He wanders off, round the other stalls, avoiding talking to anyone else. Wooden and lacquer boxes of all descriptions; books; chairs and other small pieces of furniture; prints; rugs; writing implements;

fans and hatpins and shawls. A trove of wonderful, mysterious things he could not have imagined existed. The place is crowded with people buying or browsing, haggling over prices. The alluring smell of coffee and fudge cake from the tearoom within the building. Vivaldi playing into the unconsciousness. He stops at a jewellery stall: bead necklaces dripping from stands – jet and amber, pearls, coral, lapis lazuli, opals; brooches set with blood red garnets and seed pearls, pendants, watches, rings and earrings, purses and handbag mirrors, silver and tortoiseshell vanity sets; tiny manicure sets; sewing kits, mother-of-pearl penknives and cigarette holders. A shrine for nineteenth century beauty and femininity.

He is bound to find something here. His eyes dart from one item to another. He tries to decipher the prices on the small white labels; some of the tags are ominously turned over, hinting at figures beyond his reach. And then, round the neck of a velvet-hatted dummy on the counter, he espies them: four lockets on chains, two gold, two silver. The stall holder, a heavily made-up woman engrossed in a book with a romantic cover, sips at her steaming tea and takes no notice of him.

'How much are the lockets please.'

She looks up reluctantly from her book. 'The prices are on them.'

So they are. The silver ones are £50 and £79 respectively. But the gold, which he prefers, are much more. The larger of the two is marked £210, the smaller, which is heart-shaped, £175.

'Fifteen carat,' she says from the pages of her book. They're all late nineteenth century. The chains are more modern. Probably nineteen thirties. Open them if you like.'

This is more complicated than he imagined; the catches are tiny and fiddly.

'Here. Let me do it for you.' She gives a resigned smile and sets the book down. 'Who's it for?' she asks, undoing the chains from the dummy's white plaster neck, taking them off and opening each locket in turn.

'My mother.'

'Her birthday?'

It will be in six weeks, he realises. A Scorpio. And yes, how his mother could sting in the old days. But the gift is for now.

'She's been – ill,' he replies.

The woman's whole mien changes; concern transforms her features. She lays the lockets carefully on the counter for him to inspect.

One of the silver ones and the larger gold one have initials on the inside of the lid. The heart-shaped locket contains a sepia photograph of a man. At first he is unable to make out the initials because of all the elaborate twirling. And then, with a sense of disbelief, he examines the letter on the gold locket more closely.

'L,' she confirms. 'Lily was quite a common name in those days. 'Lavinia, also.'

'My mother's name is Liz,' he says, fingering the smooth oval. Longing. Oh how he longs to buy it. But he can't afford it. Has only – *only*? when it seems like the earth – £184.50 on him. And another £4.30 back in his room. He's not very good at saving.

'You could always have her initials put in the other locket.'

'But I like this shape better. It's more . . . It's more . . .'

'Subtle?'

'Yes. And the other's so small. I mean, there's not room for a photo.'

'There's one in it now.'

'Yes I know but . . .' He already has the photograph in mind which he would put in this. Cut to size, it would be perfect. He can picture his mother's face, her joy. He is suddenly despondent: having found the perfect present, nothing else will suffice.

'Look,' – the woman watching him intently, his crestfallen expression – 'let me make a phone call. It's not my stall. It's my friend's.'

She picks up the mobile phone and dials the number. He listens to the one-sided conversation as she explains the situation. Every so often she glances across at him.

She rings off. The position is this,' she tells him. 'My friend can't do it for less than £195, *but—*' she adds quickly as Wiz's face slides into disappointment, '– is there any way you could pay back in instalments?'

'I do newpaper rounds. So I could pay it back next week.' He wouldn't take any videos out; that would save something.

'Well that's easy then, isn't it? I shall make up the difference and you can pay me back next weekend. You can leave me your name and address.'

He watches her wrapping it up in tissue paper for him, into a neat little square, speechless with gratitude. Hands over all the money he has with him and counts it out for her – too preoccupied to notice the wistfulness of a childless woman in her expression – and writes out his name and address for her in the cash book.

'I promise I'll pay you back.'

'I know you will.'

She stares after him as he heads for the exit, his step springy. Picks up her book once more, but does not go back to reading it. The cup of tea beside her, cold.

Back home in his room. Carefully measuring the photograph against the locket, cutting round it, putting it inside. He folds the tissue paper round it again, not quite as expertly as the woman did – and affixes one of his bird stickers –

a swallow – to it. There is a space for a message beneath the Latin wording: *Hirundo Rustica*. And he writes, To my wonderful mother, with my love, Wiz . . . And Ben.

She is in the library reading. Alastair is at the tennis club. She made him go. He did not want to leave her: she is newly precious to him.

Wiz stands just outside the doorway, can see her in the path of a ribbon of light from the window behind her. So thin and lost behind the wings of the chair. Wearing his father's socks. No shoes. A private little smile hovers about her lips. She looks tranquil.

In he goes. 'Mum . . .' over to her chair. Stands there awkwardly, his hand in his trouser pocket, drawing comfort from the small package in there.

'Hello darling.' She holds out her arms, and he bends to her level, relaxes against her. 'Sit down. You've grown too tall.' Pulls him onto the arm of the chair and strokes his face without saying anything at first.

He leans his head on her shoulder. He is still horrified by what she did. That she could have done it. It is so important that he raise the matter rather than pretend it did not happen. So important that he talk about the other things. Where to begin? His fingers in his pocket become clammy.

'It was you, darling, wasn't it?' she says gently, still caressing his cheek. 'The bits left around the place for me to find. The phone calls.'

'I thought you – Klaus and you—' Out it comes in a disjointed confessional. He was balancing the equation, he explains to her, as she nods, attempting to make sense of his jostling words. It seems, she gathers, he was actually trying to protect her.

'Then it all got so *complicated.*' His voice rises and he thumps his fist against the top of the chair. He tries to pull away, but she holds him tight, murmuring, 'Ssh. It's going to be fine. From now on everything's going to be fine. I promise.'

'You don't love him?'

'Who darling?'

'Klaus.'

'No.' Poor Klaus, she thinks. Poor Klaus. Has had a letter from him. From Boston. Gunning for a post at Harvard.

'And Dad?'

'I love Dad very much.'

'So – I mean, you won't get divorced or anything.'

'Not now or never.'

'And you won't ever do – try and kill yourself again?'

'I swear I won't.'

Both their eyes streaming. And all the main issues having been cleared up, he delves into his pocket and gives her his present.

'Here, this is for you. I got you something.'

Wiping his nose, his eyes on his sleeve. Watching her eagerly as she reads the little note, her mystification: 'And Ben?' she reads out loud. He is restless as a grasshopper as she first picks off the sellotape from the tissue paper, then unwraps it with slow, tantalising care. He is bursting with expectation. Finally she draws out the locket and chain.

'It's very old. Nineteenth century,' he says.

Liz, shaking her head wordlessly, holding up the chain, her chin quivering, features puckering.

'Open it.'

'I can't. My fingers are trembling too much. You'll have to.'

He opens it for her. Within is a photograph – there is only room for their heads and necks – of himself and Ben together.

'Oh no . . .' Her face crumples. Her arms haul him onto her lap – she is so bony, he can feel all her bones – and she hugs him fiercely to her. Hugs him and weeps and rocks him.

'I shall wear it always. I'll never take it off. I'll sleep in it,' she tells him when she is slightly calmer.

'It's got an "L" on the lid.' His voice is muffled against her. 'The lady in the stall at the jam factory said that in the nineteenth century names often began with "L".'

'It's all too much . . .' Liz starts hugging him all over again. 'It's all too much.'

Alastair, clearing out his Lair. From habit he had initially closed the door – then deliberately opened it wide again. Two bin bags full of travel brochures. Dave Brubeck's 'Unsquare Dance' blaring out merrily. And he whistles to it. Hasn't whistled for years. He comes across one brochure – 'Narrow Boat Holidays on the French Canals' – is about to discard it, then changes his mind; visualises rose-coloured villages and terracotta roofs, sun-wrinkled dark water. French food and wine, old churches . . . And Liz sunbathing on the deck while Wiz helps him navigate the locks and even takes the helm. And speaking of boats: what happened to his idea of buying one? Next week he will do something about that. They'll look for something together, as a family. Maybe they'll get one that needs a bit of work on it and he and Wiz can do it up ready for next summer. Where did summer go this year?

Reflects on how close they came to losing one another, to more tragedy; on how he failed not only his wife, but also his younger son. Reflects: no, things cannot revert to the same as before Ben. It cannot be as if he never existed. He and Liz will have to attend counselling sessions together again. But starting from the premise that they do still love each other, cannot be a bad thing.

A week later – and his aunt and uncle are over for dinner.

'Goodness, haven't you sprouted?' Nita says to Wiz, kissing him on the lips, leaving him unmoved. Tomorrow night he is going to the cinema with Emma.

His uncle staggers in under the weight of a huge box. 'Some wine for your father' he replies to Wiz's question as to what is inside, and putting it down with a 'phwew' in the corner of the kitchen.

A normal evening. A normal family. As though the bad was dreamed. Nita with her stories, Chris his manic staccato. His mother in a mini red tunic over black leggings; red lipstick. His father and her exchanging long meaningful looks that are a bit embarrassing. Flirting with each other. The food overcooked as usual. The Archduke chortling and plucking. Lowry beneath the table. Schrödinger on the Rayburn. General conversation about the government, about the Irish peace plan, about a new play . . .

'Shall we unveil the wine?' Chris suggests at the end of the meal.

'Wiz – open it for me, there's a lad,' his father says casually from the table.

He fetches a knife from the cutlery drawer, goes over to the box and slits along the thick tape. Pulls the heavy cardboard flaps apart. Inside is a bronze eagle. A smaller version of the one exhibited in the gallery. Wiz kneels over it.

'I made two,' Chris says gruffly. 'The life-size one and this.'

'It's incredible. Is—'

'It's yours.'

Wiz getting into his pyjamas. Tomorrow will be 1 October. He must remember to say 'rabbits' first thing in the morning. To remind himself, he writes a note in large letters and props it against the eagle at the foot of the bed.

Fancy old Chris coming up trumps like that. Adults are so unpredictable. He will not meddle in their lives again.

Liz and Alastair, their limbs wound tightly around each other. Nothing more. He does not dare touch her between her legs or make any sexual advance. He will just have to bide his time. The lamp out. Dull Oxford traffic beyond the window, which is slightly ajar. Her tummy seems rounder, the hip bones less prominent. And then he feels a hand on him, tentative, then firmer. Her fingers closing round him . . . Her face pressing down on his. Himself becoming erect. He doesn't move. Her mouth tastes of toothpaste. Her hair smells of cooking. His breath holds in his throat. He has to hear it from her . . . Her whispered, 'Make love to me.'

Wiz awakening the following morning, Sunday. Piece by piece, consciousness lapping at the shores of his mind. Then the awareness of a weight upon his feet. He is about to acknowledge Schrödinger when he spots the note against the eagle. Got there! The first time in months!

'Rabbits,' he says loudly. Then, in surprise, repeats it. 'Rabbits, rabbits, rabbits.'

What has happened to his voice? He tests it on the cat.

'Schrö-ding-er.' He starts laughing; and even his laughter is all over the place. '*Schrö*-dinger . . .'

The cat worms its way up to his neck and nestles there like a scarf.

'Testing, testing, testing,' Wiz chants, his voice shooting up and down. A strange, cracked-egg tone.

Oh halleluja, oh shit, oh thank you.

He holds a conversation with Schrödinger, and his voice returns to his own alto. He can't believe it. Gone already. Did he imagine it? He laments its moth's existence, and clambers out of bed to have a shower – stopping en route to inspect his eagle. In the shower he recites a ditty by William Blake, that Ben used to recite when they were both very young; the one piece of verse he can remember:

'Does the eagle know what is in the pit
Or wilt thou go ask the mole? . . .'

And down his voice plunges again. He had not imagined it. His voice is breaking. What will Emma say to that?

THE ORKNEY VOLE.

'The Orkney Vole has been proved to be a fraud,' he writes.

> For years this attractive rodent, which is double the size of the common vole and is not found anywhere else in the world, has been regarded as the only mammal unique to Great Britain. Now, however, it transpires that this creature actually comes from Europe, possibly Scandinavia.
>
> The fossilised remains of voles . . .